THE FUTURE HISTORY OF THE GRAIL BOOK THREE

RETURN
TO THE
GREEN LAND

I0628418

DINDRANE

J.G. FOLLANSBEE

THE FUTURE HISTORY OF THE GRAIL

Book 3: Return to the Green Land

A novel

by J.G. Follansbee

Print ISBN: 978-1-7354656-9-2
E-book ISBN: 978-1-7354656-2-3
Seattle, Wash., USA
Cover art by Christian Bentulan
http://coversbychristian.com/
Edited by Melanie Austin
https://seattle-editing.com/
Proofread by Edith Follansbee

CHAPTER 1: THE WEEPING WAY

Sir Percival Rathkeale steadied himself for another gamble. He weighed the odds of victory or defeat as he and his friends approached Camelot's western gate. For the third time, he was leaving the city on a journey with a greater chance of failure than success. He didn't know if he or his companions would return. If he returned empty-handed, his country would pass away. This was the final roll of the dice.

The footfalls of his horse echoed in the half-empty streets. Early morning sparrows flitted among piles of stone and broken lumber remaining from the Lucian occupation. He glanced over his shoulder, brushing away strands of his flaming red hair. Trailing him were retainers on horses leading pack animals heavy with supplies. Percival expected the expedition to take months.

"What's troubling you, Percival?" Sir Galahad du Lac-Corbenic rode beside him on a dapple-gray destrier. Galahad's trademark white cloak flowed over the horse's rump. "Have you forgotten something?"

"I miss my sister, Dee."

Percival's twin sister was back at the palace, probably working in the Great Audience Hall, the place where King Arturus III received important visitors and conducted public ceremonies. The king had asked Dee—short for Dindrane—to accompany Percival on the journey to Cassanti, a port city deep in the Hot Lands. At first, she agreed, but a day later, she asked him to come to the Dark Unicorn, a pub popular with students at Camelot University.

"I'm not going with you, Perce." She said this without meeting her brother's eye.

"Why not, Dee? I need you. How am I supposed to find the Grail without you?"

"You can easily find the Grail without me. Galahad knows almost as much about the Grail as Merlin. He found the False Grail. Maybe it was useless, but he found it."

"Dee, I've been on two Grail quests. One to the eastern deserts. One to Koda. Both failed. I think things would've gone better if you were with me. If I don't succeed this time—"

"That's ridiculous. I'm no expert on the Grail or the Great Machine."

"When we came to Camelot, you went to university. I went to The Keep. Until then, we did everything together at home on Mother's property. We helped each other with chores, with homework. We'd comfort each other during storms. We even, well, killed our father together."

Dee winced at the memory. "I did it to save you and me. I'm not proud of it."

"How do you know I won't need you to save me again?"

"You saved me at the Battle of the River's Bend. I'd say we're even."

"Family doesn't work like that. No one's keeping a tally."

Dee shifted in her seat. "The truth is, Perce, I want to stay in Camelot to finish my mural in the Great Audience Hall. That's my Grail, the thing I want to achieve. At first, it was just a job Mordred gave me, but now it's taken on a life of its own. I belong in front of a light tapestry telling stories with lasers and mirrors, not getting saddle sores a thousand kilometers from anywhere."

That ended the conversation. Percival was so angry and upset that he didn't speak to Dee for days. She never reached out to him; maybe she was just as angry. Arturus could not order Dee to accompany Percival. Instead, the king asked Galahad to join the expedition.

"I know I'm a poor substitute for your sister, Percival," Galahad said on the street near the western gate.

Behind Galahad, on a strong pony, rode 11-year-old Penny Corbenic, though no one knew her true surname. Galahad found her wandering the streets of Perditon as he and Lancelot traced a Grail rumor. She was now his page.

Percival shook his head at Galahad, whom he'd got to know on the Grail quest to Koda. Galahad had a bright scar on his neck from the Battle of River's Bend. "No, my friend. I'm glad you're here. And Penny as well."

Percival waved and grinned at Penny, a pretty girl whom Galahad praised as clever and quick.

She returned the smile with her own, the kind that had street knowledge behind it. In Perditon, Penny sold bulbs of water and fresh batteries to travelers, while avoiding enforcers in the corrupt city government.

As a condition for joining the expedition, Galahad insisted Penny go along. But Percival thought she might attract trouble. Though he had a plan for reaching Cassanti, no one knew the hazards of the journey in detail. No Viridian had been to the city in hundreds of years. The roads might be infested with bandits, trolls, or herds of basilisks, for all Percival knew. Penny might get hurt. She was also a liability. She would be an easy target for kidnappers or slavers reportedly operating between the border and Aurelia, the first major city on the Peaceful Sea south of Camelot. Percival planned to stop there before heading to Cassanti further on.

On the streets of Camelot, a few people watched Percival's party, unimpressed. When his first expedition left for the desert nearly two years in the past, hundreds cheered or waved handkerchiefs to wish him good luck. Now they appeared sullen and resentful. Dozens queued up on a bread line. Schools were refugee centers. Tents hugged houses and apartment buildings broken by the war.

On the news chans and com boards, people argued that the money spent on the expedition was better spent on housing refugees and rebuilding Camelot. The Lucians had destroyed grain silos and burned crops, but the failing climate had also hurt harvests. Maybe Merlin could find another solution to the climate problem. Percival sympathized with those demanding help, but he disagreed with them. Yes, all of the Grail expeditions so far had failed in one way or another. But Camelot's knights had to follow any hint of a working Grail to fix the Great Machine. That was the best way out of the crisis.

Even so, Percival's confidence wore thin. "Are we doing the right thing, Galahad? People are hungry. The money we're spending could feed thousands."

"You know what's at stake, Percival. Nothing less than survival."

He didn't need to be reminded. "That's not really an answer, my friend."

"How would history judge us if we didn't try?"

"People say we're following ghosts and fairies. They think Arturus has gone mad after nearly losing everything to Lucanus. They're turning to Lord Mordred."

Mordred, Prince of Lothia, did nothing to dissuade people from singing his praises. He was still in Arturus' government, so he couldn't speak publicly about his grievances with the king. Instead, he wheedled toadies at the Round Table and sycophants on the news chans and the com boards to press his case. Viridiae had a deep history of freedom of expression, but even Percival wondered if the stand-ins for Mordred didn't commit a petty kind of treason by promoting the prince as a candidate for monarch should Arturus suffer an early death. They winked, in a manner of speaking, when they said this. It made Percival's blood boil.

"Not everyone loves Mordred," Galahad said. "He's a great general, but he thinks too much of himself. His kind of arrogance may win victories sometimes, but it also courts disaster. Losing a bet on him could cost you your life."

Percival hoped he'd never suffer the same fault as Mordred. He wanted only one thing: the find the Grail and bring it home. Percival checked himself. He realized he wanted something else:

Lina.

They'd met briefly before the war. She'd worked at the art gallery where Dee had her first important show of her light tapestries. Blond-haired and gray-eyed, Lina was sweeping the gallery's floor when he first saw her. He'd thought about her a few times during the journey to Koda and in his cell in Lucana.

When he returned to Camelot, he learned the she and Dee had become close friends. When he met Lina again, the spark turned into a flame. Within a few days, they'd spent all their spare time together, even as he scrambled to pull together the expedition. Percival reached into his tunic and removed his com reader. He scrolled through a few texts until he came to Lina's.

I'll think of you every day. I know you'll succeed. I'll wait for you.

Only 14 words, but each of them were like diamonds. If he survived, Percival thought, he'd find a way to preserve them forever.

"News?" Galahad said. "You're staring at your com as if you got the last message you'll ever receive."

Percival tucked the device back in his pocket. "What if we don't come back, Galahad? Will people remember us? Will they think about us?"

"People generally forget failures, except glorious failures."

The gated portal through Camelot's outer defensive walls came into view. Before the Lucians reached the city during the war, tens of thousands of refugees had fled through the gate, which led to Camelot's suburbs and forested hills beyond. Over the decades since its construction, water collected between the stones and dripped down, creating the illusion of tears. Camelot's residents called it the Weeping Way.

As if offering reassurance, a temple to Gaia stood to one side of the gate. Percival's mother, Eleanor, a secular woman who home-schooled her children, taught Percival and Dee to value facts and reasoning. She treated religion as an annoying curiosity. Percival, however, had seen first-hand the power of the unseen. His sister had inherited an ability to kill at a distance with nothing more than her will. Was it strictly an unexplained natural phenomenon? Or was it supernatural? He didn't know, but he knew enough to respect a possibility: Gaia, the Mother of All Life, was real, even if you couldn't touch or see her.

"Let's take a break before we leave." Percival dismounted and climbed the steps into the temple, which the Lucians had left untouched. Both cultures honored the Mother, though they argued over which honored her more devoutly. They hadn't fought any wars over religion, at least not yet. Percival didn't expect his companions to follow him inside, but they did. They meant it as a gesture of loyalty, which he appreciated, and it reminded him of his responsibilities.

Their gear and animals were safe outside without a guard. That would change once they left the city.

Percival passed through a circular colonnade into a room protected by a dome with an oculus at its apex. Sunlight streamed through floor-to-ceiling windows, highlighting dust floating in the air. Fresh flowers from the People's Preserve filled vases attached to the walls. A bronze brazier with a small fire burned in the center of the temple. The fire was the only plasma fire allowed by Viridian law. Burning wood or incense released carbon dioxide into the atmosphere, breaking an ancient taboo, but the fire tradition was as old as humanity and believers insisted on it. The temple could hold fifty or sixty people. On the solstices, priests and priestesses led all-day ceremonies. On this day, the only devotees were Percival and his party.

Percival took a seat on a stone bench. He liked the peace he felt below the wooden vault. Two-dimensional paintings on the temple walls celebrated the forests, mountains, and wild coasts of Viridiae. They showed why some people preferred calling their country "the Green Land." Small twittering birds flitted among the rafters. People said the birds carried messages to Gaia.

Galahad, dressed in a dark green tunic and trousers the color of loamy earth, approached the brazier. He drew his sword, the weapon singing against the metal of his scabbard. He dropped reverently to one knee, bowed his head, and held his weapon before him. Penny looked on, wonder in her eyes. After a few breaths, Galahad stood and stepped back, deep in thought.

Outside at the temple gate, when the party remounted their animals, Percival said, "Were you praying in there, Galahad?"

"I don't really understand what people mean by prayer, but I thought about our quest and how Viridiae is depending on us. I offered my service to Gaia and our country. There are things larger than ourselves. Do you think I was silly?"

Percival didn't think so. Although he didn't feel the need for a ritual gesture, a thousand thoughts filled his mind. He worried about his ability to fulfill his task, especially without his sister. Twice he'd lost the Viridian Grail, the only thing that could save his country from a slow death. He lost it on Koda and on the trek back from Lucana. The odds were he'd fail again.

He longed to atone for what he'd done in the war. He'd murdered a man out of hatred and frustration. How do you repay the taking of a life? He'd also lost his nerve at River's Bend, when every fighting man in Viridiae challenged an army bent on destroying Camelot. He was needed, but he ignored the call. Arturus had given him a chance to redeem himself by finding what people started calling the "Last Grail," but Percival wondered if redemption was possible.

Remounting their horses, Percival and the expedition rose slowly toward the Weeping Way. Recent rains had recharged the cracks between the stones. They passed under the gate's wide arch, and drops of water hit Percival's checks and dribbled down his neck. It was easy to believe the walls of Camelot shed tears of farewell and wished godspeed.

CHAPTER 2: A RARE DISEASE

Dindrane Rathkeale sat against the headboard of her bed, her knees to her chest, her heart unable to let go of its sadness. Her mind wouldn't stop going over her argument with Percival at the Dark Unicorn. Everything she said and he said replayed like an unpleasant recording. She had upset him terribly, and though she knew her decision to stay in Camelot would be difficult for him to accept, her feelings of guilt nearly made her change her mind and race after him.

But he was already two days ride away. Sir Galahad had joined the expedition in her place. Making amends would have to wait until Percival's return.

"I know I made the right decision for myself, Lina. Why do I feel so terrible?"

Edlina Catalpec, her friend and assistant on the light tapestry commission in the Great Audience Hall, offered a sympathetic ear. "He's your brother, Dee. Percival told me how close you are. It's natural to feel bad now that he's gone. But people are really excited about your work."

Dee now spent so much time on her commission that Queen Guinevere arranged a room for her in the palace. The room was small and cold with a kitchenette and a bathroom, but Dee liked the view of two of Camelot's nine towers undergoing reconstruction. It reminded her that things were getting better, at least on the surface. Before the Lucian War, Lina worked at the gallery run by Judson Ball, the man who took the first chance on Dee's talent as an artist. The shared trauma of the conflict led to a bond between the two young women when Dee returned from the mission to Villafroide. Lina was the kind of friend who supported you even if she was skeptical of your decisions and behavior.

Dee knew of Lina's budding love affair with Percival. She saw how her brother looked at her. He'd had a few short affairs, and Dee was quick to give her opinion—mostly negative—about his choices. This relationship was clearly different for him. He smiled and laughed more when Lina was in the room. Dee approved.

She envied how Lina's blond hair framed her oval face. It had a prettiness tempered with maturity. "Do you miss him?"

Lina gazed out the window, which looked on the gardens behind the palace. "Yes, Dee, more than I thought I would."

"Have you heard from him?"

"He's at Sir Galahad's estate. There's rumors of bandits across the border. They've decided to wait until its safe to cross."

Dee sensed Lina's worry. "You should go visit him. He'd be thrilled to see you."

Before Lina responded, a page knocked on the door. Guinevere wanted to see Dee immediately. She rushed to the mirror for a quick cleanup. Lina gathered her jacket to leave. She lived with her parents in an old neighborhood inside the city's main defensive wall.

"Aren't you coming with me, Lina?"

Lina nearly dropped her jacket in surprise. "I've never met the queen before. I've never been introduced. I'm not wearing anything appropriate."

"Don't worry. I've got this."

Dee took Lina's hand and they followed the page down a long hallway to Guinevere's office. The queen stood at a table strewn with papers and tablets. A lady-in-waiting had pinned her braids tightly to her scalp. Her sleeves were rolled up to her elbows.

"Dee, thanks for coming so quickly. Who's your friend?"

"This is Lina Catalpec, one of Ganieda's students. She's assisting me with the commission."

Lina tried an awkward curtsy.

"I'm so pleased. Maybe Lina can help me as well." Guinevere gestured at the table. "These are the latest designs for the next Camelot Festival of Science and Technology. This is the first festival since Viridiae's liberation. I'm trying to find a balance between a tight budget and the need to lift people's spirits. What do you think, Dee?"

"Nothing too expensive-looking, my lady. Times are hard. People won't like extravagance."

"How about you, Lina?"

Lina studied the brightly colored geometric design of the logo and the stationary for special invitations to the field day, when inventors and scientists demonstrated their inventions and discoveries. Dee saw Lina's nervousness. Maybe she should've given Lina a chance to prepare. She gave her encouragement with a light nudge.

"I think you've struck a good balance, my lady. Perhaps a slightly more modern font would suggest an eye to the future?"

A flash of fear washed over Dee when Lina mentioned the future. What if she and her brother had no future? What if he was gone forever?

Guinevere picked up one of the proofs and studied it. "You've both made good points. I knew I was missing something. I'll discuss it with the designer."

Dee sighed.

"Are you alright, my dear?"

"I'm sorry, my lady. I was thinking of Percival. I miss him. If this were any other time, we'd probably go to the festival together."

"I hope you're planning to go anyway."

"Of course. I'll probably go with Ganieda. She likes the art exhibits."

"Lina?"

"If my little brother is healthy enough, and I'm not needed at home."

"Oh?"

Lina shifted her feet. "Please, my lady, I don't want to trouble you with my family problems."

"I'm interested. Go on."

Lina cleared her throat. "My brother Kenric suffers from a rare blood disease."

The disease had a long, complicated name, but it stopped Dee short. It was familiar, but not in a way Dee liked. The details were woolly.

"The illness is debilitating, and sometimes he needs extra care," Lina said. "Other days, he's like any other 10-year-old, rambunctious and annoying."

"I hope he recovers soon."

Lina opened her mouth to speak, but she looked at the floor instead.

Dee felt as if she wanted to excuse herself, but she didn't move.

Guinevere picked up Lina's sadness. "I'm sorry, Lina. What can be done?"

"We need a donor, but they are extremely rare, and most people who could be donors don't know it."

Because of her own unique genetic history going back to experiments before the Dissolution, when the world fell apart, Dee knew a lot about her genome. As soon as Lina mentioned her brother's illness, she remembered a report her sage-physician had given her after a visit. It said something important related to this disease, but Dee couldn't quite recall. She'd re-read the report later.

Guinevere rescued her by changing the subject. "I know how Dee feels about Percival, at least when she says she misses him. When I was in Villefroide with Dee, waiting to see Queen Jarnay, I missed Arturus. It was as if one of my limbs was missing. When I was reunited with him, I felt whole again. And like your brother, Lina, my husband has his good days and bad days, health-wise."

The whole country worried about Arturus' slow decline, but Dee wondered about Lancelot and Guinevere's relationship.

Word around the palace was that the affair with Lancelot was truly over, but did great loves die in the same way people departed the world?

"Your last name is familiar, Lina, but we haven't met before today."

"No, my lady."

Guinevere picked up a tablet and scrolled through a document. "I don't see your name, but your parents are Reuben and Isra Catalpec. Is that right?"

"Yes, my lady. My father runs a large construction company, well-known in the city. He's very busy with rebuilding projects. He's repairing two of Camelot's nine towers."

"He's doing the city an enormous service. I'd like to send you one of my invitations to the festival."

Dee caught Lina's glance.

"I'd like you to be close to my lord husband and me in the royal box. Any friend of Dee's is someone I want to know better."

"Of course, my lady. I'm honored." Lina could hardly contain her amazement.

"Good," Guinevere smiled. "Look for the invitation in the next few days, probably with a new font."

* * *

Two weeks later, the sun promised a hot day on the tournament grounds, just outside Camelot's battered walls. Dee spent the morning with Lina and Ganieda perusing the exhibits, gathered under vast tents outside the main field. Thousands of people gathered to see the newest gadgets, watch traditional games, and stuff themselves with unhealthy food. Dee loved the noise and activity.

Lina stopped to read her com.

"Trouble?" Dee said.

"It's from Percival."

"He's starting to send messages to you before me. That's a bad sign." Dee grinned to show that she was joking.

"Border security says the bandit threat has eased. The expedition is leaving in three days."

"There's more?"

"Percival wants me to visit him." Lina fell silent.

"Well, are you going?"

Lina walked ahead of Dee and Ganieda, her face full of worry. Dee decided not to pry.

In the main exhibit tent, the hottest technology from Perditon amazed Dee and every other attendee. The entrepreneurs and engineers in the country's second city constantly invented new ways to reuse ancient technology discovered in the recycling mines. They repurposed devices from the days before the Dissolution for modern needs.

One exhibit showed how intelligent public cars could be used during a mass evacuation in case of another Lucian invasion. They almost acted like cells in the blood stream, picking up and transporting frightened refugees to safety, at least in the demonstration video. Another product sped the reconstruction of stone buildings by using robots to lay bricks and apply mortar.

"My father should see this." Lina hid whatever discomfort Percival's invitation had caused. "Dad is always complaining of a shortage of skilled workers."

"Maybe a machine could take up the slack, if the bricklayers guild would agree," Ganieda said.

Though the festival was devoted to science, Guinevere made sure artists such as Ganieda weren't forgotten. One pavilion featured new work from Viridiae's established artists. The centerpiece was a huge, three-dimensional light tapestry depicting Arturus' defeat at the River Colum. The main composition showed Arturus and his closest knights—Lancelot, Bors, Galahad, and Percival—about to clash with Robert Dardarius' legions. Artists had already seized on the battle as symbolic of the nation pulling together, because the Viridian army was a scratch force made of bits and pieces from all over the country, including civilians, some carrying nothing more than single-shot hunting rifles.

"Ganieda, what do you think about this jumble?" Dee wrinkled her nose in dismay. "Some people think it's too soon to interpret such a major event. It's only been a few months since the end of the war."

Ganieda stepped around the work to get different views. "It's true that interpretation needs distance to get to the moment's meaning. On the other hand, others wanted to strike while the emotional iron was hot."

"I'm not sure the timing matters," Lina said. "Look at how the artist has rendered the figures. I love the image of Percival sitting on his warhorse waiting for orders."

"I think Lina has lost her objectivity about Percival." Dee giggled, intending to tease Lina, but her friend didn't react.

"This is charming." Ganieda hovered near a table.

"The artist is from the town where my mother owns property," Dee said.

The bronze, ten centimeters tall, was a simple, expertly cast depiction of a puppy licking the face of a laughing girl. No one could look at it without smiling.

"So much less ponderous than the battle scene," Dee said.

Ganieda bent over the table scribbling on a piece of paper. "It's a silent auction. I'd love to have this piece."

An announcement over the festival loudspeaker reminded the women to head toward the tournament ground's grandstand. As they made her way to the VIP entrance, they passed food booths smelling of barbecued beef, deep-fried sliced potatoes, and the cloying smell of cinnamon sprinkled on pastries.

Dee stopped in mid-bite of the buttery bread. She heard a muffled cry from a small tent near the tourney field gate. An elderly man lifted one of the tent flaps and called to a worker.

"It's Merlin," Dee declared. "Should we go visit him?"

Ganieda shook her head. Merlin was her younger brother. "He told me about his demonstration. I think we should leave him alone."

Dee heard the cry again, but it didn't belong to a human, nor any animal she could think of. The security guard at the entrance shunted Dee and her companions through before she could catch a glimpse of the creature inside the tent. Or was it something else she saw?

CHAPTER 3: A PROVOKED ATTACK

Ushers guided Dee, Lina, and Ganieda to a section underneath the grandstand's canopy. The promised heat had arrived, but Dee didn't remove her sun hat or glasses. She came prepared with a flask of water, but a craving for sugar forced her to order sweet-water drinks from a vendor for Ganieda, Lina and herself.

Normally during the tournament season, Arturus and Guinevere sat in a special box at the edge of the parade ground so they could speak to jousting knights before and after their competitions. Today, the box was several rows back from the field's edge. Dee's assigned seat was three rows below the king's box, and she had to strain to see its occupants. Neither he nor Guinevere was in the box.

Dee caught the attention of Ganieda. "Isn't that Lady Morgause?"

Ganieda strained to see the mother of Lord Mordred Lothian, fanning herself, almost hiding in the back row of the royal box. "Yes, it is." The way Ganieda said it, you'd think that she was disappointed to see her old friend from her youth.

"She's looks miserable," Lina said.

"No doubt planning something to make us all miserable," Ganieda remarked.

Lina looked at Dee quizzically.

"They have a history together," Dee whispered. She'd tell Lina later about Morgause's ejection from the Theurgist's Society for toying with dark magic.

"Sometimes I think that woman is determined to test us,

maybe test the country. I don't know who can stand up to her, except maybe…" Ganieda didn't seem willing to finish the thought.

Dee said, "Do you think she's helping her son with dark forces?"

Ganieda grew quiet. "I'm almost certain. Somehow, I feel like she and I are going to—I don't know how to put it."

"Fight?"

"Confront one another, though maybe not face to face." Ganieda relaxed and patted Dee's arm. "But not today."

A trumpet fanfare blew over the loudspeakers, and a voice asked the crowd to rise for the king and his consort. The grandstand was packed with people from all over Viridiae, as well as ambassadors, foreign merchants, and military attaches, some in uniform. The most distinctive were the Ontarii, with their unique striped pigment on their faces, a legacy of a pre-Dissolution experiment in human genetic engineering. They organized themselves into clans based on the width and number of facial stripes, and by the look of the group, they had representatives from all the clans. On the south end of the tournament field, now empty of horses and knights, was Observation Hill, a grassy knoll covered with the blankets and small pavilions. The balance of the audience sat on benches on the opposite side of the field from the grandstand.

A cheer and applause rose from the spectators. Stepping through a private door in the rear of his box, Arturus, dressed in light trousers and a short-sleeved shirt, acknowledged the crowd's subdued adulation. Guinevere stood next to him in an off-white, billowy dress that was neither too modest nor so loose-fitting that the breeze might turn it into a sail and carry her off. She smiled in Dee's direction, but Dee couldn't tell if it was meant for her or for the entire crowd of invited courtiers that surrounded Dee on the benches.

The announcer again called for the audience's attention, describing the purpose of the show. The festival's Field Day was just one of several competitions; they ranged from research papers to the science-fair style exhibits Dee examined earlier in the day. But everyone looked forward to the grandstand event, because the entrants were judged on showmanship, as well as technical prowess.

The announcer introduced the first entrant, a delivery company that claimed it could deliver anything, anywhere, anytime, no matter the roads, weather, or remote location with a flying machine. Another entrant fired a rocket that returned sharp images to a large screen on the north end of the field. The engineers claimed they had reached the edges of space and would soon send a small satellite into orbit. A third team laid out what appeared to be nothing more than flat sheets of a building material. Within seconds, the sheets had unfolded into a fully constructed building in the shape of a large shed. The team described their invention as an instant shelter, sturdier and more long-lasting than a tent. A moment later, the building refolded itself, and the engineers loaded the object into a trailer.

Finally, the last entrant was announced. Everyone gasped and cheered when they heard the name: Merlin. A large, fully enclosed white van drove to the center of the field, and the sage-scientist emerged from the passenger side of the cab.

"Your Majesties, my lords, ladies and gentlemen." Merlin's crackly yet melodic voice echoed across the field. He wore a long white coat that heightened his thin physique. "For more than 10 centuries, humanity has lived with the legacy of the Old Civilization. The scientists and engineers of that time achieved amazing things, which we're only now rediscovering. They pushed the boundaries of science, some say too far, particularly when it comes to the building blocks of life. Among their achievements, or follies, depending on your point of view, were new species created by combining the DNA of one species with another, often several species together. In some cases, they started with even more elemental blocks, and designed whole new species.

"Most of the latter creatures were microscopic and purpose-built, perhaps to fight disease or cure a genetic anomaly. One, however, was a large animal, a legendary animal so rare that our knightly class often goes in search of one. To do this, they need special approval from the monarch."

Dee held her breath, anticipating something wonderful. She set aside her suspicion of the Old Civilization's penchant for toying with everything; her own DNA was tainted by their experiments.

"As a scientist," Merlin said, "my goal is always to discover new knowledge. In this case, I have relearned old knowledge, and taken it a step further."

Merlin stepped away from the truck and gave a signal. The sides of the van fell away, revealing an aluminum cage. In one corner, cowering like a frightened dog, was a creature Dee had only seen in illustrations. A few photos existed, but the images led to more questions than answers. A few bones were exhibited in Camelot's natural history museum. A dead one was found on the island of Koda. And Percival had famously recorded its call in the King's Forest before he was rescued by Lancelot after his first expedition to find the Grail.

"My lords, a Questing Beast."

As if on cue, the frightened beast called out, and Dee recognized the noise as the same one she'd heard while waiting to get into the Field Day. The crowd was stunned and fascinated. Lina and other audience members applauded, while Ganieda looked skeptical. The beast called again, a different noise, full of anxiety, and it looked about, as if searching for someone. When it saw Merlin, it relaxed a little, and moved closer. Merlin put his hand between the bars and touched the beast's snout. The rear door of the cage opened, and Merlin coaxed the four-legged beast to hop down to the grass.

Dee's heart raced. She saw no leash or chain on the animal, which was at least three meters long from head to tail. She guessed it weighed around a thousand kilograms, a little bigger than a strong warhorse. The scaly skin was the gray-blue of winter clouds, while its eyes were the fiery orange of the evening sun. The snout curved into a meat-tearing beak like an eagle's, and its teeth were ivory-white. The tail ended in a broad paddle. Dee wondered if the paddle helped it swim. Merlin led it away from the cage. It followed him like a puppy, barking and hopping on its forelegs, as if ready to play.

"A brief explanation, my lords and friends," Merlin said. "We've known that the Old Civilization modified human and animal DNA to cure disease and lengthen life. Just before the Dissolution, when the world fell apart, one geneticist worked on creating large life forms from scratch. He succeeded, and the modern questing beasts are descendants of that effort. A few years ago, I discovered and deciphered documents that described the methods, and today, I offer my results."

Merlin bowed, and the crowd roared. The beast raised its head and looked about, clearly aware of the noise, though it appeared anxious. Merlin stroked its snout again, and the beast calmed.

Dee turned to look at the royal box. Arturus and Guinevere stood and applauded in polite restraint. Guinevere's eyes beamed with joy, while Arturus' smile signaled his pride. Others in the royal box were less restrained, but Dee noticed Morgause's seat was now empty, as was the seat next to hers. Was it intended for Mordred?

A bright flash nearly blinded Dee. An instant later, it disappeared, but she saw a strange man in the hat and sunglasses holding something reflective above his shoulder. He stood near the royal box, but far enough away to appear inconsequential. He was too far away for Dee to make out the object he held, but another, less intense flash reminded her of a mirror held up to the sun.

Her attention returned to Merlin and the beast. A distorted reflection played on the grass near the scientist and his creature, which was enamored of the light's playful movement. The reflection vaulted onto the beast's face, and it closed its eyes, crying out. It bolted forward knocking Merlin down, and sped toward the grandstand.

With the speed of a predator, the beast leaped into the grandstand. The crowd below the royal box panicked, pushing each other aside to get out of the way. Dee froze, directly in the path of the bounding beast. She had nowhere to go and no defense. Lina dropped to the wooden floor, while Ganieda held out her arms to ward off an attack. The beast's claws clacked on the wooden backs of chairs as it climbed toward them. At the last second, it leapfrogged all three, landing on a set of empty seats. It clambered toward the royal box.

The beast, angry and frightened, reached the box, but at the last second, a guard closed the exit door, leaving him alone with the creature. He slashed at the creature with his sword but missed. The beast chomped down on the guard's sword arm, severing it. He screamed, matching the beast's cry. More security men and women scrambled into the royal box from above and below. Dee heard several shots. Silence. No movement. Dee imagined the creature was dead, but she swallowed her sadness. A moment passed, and the crowd breathed a collective sigh.

Where was Arturus and Guinevere? A shout, and Lina pointed upward. The king and queen had emerged from a portal into the grandstand. Flanked by guards with swords and single-shot pistols at the ready, the couple waved, apparently uninjured. Lina cheered, along with the crowd.

An ambulance's siren sounded. Merlin was prone on the grass.

* * *

After the security detachment at the tournament grounds cleared the three women, Lina took Ganieda home, and Dee ran back to the palace. She needed to talk to Guinevere. She had to tell her what she'd seen.

The palace was in an uproar. To Dee's eye, people appeared to be running about with no destination or purpose, though she didn't sense any panic. Maybe the various aides and courtiers had jobs in a crisis. She certainly didn't, but her instincts drove her toward the royal couple's apartment, until she was stopped by more armed guards. She caught a glimpse of Guinevere.

"My lady! My lady! I need to speak with you."

Guinevere ignored Dee.

"My lady, please. I saw something. Please let me tell you."

Guinevere looked up and spoke to an assistant, who ran off.

"Dee, I don't have time to talk with you now."

"I know, my lady. But I saw something. It might help."

"Alright, quickly then."

"It has to do with Lady Morgause."

The mention of Mordred's mother stopped Guinevere in her tracks. "You're sure?"

"Yes, ma'am. While I was watching the demonstration—"

Guinevere held up her hand. "Not here." She ordered the guards to stand aside, and she led Dee into her office. "Talk to me. I don't have time for gossip."

Dee told Guinevere about the strange man, and Morgause's absence from the royal box.

Guinevere worked her jaw, chewing over the information. "Come with me."

Guinevere led the way through the office's back door down a narrow, poorly lit passageway. A moment later, they came out into a large office, big enough for a dozen people to meet. Dee blinked at the bright sunlight pouring through the windows. Standing with a half-dozen men and women with determined, stoical expressions was Arturus.

"My lord husband," Guinevere said, "I think you should hear this."

All eyes turned to Dee. "Sire, I saw something. Two things, really, that struck me as strange."

"Go on."

"I saw a man in the last row of seats next to the royal box. During Merlin's demonstration, he pointed something toward the questing beast. It might've been a mirror reflecting sunlight. Why would someone do that?"

"Indeed. Why would they? You're confirming what others saw, Ms Rathkeale. What else did you see?"

"Well, just before you arrived to watch the demonstrations, Lady Morgause was in the royal box. I assumed she was just waiting for the show to start."

"Was she alone?"

"Yes, sire. But I noticed that she was gone right after the beast attacked the box."

"You mean you saw her leave before?"

"I'm not sure, sire. Did she leave with you?"

"That's privileged information, but... No, she wasn't with us."

Dee realized the implications. "That means... Dear Gaia, if she left before the attack, she might have known it was coming."

"That's what we're trying to discover, Ms Rathkeale. She hasn't been seen since the incident. And Mordred is nowhere to be found."

Guinevere said, "She told me a few days ago that he was in Lothia on business."

"That's true," Arturus said, "but we know he returned to Camelot last night, unannounced."

"I don't understand," Dee said. "The strange man wasn't Mordred. I'm certain of it."

"No, he was only an agent." The voice was Merlin's. He stepped out from among the advisors, his arm in a sling. "One of Morgause's agents."

"Sir?"

"The Lady Morgause has long been a supporter of my research. She knew about my experiments with the Old Civilization's DNA splicing technology. She's also a scholar in her own right, something she's doesn't talk about much. She knows as much or more about questing beasts than a lot of knights who go after them." Merlin glanced at the collection of advisors.

"One of the few facts most sources agree on about questing beasts is this: They love shiny objects. They collect them, something like the bower bird. Do you know about those, young lady?"

"Yes, I do. In some species, the males collect interesting, colorful objects that could attract females."

"Very good. Well, questing beasts can't resist shiny things. Sets them off like a match. I'm guessing that Morgause knew this, and thought she could get my questing beast to go after a flashing light, thinking it was a bauble or something. It seems to have worked."

"But the beast was killed before it could hurt the king," Dee said. "It didn't mean him any harm. It was just after a sparkle." Dee felt sad for the beast, which had only followed its instinct, and died for it.

"That's the best hypothesis we have at the moment," Merlin said. "Perhaps she was counting on His Majesty getting trampled, or bitten. Maybe she or the agent would finish him off when he no one was looking." He raised his hands, then winced at the pain in his arm.

Guinevere said, "Dee, you've confirmed that Morgause was in the royal box prior to the attack, and disappeared after. You're also the best witness to the plan for getting the questing beast into the royal box. It was clearly deliberate."

"Are you sure, my lady? What does the Lady Morgause say?"

"Once we find her, we'll ask."

"What about Lord Mordred? I know that he's... I mean..." Dee was reluctant to say what everyone knew: that he hated the king.

"Lord Mordred," Arturus said, "has tried my patience for too long. I believe he planned to take my throne if I was killed or injured in the attack. Obviously, that didn't happen, and he's already been seen on the road heading back to Lothia."

"Will you arrest him, sire?" Dee said.

"That would be difficult. He has an army waiting for him there."

"What?"

"It's his backup plan, in our opinion," Guinevere said. "He's planning to march on Camelot, if he hasn't already."

"Attack Camelot?" Dee couldn't believe her ears. "But he saved the country. He defeated the Lucians. Why would he attack his own home?"

"He feels he's been wronged," Arturus said. "And he thinks war is the only way to get what he wants."

CHAPTER 4: A VISIT WITH PERCIVAL

Lina approached the front door of the manor house, unsure if she was doing the right thing. Ganieda had suffered a major fright at the tournament grounds, when the claws of the questing beast tore out a chunk of the bench beside her. A few millimeters closer, and the elder might have suffered a brutal injury. Just as Lina finished making Ganieda a pot of tea in her studio, she received another text from Percival asking if she would come to Sir Galahad's estate.

Ganieda assured her she was fine. "You should make the most of time with Percival. You don't know when you'll see him again."

Lina took a shared car out of the city. She rarely took trips to the countryside, preferring to spend time in Viridiae's larger cities or on its rugged coast on the Peaceful Sea. On the drive to Galahad's home, the sun dipped below the western mountains. One of the peaks was Apparatus Montis, where Merlin worked on the Great Machine. Yellow and orange light caromed off the broken clouds above the mountains. The car dropped her off at Galahad's front door around midnight. Lina pulled the bell and a young girl answered.

"Hello, I'm Lina Catalpec. I'm here to meet Percival."

The girl yawned and let Lina into the foyer. "I'm Penny. Percival told us you'd be coming. You can put your jacket on the peg."

A staircase with a simple wooden banister rose from the foyer. Heavy footsteps pounded down the carpeted stairs and stopped. Percival appeared, and Lina's body warmed. Gaia in Heaven, she thought, what a beautiful man. His long flaming-red hair flowed down his neck as he poked his head around a column where the stairs turned. He descended, never once taking his eyes off Lina. He stood next to her, but didn't reach out.

"Hello, Ms Catalpec." Galahad arrived from an adjacent room. "Was your ride comfortable?"

"Yes, sir."

Galahad wore slippers, pajamas and a house robe with satin lapels. "Forgive my dress, but we weren't sure when you'd arrive."

"It's alright, sir. I'm sorry if I kept you up."

The Ermine Knight, which some people called him because of his fondness for elegant things, shifted his gaze between his guests. Galahad spoke to Percival, who floated, it seemed, next to Lina. "You are right, my friend."

"I'm sorry?"

"She's as beautiful as the sunrise."

Penny giggled.

Percival flushed red.

Lina cupped Percival's cheek in her hand. She laughed. "The earth has probably mistaken that head of hair for the sunrise at one time or another."

"You're supposed to kiss her, Percival." Penny pushed him forward.

Their kiss was deep and long. Though he'd only been gone a few days, Lina wanted every moment with him to linger. Every second was precious, because she had no idea how long she'd have to remember the moment until he came home. If he came home.

"You're not supposed to suffocate each other!" Penny said. "Galahad, can we have pie now?"

"Lina, we thought you might want a little snack after the long drive," Galahad said. "My cook made some fresh apple pie this evening. Would you like some?"

Lina almost didn't hear him as she kept her gaze on Percival. "I'm a little hungry."

"Me too." They were the first words Percival had said since Lina arrived.

The kitchen was spotless, if a little dated. The butcher block working table was cut and stained with the juices of thousands of meals. Copper pots and stainless steel utensils hung from a rack. Lina could almost smell the soups and sauces prepared on the gas stove.

"My grandfather Pellas built the house for my grandmother after the civil wars," Galahad said. "I haven't done much updating since my father died. I've been too busy on research trips or quests. Not to mention wars against the Lucians."

Lina got the impression that Galahad liked well-kept dilapidation.

Penny opened the ancient icebox and pulled out the pie and a pitcher of milk. Galahad found plates and forks. The four sat at a wooden table in a nook. The pie tasted of cinnamon and butter. The apples were perfectly cooked: crisp, but not crunchy. Lina wondered if her mother Isra would like the recipe.

Penny wolfed down her slice and asked for more.

The conversation turned to Camelot. Galahad asked about the mood in the palace.

"I can't say, sir. I'm usually just in the Great Audience Hall working with Dee on her commission. I live with my parents, so I don't hear much gossip, although I did meet the queen just the other day."

"How does she seem?" Percival said.

"Busy with trying to get things back to normal."

Galahad said, "Percival told me you were at the tournament grounds, that you saw the incident with the questing beast."

"I was. It was frightening."

"Do you mind telling us?"

Lina recounted her experience. "There also something odd about it."

"Oh?" Galahad picked up the plates and put them in the sink.

"I was looking at some of the news chan reports. The whole experience seemed unreal at the time. But Dee pointed out Lady

Morgause in the royal box to me just before the incident. I saw the beast go in, but the lady wasn't there."

Galahad glanced at Percival. "Maybe she escaped."

"Possibly, but it happened so fast. Could she move that quickly? It just seemed odd to me."

"Fear and terror can sometimes push people to do what they never thought possible," Percival said. "I learned that in Lucana."

"There's another thing. I haven't found a news report yet that mentions Lady Morgause. It's as if she was never there. Nothing about whether she was injured, or escaped, or anything."

"Morgause has tremendous influence in Camelot. Being the mother of Mordred allows that," Galahad said. "It's conceivable that she told her media contacts to play down or ignore her presence."

"Why would she do that?" Lina said.

"She wants to cover up something," Percival said.

Lina shrugged. "I'm no expert on palace intrigue. I just help Dee prep her equipment and clean up. She's also letting me work on some of the landscape sections. Flowers are my specialty."

Penny yawned again and lay her head on the table. Lina found Percival's hand under the table. He squeezed back.

"It's very late, and we have our own prep work to do before we depart again for the border," Galahad said. "We've prepared a room for you next to Percival's, Lina. I hope it's comfortable."

Lina almost said she didn't need it, but she understood Galahad's need to look as if Percival and Lina were casual friends only. "Thank you, sir."

Galahad said his good nights, and led Penny by the hand out of the kitchen. Lina looked at Percival again, and her whole body flamed with desire. "Show me my room, Percival?"

Percival took her hand and led her upstairs. The house was already quiet. One room had an open door, and Lina could see open bags and a stand holding Percival's light body armor. The next room was empty, though the bed was ready and the room clean. In the blink of an eye, they were making love. It was not the first time they had shared a bed, but the unfamiliar room and the chance that she might never see Percival again infused their coupling with the energy of making up for time they might never have. Afterward, she lay with her head on Percival's powerful, scarred shoulder. He'd only just regained the weight he'd lost while a prisoner in Lucana.

Lina thought it was time to say the thing so fraught with risk. "I think I'm in love with you, Percival."

He let out a breath, as if he'd been holding it for hours. "That's wonderful. I've been thinking the same thing, but I was afraid to say it."

Lina looked at him. "Why?"

"Because it scares people away. I don't want to scare you away."

She kissed his shoulder. "I'm not scared now."

They lay together, just breathing, for several minutes. The house was silent.

"What's the story with Penny?" Lina said.

Percival told a short version of Galahad and Lancelot's discovery of the False Grail in Perditon. Before Galahad returned to Grey Harbor and the ship that would take his first expedition to Koda, he sent the False Grail home with Penny, who was a street urchin with no family.

"Galahad intended to find her a good family in Camelot, but he began to think of her as his responsibility. He has no partner and his immediate blood family are all dead. I think he's lonely here."

Moonlight streamed through the window. Even though it was the small hours of the morning, Lina didn't want to sleep. "Are you still awake, Percival?"

"You can call me Perce, if you like. There's only two other people I let do that: Dee and my mother."

Lina stroked the skin of his neck. "I can't get Lady Morgause out of my mind."

"It's best not to think about her."

"Really? I don't know much about her. I'm new to the palace, but I hear whispers. She's Lord Mordred's mother, and she lives in the palace. It's said she wants to be queen."

"When I came back from my first expedition, I was convinced that Mordred sabotaged it somehow. Now I think it was his mother. She arranged for clues to distract us from finding the Viridian Grail after someone, probably Gawain, took it from Merlin. Arturus told me once, 'The man or woman who has the Grail owns the nation.' She wanted it, but more for her son, so he could lay claim to the throne. Though no one talks about it, everyone believes Mordred is Arturus' illegitimate son by Morgause."

"But there's no proof. About Gawain, that is."

"Not definitive proof. But Gawain is Mordred's half-brother, and blood means everything to aristocrats like the Lothian clan."

"But the Viridian Grail was lost during the war. What does she want now?"

"Probably the same thing, the throne for her son. But Arturus and the country are so weak, she doesn't need the Grail for legitimacy any more. Ordinary Viridians are splitting, some for Arturus, some for Mordred, though most just want stability and a chance to rebuild their lives. Arturus wants the Grail, though. He takes his duty to heal the country seriously."

"Would Morgause try something as crazy as getting a questing beast to attack Arturus?"

"She's as single-minded as anyone I've known. I think it's possible."

Lina had a hard time grasping the machinations of the powerful. Her family was as middle-class as they come. Her father built a business that was flowering due to the need for Camelot to reconstruct itself. Lina's mother Isra was the youngest daughter of an important landowner, and she'd spent time in the royal court, but she had no stomach for court intrigue. She wanted a family, and she was a perfect match for Reuben Catalpec. The only blemish on their idyllic family life was Kenric's illness. The future looked dark for him.

"How is your brother doing?" Percival said.

"We take it day by day."

"You never told me about his illness."

"His body can't make a certain blood protein. It's a genetic mutation." Lina named the disease. "He needs a donor, but we can't find one."

"That sounds familiar for some reason." Percival moved to face Lina. "You should talk to Dee. She has a genetic mutation, and I swear I've heard that word used."

"But she's not sick, is she?"

"Not that I know of. But she might have some information that could help. It wouldn't hurt to ask."

Lina and her family had tried for years to find a donor for Kenric. Could Dee offer some hope? Lina promised herself to ask Dee as soon as she returned to Camelot.

CHAPTER 5: THE SEEDS OF DOUBT

Dee slept fitfully the night after the incident with Merlin's questing beast, feeling as if the world had slipped backwards into the chaos everyone thought was behind them. The thin walls of her room let in muffled words and heavy steps of worried people. The noises died down after midnight, but Dee could only snatch two or three hours of sleep, before she gave up and rose an hour earlier than normal.

She'd done this before, but only when images and ideas came to her like the staccato of gunfire, and she could no longer resist their energy. On this morning, while it was still dark, she bathed, dressed in work clothes, and made coffee. For all the hubbub of the day before, the corridors were mausoleum quiet, the guards still as urns holding half-dead plants. In the Great Audience Hall, her footsteps echoed among the columns and walls, exaggerating her sense of solitude. Basilicas had the dual effect of making you feel embraced and alone.

She pulled aside the curtain separating the mural workspace from the rest of the interior and found Lady Morgause sitting at a work table. Shocked, Dee held the curtain open for a moment before stepping into the workspace. Was it really her? "My lady, I'm surprised to see you here."

"And why would that be?"

Dee's surprise gave way to a simmering anger. "People are looking for you. You disappeared after the incident at the tourney grounds."

Dee barely held back from accusing Morgause of trying to kill

Arturus. Staring at the black-clad woman, hair hidden under a wimple, Dee stayed out of Morgause's reach. It was silly to think the elder would attack her physically, but her instincts told her to keep her distance. Dee glanced about, but she didn't see any retainers.

"An old woman has physical needs," Morgause said. "I wasn't about to embarrass myself in public."

"So you didn't have anything to do with the attack yesterday?"

"Is that what people are saying?" Morgause said.

"If you simply left at that moment to take care of bodily functions, why didn't you come back?"

"It was mayhem. Why would I wade into that? I'm defenseless."

Dee stifled a laugh. "You're as defenseless as an armored knight."

Morgause threw a cold gaze on Dee. "Do you see any weapons on me?"

"Your weapons are guile and deceit."

"Watch yourself, child, or you may be stung to death by them."

Dee took the woman's threat seriously. She was a guppy swimming in a sea of sharks. According to Ganieda, Morgause wielded the insidious weapons of the theurgist who practiced dark magic, signaled by the garnet and obsidian ring on her left hand. Nonetheless, Dee's disgust overrode her judgment.

"Merlin believes you took advantage of a natural instinct in questing beasts to endanger the king and queen."

"I've read the media reports. I wasn't the one holding the mirror."

Dee couldn't hold her laughter back this time. "All you had to do was put someone up to it."

"That's pure speculation. No one can prove it. Have they found the man who supposedly excited the beast to jump into the grandstand?"

Dee folded her arms. "I don't know."

"The whole theory is ludicrous. Maybe Merlin prodded the beast to attack. What a fool. His opinion of himself knows no boundaries. Letting an unpredictable animal—a genetically engineered animal—run loose like that was irresponsible. Anything could happen."

Morgause's alternate theory raised doubts for Dee. "Why would Merlin be so reckless?"

"He's always been less than he makes himself out to be. How is that he's failed to repair the Great Machine after all these years?"

"Because the most important part is missing, the Grail." Dee's chest tightened at the mention of Percival's quest.

"That's what he says, but how do we know it's true? We're going by his word only. Somebody really ought to investigate that man and his so-called expertise."

Dee felt lost. What were they talking about? "You still haven't explained your absence during the attack."

"I told you. I was in the ladies room. Besides, I don't have to answer to you."

Dee clenched her fists to beat back her frustration.

"My lady, why are you here?"

"I want you to give a message to Guinevere. I want you to tell her that she is the traitor, not I nor my son."

"I can't possibly say that to her. She is as loyal to Arturus and Camelot as anyone."

Morgause grinned with the cynicism born of decades of palace intrigue. "You are a babe who knows nothing."

"I'm not stupid. You're making accusations which don't have any truth to them. You're trying to lead me away from the real conspiracy, your son's, and probably yours, to usurp the throne by force. Everyone knows that Mordred is amassing an army in Lothia."

"If I had time to explain what's happening, I would. I'm not sure you'd get it. I will ask you this: Who gains from a usurpation? Think about it, Dee. Guinevere comes from a family as powerful as my own. Arturus married her as a sop to her Camiliard people, who believe they are the rightful heirs to the Viridian throne. Guinevere is their leader by blood and law. Maybe Guinevere is the one who plans to take Viridiae for herself. My

Return to the Green Land

son Mordred is trying to prevent that. If Arturus is in his way, so be it."

The doubts gnawed at Dee. "You're saying the real conflict is between you and Guinevere? I don't believe it. She's a kind, loyal, amazing woman."

"I agree with you, Dee. She's all those things, although she's mostly loyal to herself, as we all are."

Is that true? Is everyone ultimately selfish, when push comes to shove? "I don't see it, Lady Morgause. People are known by their behavior, and Guinevere has done nothing that seems treasonous."

"That's what makes her such a formidable enemy. If you expect to survive in the palace, my child, you have to understand that nothing is ever as it seems. You've barely noticed what lies beneath the surface. I've spent my whole life tunneling to the core. Do you know what's there?"

"No, my lady."

"The desire for power. The desire to rule. Nothing more."

Dee wasn't ready to accept such a bleak assessment of human motivation. She understood that politics was sometimes a contest between egos, and that some practitioners were only interested in glory and adulation. Nothing in Guinevere's attitude toward her suggested these things, though she admitted to herself that Guinevere kept many secrets. Morgause knew the queen far better, but Mordred's mother had an agenda that colored her assessments. She had reason to persuade Dee to her side. Was that what she was doing, trying to turn her loyalty?

"Madame, I'm uncomfortable here. I have work to do. I don't want to report you to the guard."

Morgause laughed. "Half the palace guard belong to me or Mordred. You wouldn't get very far. Nonetheless," she rose stiffly, "I have no desire to cause discomfort. Please give my message to the queen, and think about what I've said. My son and I want only what's good for the country. Can Guinevere say the same?"

Dee rose with Morgause. She held the curtain so the elder

could pass. The lady nodded in thanks and disappeared in the looming twilight of morning. Dee's shoulders and neck hurt from the tension. She felt as if she'd sparred with a master swordsman, and lost badly. She tried to work, but she set down her tablet and projectors after only a few minutes. A wave of exhaustion came over her, and she returned to her room. She had to reset before speaking to the queen.

* * *

In the late afternoon, Dee found Guinevere in her office with an aide watching a news report. The aide was near tears, but Guinevere stared at the screen with barely a hint of emotion. Dee moved in behind the pair, taking in the report over Guinevere's shoulder.

The camera panned over a field of smoldering ruins and bodies. Some of the images were fuzzed out to hide the blood and wounds. The vehicles, horses, and men-at-arms belonged to Viridiae, though a few carried the Lothian crest. The anchor spoke in quiet tones, describing a skirmish on the border between the land governed directly by Camelot, the royal demesne, and Lothia. More than a dozen troops loyal to Arturus were slaughtered, with five killed on the Lothian side.

"The war we all feared has started," Guinevere said evenly. "Mordred must be stopped."

Dee's heart broke. Only the day before, the country was at peace. The future looked bright. Camelot and Viridiae would soon be whole and strong again. She imagined Percival and Galahad riding into the palace main gate, carrying the Last Grail in triumph. Within days, the Grail would be installed and the Great Machine and the world would be perfect again. She'd finish the grand mural in the Great Audience Hall, and the whole nation would celebrate.

Instead, a new nightmare had come to Viridiae.

"What will happen now, my lady?" Dee said.

"A slaughter."

"My lady?"

"You know your history, don't you, Dee? Arturus' grandfather founded a nation at the end of a civil war. He was as blood-thirsty as the worst of his enemies. Hundreds of thousands died. Brother against brother, sister against sister, family against family. Civil wars are always the worst kind, because there are no rules."

"But Mordred can't be allowed to win, my lady. Arturus is our elected king. He belongs to the people. Mordred belongs only to himself. He wants to turn everything on its head."

"You're correct, Dee, but it won't be easy. Mordred's grudge against his father is deep and it has festered all his life. Only blood will cure it, as far as he's concerned."

"We will win, won't we?"

Guinevere's expression did not give Dee the reassurance she sought. "Arturus has departed Camelot at the head of a division of his knights. Fortunately, this time, we're better prepared than before the Lucian invasion. Arturus wants to nip Lothia's rebellion in the bud. Tell me, why did you want to see me?"

Dee relayed Morgause message, embarrassed that she had to deliver it at such as vulnerable moment.

"Who is a traitor, but someone who loves her country too much?" Guinevere sighed. "Morgause can insult me all she wants. It doesn't mean a thing. My job is to rally the country. We need every man and woman who can fight. If only Lancelot would answer my calls. The country would rally around her faster than they would me."

"The country loves you, my lady," Dee said.

"I may be a member of the Round Table, and Arturus' wife, but I'm not a warrior. We need Lancelot's popularity and charisma."

Dee wanted to ask why Lancelot wasn't returning Guinevere's calls, but she could guess why. The break had occurred a month after Arturus reoccupied Camelot. Guinevere organized a reception for close aides and veterans who had played an important part in the victory. Mordred showed up drunk. He and Arturus argued, with Mordred publicly calling for Arturus to resign. Dee could almost taste the shock in the room.

On her way to her room in the royal apartments, she heard familiar voices: Guinevere and Lancelot. Dee was reluctant to witness more drama, but she couldn't help herself. She hung back, hidden by a potted tree.

"Mordred's stepped too close to the line this time," Guinevere said.

"Is he still pressuring you to align with him?" Lancelot held the remnants of a cocktail in her hand.

"He hasn't learned his lesson," Guinevere said. "I'm not interested in helping him. One coup attempt is enough."

"And you still have your own ambitions for the throne?" Lancelot swallowed the rest of her drink.

"That's a lie."

"It's not. Arturus sent you away after Mordred's try for the throne before the war. Everyone took it to mean that you were supporting Mordred, even working with him. He offered to marry you."

"Even if it were true that I wanted the throne," Guinevere said, "which it's not, I'd never try to force Arturus out."

"Sometimes I wish he would die so I could marry you," Lancelot said.

Dee almost put her hands over her ears and ran, but her feet were riveted to the paving stones.

Guinevere lowered her voice. "Don't ever say that. We may have free speech in this country, but saying that in the palace could be heard as a threat. You could be charged with all sorts of crimes."

"It's just a figure of speech, an off-hand sentiment."

"And you need to get out of your head that we're ever going to be more than back door lovers."

Lancelot's face twisted in pain. Guinevere had pierced her heart with the words. "Is that what I am to you? A sneak-around girlfriend? I thought we were more that that."

"Honestly, Lancelot, your infatuation with me is starting to get on my nerves. I'm Queen of Viridiae, not an exotic toy you're forbidden to play with and hoping to not get caught."

Lancelot cried. "I can't believe you're saying this to me. Have I done something wrong?"

Guinevere shushed her lover. "It's just that things have changed since the war ended. I'm not the same person. You're not the same person. Arturus is still himself, a man on a slow decline, like the climate. Something's going to happen, something big, and I need to be ready for it."

Dee thought back to Mordred. If anyone had made a threat, he had, when he said Arturus should resign.

"Wait a minute," Lancelot said. "Are you telling me to go away?"

Guinevere took the dame knight's hands. "My dear Lancelot, I will be your friend forever. But I think it's time we go our separate ways, as lovers, I mean."

Lancelot withdrew her hands from Guinevere's, looking at her fingers as if they'd been held over a flame. Dee had never seen Lancelot grow pale with fear, even in the cool light of a security lamp. Dee had endured her share of breakups, but the love between Lancelot and Guinevere was legendary. Perhaps it wasn't as strong as people believed. Maybe it was just like any other relationship, only as strong as the least-committed partner. Was Dee really witnessing its end? Or was this just a fight between two tired, stressed individuals who truly adored one another?

"You can't do this to me, Guinevere. I've done nothing but love you and fight for you. What did I think about before going into battle? You, always you. Arturus was my leader, but you were my inspiration. I killed for you."

Guinevere winced. "I wish you would leave me now. The thought that you killed other people, even the enemies of Viridiae, for my sake, disgusts me."

The white light of the overhead lamp reflected off Lancelot's tears. Guinevere also cried, but she held her head up, underlining her determination to end the relationship with the dame knight. Dee's own heart broke. She felt for both of these women who cared for each other. For the queen, though, the politics of the moment didn't have space for an illicit affair, no matter how many people knew about it or tolerated it.

Guinevere had sent her lover away, and who would want to answer a call from someone who had caused so much pain? She imagined the call to Lancelot was as painful for Guinevere, perhaps even more so, because she needed Lancelot, but not in the way Lancelot wanted. It was a difficult moment.

"Perhaps you should go see her, in person, my lady. She couldn't refuse you a welcome. Hospitality would demand it. You are the queen of Viridiae after all."

Guinevere thought a moment. "Would you go with me, Dee? Just you and me? We don't have time to assemble a train, security, and all the rest."

"But we're at war, ma'am. If something should happen, I can't defend you."

"We'll take the chance."

CHAPTER 6: AN UNWANTED REQUEST

Dee had pulled out her traveling bag when Lina knocked on her door.

"Where have you been?" Dee said.

"To see Percival."

Dee stopped stuffing a sweater into the bag. She remembered that her brother had invited Lina to see him while the expedition was at Sir Galahad's estate. Lina didn't strike Dee as the type to drop everything and go on a trip. Dee promised herself to contact Percival as soon as she had the chance for a full report.

"You must be serious about him."

"I think so. What did I miss?" Lina glanced at the bag.

Dee brought Lina up to speed on the skirmish between Lothian and Viridian troops. Guinevere thought Viridiae needed Lancelot's presence. "Guinevere thinks she can persuade Lancelot away from Joyous Gard."

"What do you think?"

"Can loyalty to a flag and country overcome a lover's quarrel?" Dee shrugged. "We'll find out."

"Do you need any help?"

"With packing? Sure." Dee pointed to her dresser.

Lina gathered a few things. With Dee's approval, she put them in the travel bag.

"The expedition is leaving tomorrow from Galahad's lands for Ash. It's a small border town. The border police believe its safe now to travel to Aurelia."

Dee would not have used the word "safe" when traveling beyond Viridiae's borders. She remembered the encounters with a basilisk and hostile Lucians during the embassy to Villefroide. But Dee didn't want to upset Lina, who had fallen for her brother. Though she hadn't talked to him about the affair, she guessed he felt much the same way.

Dee zipped her bag. "There. All ready."

"You're leaving right away? It's going to be dark soon."

"Guinevere's anxious to go. Something wrong?"

Lina sat on the edge of the bed. She fussed with her hands, as if she had trouble forming the words. "I talked with Percival last night. About a lot of things."

"More than pillow talk, I take it."

"You know about my brother, Kenric, right? He has this blood disease."

Dee already knew where Lina was going. Percival had told Lina about her unique genetics.

"He didn't know the details, but he said you might know more. You see, my family's been looking for a donor for years."

"And you think I might qualify?"

"I don't know, but I have to ask. Can you tell me what you know?"

Dee sighed. "Sometimes I hate the Old Civilization."

"I'm sorry if I brought up something you don't like to talk about."

"You're fine, Lina. Really." Dee bit her lip. "A few months ago, I was having these headaches, and I went to Guinevere's sage-physician. She's the best in the country. It turns out that it was just stress, but she did some blood tests just to be sure."

"She found something."

"Um-hmm. Manipulated DNA."

"You're not a troll, are you?"

Dee laughed. "Hell, no. Guinevere's doctor found modified DNA in my genome that might explain certain, um, abilities I have. I can see future likelihoods. And I can manipulate nature if I'm riled up."

Lina looked askance at Dee, as if she suspected a lie.

"I know it sounds crazy, but trust me on this." Dee thought of the lightning bolt she conjured that killed her father, Sir Adnan de Grosse, near the Lake of Souls. Her genome gave her unique power, but it caused her trouble. On the other hand, she never thought she might have the power to heal a young boy.

"What does this have to do with Kenric?"

"Ken has a genetic disease, one of the few that the ancient scientists didn't stamp out. Ken is dying, Lina. I can see it."

Tears well up in Lina's eyes. Dee didn't want to hurt Lina, but she felt that revealing what she knew now might make things easier down the road.

"There's more to it, Lina." Dee's eyes fell to her lap. "After hearing you talking about Kenric's disease to Guinevere, I went back and looked at the test results. Here, I'll show them to you."

"You don't have to. They're private."

Dee touched keys on her tablet, which downloaded the document from her medical record. She found the relevant page and handed the tablet to Lina.

Lina looked up at Dee in shock. "I know what this means. I'm not a doctor, but I know as much about this disease as any sage-physician. Our family hardly talks about anything else. Dee, your body creates a protein that Ken's body cannot and that can't be synthesized."

"That's pretty much what I thought."

"Dee, I'm coming to you as a friend who's also a sister with a brother. One day soon, Kenric's going to have a medical crisis, and I might ask you for help."

"There's a problem, Lina. If I try to save his life, I might die."

To save Ken's life, Dee might have to give up her own. It wasn't a straight trade, her life for his, but she might not survive a procedure to help Kenric.

Lina's look told Dee she grasped her dilemma. "I didn't know that part. I couldn't ask for that."

"I hope you don't have to, but I can't say for sure whether I'd say yes if you do. I'm sorry."

CHAPTER 7: FINDING LANCELOT

Dee and Guinevere's ride to Joyous Gard, Lancelot's estate, was a half-day from Camelot, but Guinevere's desire to travel incognito added another half-day as they avoided the direct route. The journey took them through a countryside still distressed by the aftermath of the Lucian war. The road went through some of the most contested land, past burned-out farmsteads and small towns with few businesses and fewer people to patronize them. Another war would be a death-blow to some of the communities, if the battling armies came through again.

Layered underneath the scars of battle was the slow decay of the climate, no longer under control by the Great Machine and its missing Grail device. Everywhere, Dee saw evidence of stunted plants and dying trees. The carcass of a deer lay in a ditch. The effects of the climate's deterioration were uneven; some regions of Viridiae had experienced little change, but the sage-scientists who tracked the decline found evidence that even the healthier areas had not escaped at least small changes. Sooner or later, if the Great Machine was not repaired, the entire country would feel the pain. A civil war did nothing to help matters.

The two women approached the stone gate to Joyous Gard on their horses. The queen let out a sigh of dismay.

"Lancelot may be a warrior first, but she was proud of her property. Last time I visited, everything was immaculate, down to the height of the grass."

The grass had grown to ankle height, not the trim shortness

of many lawns around Camelot. Dandelions and other weeds marred the lawn like a teenager's acne. Dee pushed open the iron door, which squeaked as if it hadn't been oiled in years. Passing under the arch festooned with Lancelot's coat of arms, the portico of the main house looked drab, even tumbledown.

Dee dismounted and knocked on the door. Her com showed no welcoming message nor instructions if no one was home. After a moment, an elderly man, stooped over but shaven and well-groomed, opened the door.

"Good evening, sir. I am Miss Dindrane Rathkeale, and this is Guinevere, wife to our lord king, Arturus."

The man bent up as far as he could to see the beautiful woman on a destrier. His eyes went wide as apples. He took a breath. "Your Majesty! I had no idea... I wasn't expecting..."

"It's alright, Marsdon. I didn't tell your mistress I was coming. We're here on an urgent matter. Is Dame Lancelot available?"

The old butler's face fell, but he collected himself. "You look tired and dusty. I can have rooms and a meal ready in a few minutes. The food will be cold, I'm afraid. The groom is... not available just now. You can tie your horses on the post, there." He pointed to a pillar.

Guinevere dismounted and the visitors followed the old man's instruction.

The foyer was large, but simply furnished. Paintings of ancestors lined one of the walls, while empty suits of armor guarded a large door to a sitting room. The air was musty and the light poor. Several of the light globes were burnt out.

"If you'll excuse me, ma'am. I'll see to your usual room. Your servant will have the room next door."

Dee realized that Guinevere and Marsdon must know each other because of Lancelot and Guinevere's long history as secret lovers.

"Marsdon, before you leave us," Guinevere said, gently, "is Lancelot here?"

The butler rested his hand on the back of a velvet-covered chair. "I'm sorry, ma'am, she's not."

"Do you know where she is?"

Marsdon shook his head. "I do not." Dee perceived tears forming in his rheumy eyes.

"Please, sir, sit and tell us," Guinevere said.

"Thank you, ma'am, but I prefer to stand in your presence. I'm rather old-fashioned, you see." He cleared his throat. "As to Mistress Lancelot, she's been gone these past weeks. She came home one evening as distraught as I've ever seen her. Within an hour, she'd departed the house. She instructed myself and the other servants not to look for her. I haven't seen her since, though I believe she's nearby."

"How do you know?"

"She left her favorite horse in the stable, as well as all her other horses."

"Did she take anything else?" Dee said. "A backpack, maybe?"

"Only Arondight, her war blade. She goes nowhere without it."

Guinevere said, "Do you have any idea where she might have gone?"

"No, ma'am, thought it's possible she went to a run-down cabin on the edge of the estate. She used to go there as a child, but it's been abandoned for many years."

"What about you, sir?" Dee said. "Is anyone else here?"

"Everyone was so frightened by the mistress's behavior, they ran off within a few days of her disappearance. I'm the only one here, hoping that she'll come back soon. I keep a pot of soup on the stove, and fresh linens on her bed." He perked up as he said this, expressing his hope for Lancelot's return.

"It's nearly dark, too late to start a search," Guinevere said. "Dee, let's not impose on Marsdon's hospitality too much. A little soup, perhaps some bread, and we'll sleep. We'll ride to the old cabin in the morning."

* * *

Dee rose at first light, enjoying the morning birdsong coming from the woodland a few meters from her window. She marveled at the lush green of the hills surrounding Lancelot's estate, which reminded her of the land near her mother's cottage on the edge of the King's Forest. She looked forward to exploring the land surrounding the manor house.

Dressing in tough riding pants and a jacket borrowed from Lancelot's closet, she joined Guinevere in the kitchen, who was already sipping coffee.

"I wondered where you were," the queen said. "We don't have much time to waste."

"The bed was wonderfully warm and comfortable. Thank you, Marsdon."

The old man grinned and laid a bowl of oatmeal in front of Dee. "The boiled eggs are fresh, as is the cream."

The tangy taste of fresh orange juice again reminded Dee of home. She hadn't spoken to Eleanor, her mother, for weeks. She wondered if she knew about Percival's new expedition, or about his new love, Lina. She vowed to call her as soon as she returned to Camelot.

Thoughts of the crisis raised a new fear. Dee's project in the Great Audience Hall was sponsored by Lord Mordred. What would happen to it, and to her, now that he was rebelling against the king and the government? She pushed it out of her mind for another time. She couldn't do anything about the problem now.

Dee helped Marsdon with the dishes while Guinevere saw to their horses. She borrowed two of Lancelot's riding horses. She decided to bring along a third, in case they encountered the dame knight on the road, and she was fit to ride. Marsdon found a small tent and camping gear for a stay in the woods overnight.

Soon Dee and Guinevere's horses clopped on worn concrete. Marsdon had given them a map, which showed the old road to the cabin. Within a mile, pavement turned into loose gravel with a hump of overgrown weeds in its center like a backbone. The long branches of fir and hemlock trees arced over them, at once embracing them and almost suffocating them with their dense fragrance.

As the sun reached its zenith, Dee spotted a dilapidated, one-story building. The women picked up their walking pace, but when they reached the structure, they found no one. Guinevere called out Lancelot's name twice, but the forest absorbed the sound like a sponge, and they heard no response. Dee circled the cabin, looking for any indication of recent habitation or visit.

"My lady, come see. I've found something."

Guinevere rushed over.

"This blanket hasn't been here very long. And here's some food packages. Could it be Lancelot?"

"Or bandits. Or a troll."

Dee stiffened. She hadn't thought much about trolls on the journey. People said they were everywhere normal humans weren't, but she'd never seen one in person.

"You didn't think to bring a weapon, did you, Dee?"

Dee gulped. "No, ma'am."

"Not to worry." Guinevere showed Dee the dagger slipped into her boot. "I know how to use it."

"What do we do now?"

"Lancelot is nearby. She might have seen us and hidden herself."

"If she wanted to be found, she'd show herself, don't you think? From the behavior Marsdon described, I'm not sure Lancelot is, um, stable."

Guinevere considered. "Maybe so, but I'm not stopping now." She turned on her heel and took her horse's reins. Dee jumped after her as Guinevere led the way further up the road, which quickly deteriorated into an almost invisible trail.

All the while, Guinevere called out "Lancelot! Lancelot! I want to talk to you!" The sound of her voice made Dee wary, as if Guinevere implored a supernatural being to materialize in front of her.

The trail ended at a wall of bramble and large stones. The nervous horses swiveled their ears at every rustle in the grass or call of a forest bird. Slivers of sunlight penetrated the deep green, alighting on tiny purple flowers. Dee wished she'd brought sketching materials.

"Let's eat something." Guinevere leaned on one of the moss-covered rocks. "I'm ready for a nap, too."

Dee picked up the horse's anxiety, and as she broke off a chunk of bread and laid a slice of cheese on it, she couldn't imagine closing her eyes in such a weird environment.

"Do you still believe Lancelot is nearby, my lady?"

"Well, she hasn't made herself easy to find. I have trouble imagining where else she would go. This is her property. She'd feel safest here, but finding her might be harder than I thought."

The meal worked its will on Dee, and she dozed in a warm shaft of sunlight. A horse's whinny startled her awake. Dee felt the hairs on her arm lift.

"We need to get back," Guinevere said. "I really don't want to camp out tonight."

"No argument from me, my lady."

The trolls appeared from behind an ancient tree and a clump of rocks. One grabbed Dee and held her tight. He put his hand on her mouth, and she could feel his scaly skin. She nearly retched at his sweaty smell. Dee tried to scream for help, but the troll's grip was tight.

The other troll had less luck with Guinevere. She twisted away and unsheathed her dagger. Dee had never seen a troll before, except in pictures. The one facing Guinevere was young and muscular with eyes the color of dirty coal. He wore almost nothing. He grinned, as if certain he could best the queen if he was patient enough.

"Touch me and I'll kill you and your friend," Guinevere said.

"An empty threat. I could snap you like a twig."

"What do you want?"

"What trolls always want. Food, clothing, medicine."

Dee felt the older troll tighten his grip around her waist and shoulders. He said nothing, but his breathing was harsh and intense. He was frightened as well.

"We have some camping gear and food. They're on the pack horses, which you managed to scare off."

"We'll find them. But first, we have to take care of you."

The younger troll lunged at Guinevere, and she stepped aside. Her foot landed on a root and she slipped. Her opponent grabbed her wrist, and she yelped in pain. She dropped her dagger and the troll pulled her toward him, grasping her from behind like the older troll did Dee.

Dee's breath caught. She was certain death was moments away.

A flash. An odd muffled sound, like a object dropped on a thick carpet. An object rolled in front of Dee. It was the head of the troll who held Guinevere.

Dee vomited, and her troll let go. It ran into the thicket, but something metal flew at the troll, piercing its back. It dropped to the ground without a sound. A human form, tall with hair flying, dove into the thicket. Dee saw the person pull the sword from the troll's back and disappear. In Gaia's name, was that Lancelot?

"Dee."

Guinevere's voice brought Dee around. The queen was on her knees, her hair and back covered in blood. The headless corpse of the troll was sprawled before her.

"Lancelot," Guinevere said. "She's here."

"She ran away. I saw it." With a napkin left from lunch, Dee wiped blood from Guinevere's face and neck.

"She's watching us. I know it."

Dee had nothing to clean the vomit off her chin. She used her sleeve, hoping Lancelot would forgive her, if they ever spoke.

"What do we do?"

"I think she'll come, if we wait."

They sat for an hour, hoping for a sign from the dame knight, but they saw and heard nothing. Flies gathered around the severed neck and head of the troll, its mouth agape and eyes rolled up. One of the women's horses made its way back, and Dee found more napkins and a small hand towel. The two cleaned themselves as best they could. Together, they dragged the corpse into the thicket. Dee used a long stick to push the disgusting fly-blown head behind a tree. She didn't want to check on the other troll. The stink of death glued her to Guinevere's side.

Darkness descended on the women, and Guinevere decided they had to stay. She still believed Lancelot was near, and traveling at night was too dangerous. Trolls were solitary, more or less, but they sometimes cooperated in small groups. Lancelot might not stick around to protect Dee and Guinevere.

They pitched the tent, but slept fitfully. Dee dreamed of Percival, but he was angry and upset. Dee couldn't perceive why. When she awoke, her heart pounded.

The women rose with the first inkling of light and bird song. Guinevere set up the battery-powered stove and warmed water for coffee. Dee made breakfast with the oatmeal provided by Marsdon. Sunlight on the highest leaves of the trees signaled the sunrise, and Dee helped pack up.

Guinevere studied the forest around their campsite. Their eyes could only penetrate a few meters into the brush. She worried out loud that the troll's bodies would probably attract scavengers.

"I thought Lancelot was near and might even show herself," Guinevere said. "Maybe I was wrong."

"You tried to reach out to her." Dee resisted the urge to comfort Guinevere with a touch. But she was the queen, and her person was inviolate. "She doesn't want to talk."

"She could've done nothing and let the trolls rob us or kill us. But she saved us. Why?"

"She's a knight, sworn to serve Arturus and you. She believes in the old values of protecting the helpless. Maybe that's why."

On foot, Guinevere led her horse down the path toward the ruins of the cabin. She could've ridden her horse, but she wanted to linger. They walked for a kilometer or so when Guinevere stopped.

"What is it, my lady?" Dee said.

"Lancelot."

Ten meters ahead, illuminated by a shaft of sunlight, the most famous knight in Viridiae blocked the way. She looked as if she had left civilization behind. Bits of grass and dead leaves snagged her hair, which cascaded down her shoulders and breasts. Her clothing was torn and dirty. Her feet were bare, and she wore no gloves, despite the gleam of Arondight in her right hand. Her face expressed the emotions of a witness to a horrible crime, disbelieving, disgusted, and frightened. She was too far away for Dee to see her eyes clearly, but she believed they brimmed with tears, whether of joy or fury, Dee couldn't imagine.

Had Lancelot lost her sanity? Why did she appear like this, resembling a wraith, rather than a human? Was this what grief did to a person, who had loved someone so deeply that the end of it made you completely crazy? Dee glanced at Guinevere, whose emotions fought their own battle behind her stoic mask. Her jaw muscles and pursed lips worked to hold in her feelings.

"I knew you stayed near." Guinevere spoke to her former lover.

"I did so more for Dee, than for you."

Dee's face flushed. Lancelot wanted to protect her.

"Do you hate me so much?" the queen said.

"Not so much that I'd want you to die at the hands of vermin. They were trespassing on my land, in any case."

"But you hate me, Lancelot."

"If you say so. It doesn't matter. I want you to leave my property."

Guinevere handed her horse's reigns to Dee and took a step forward.

"No further." Lancelot seemed to lean back, as if fearful, but she didn't take a step to avoid Guinevere. "I asked you to leave."

"What's happened to you?"

"I'm not interested in this world, your world, any more. I've always loved the forests around my house. I feel more at home here than anywhere else now. I can thank you for that." If there was bitterness in Lancelot's voice, Dee didn't detect it.

"The world needs you, Lancelot."

"No, it does not. You rejected me. If you needed me, you wouldn't have sent me away. All you care about is yourself."

The conversation became painful for Dee to hear. It was a replay of the spat after Mordred's threat to Arturus. Dee didn't want to take sides.

"I didn't come here for myself. I came here for Arturus."

"I don't care about Arturus."

"I came here for Camelot and Viridiae."

"I don't care about those either. They're empty dreams."

"Arturus and Camelot need you. Mordred has made his move. He's gathering an army. There's already been fighting on the Lothian border."

Lancelot didn't respond, but Dee sensed she was thinking. "There's nothing I can do about it. That's your world now, not mine."

"Arturus was your best friend. I hurt you, but he hasn't. He needs his best warrior. Without you, Camelot will fall, and who knows what will happen to Viridiae after that."

Lancelot let the tip of her sword fall to the ground. "It won't touch me here. I might even be dead by then. You can survive on roots and grubs only so long, but I don't care. Life in your world is nothing but hell. In the forest, I'm someone else, completely free. No love, but no burdens. Only myself."

"You would abandon your friends so easily? Arturus, Bors, Galahad, even Percival?"

At her brother's mention, Dee's heart skipped. She didn't dare speak, but even if she didn't want to get involved in the women's love affair, she felt that Lancelot had to help her country and save her friends.

"Shut up, Guinevere. You know nothing of friendship. You abandoned me like a sick dog."

The hurtful accusation hit Guinevere like an arrow. She struggled to contain her frustration and her tears. Dee wanted desperately to leave for the manor house.

"I'll ask you once more, Dame Lancelot du Lac. Come with me. Fight with Arturus to save Viridiae."

Lancelot shook her head. "I'm my own country now." The proud warrior backed away into a shadow. Dee blinked, and the knight was gone.

"Lancelot!" Guinevere called, but no response came. That's when Guinevere's tears fell.

"My lady, Lancelot is gone. I don't think she's coming back. It's time to leave."

Guinevere sniffed and brushed away her tears. Lancelot was lost to her and to Viridiae. Dee gathered the horses' reigns and with Guinevere's hand in hers, started down the path.

CHAPTER 8: A DECISION TO CROSS

A slow drizzle welcomed Percival and his expedition to the village of Ash, a few kilometers from the border with the Hot Lands. He wanted the latest intelligence on the journey ahead, and Merlin had promised to meet him with the newest information about the Grail. With his companions beside him, Percival eyed the storefronts of the one main street, which included a market, an implements store serving the local farmers, and a public house. He was looking for the office of the Viridian Border Service.

His mind wandered, as it had throughout the journey from Sir Galahad's estate. Each step of his horse, each droplet of rain on the brim of his rain hat, brought him back to Lina, and a fantasy. He missed her voice, the downy softness of her cheeks, her penetrating gaze that unpeeled the layers of his soul. For the first time in his years as a knight of the Round Table, he had found something more important than discovering and returning the Grail.

What if he dropped all this questing? What if he put Galahad in charge and rode back to Camelot straight for Lina? He could resign his Round Table commission and slough off his responsibility like a wildcat sheds its winter coat. Other knights had given up their sword and armor for a woman. What if he took Lina to some empty castle in the Range of Needles? He knew of one or two. No one would bother them.

With Lina to help him build a different life, he could forget a lot of other things that woke him at night. He could set aside the memories of starving soldiers on the death march to Transietum. He could blot out the face of Adrian Dardarius as he slipped the Lucian's gladius into his heart. He could hide his shame at his failure to fight during the Battle of River's Bend. Everything seemed so pointless, now that Lina filled up the empty spaces in his heart.

But quitting was impossible. It would mean giving up his chance at redemption in Arturus' eyes, as well as the country's. He was certain Lina was disapprove.

And then there was Dee. And Lancelot. And Guinevere. And Bors. His mother. And all the other people who loved him.

He shook his head at the thought of forsaking his mission. He wasn't quite ready yet to give up everything for Lina, but he was tempted. How long could he resist?

A sodden Galahad pointed out the Border Service office next to a diner. Suddenly hungry, Percival invited everyone out for lunch. He didn't know when they might eat a home-cooked meal again. The family-run restaurant had a warm fire and cold beer.

After eating, Percival and Galahad left Penny and the retainers at the diner. They sought out a commander named Gereon at the Border Service office. An affable man, his khaki uniform was pressed and trim, and he looked as though he kept himself in good physical shape. He had a hint of gray on his temples.

"Ash has become more popular with Round Table knights over the past few years," Gereon said, shaking Percival and Galahad's hands. "We saw Sir Galahad during the war on his way to cause trouble for the Lucians in the south. How is Sir Bors?"

"Thank you again for your escort to the border, Captain Gereon," Galahad said. "Sir Bors is back on his farm, which is doing well, I'm told."

Gereon turned to Percival. "I've studied your plans, Sir Percival. I have a short presentation prepared for you."

The officer showed them to a conference room. "Before we get started, may I ask about His Majesty? How is he?" Gereon showed sincere concern.

"We met with him on the day of our departure from Camelot. He's doing well."

"I hope you'll find a way to relay our regards," Gereon said. "We feel a little, well, lonely out here. Except for the visit by Sir Bors and Sir Galahad, the war barely touched us, but we had to guard this part of the country nonetheless."

Percival sympathized. Virtually all the major actions happened far to the east. "I'll tell him that we were warmly welcomed and suggest he visit on his next royal progress around the country."

A younger guardsmen brought in filtered water and coffee. Gereon grinned as he poured himself a cup of the hot liquid. "By virtue of my position, the locals look to me for a certain amount of leadership, even though there's an elected council and a few other government officials. There wasn't any fighting around here, but the economy has suffered, and then there's the climate." Gereon's voice trailed off.

Percival accepted a cup. "That's what we're hoping to fix, assuming we find the Grail, Captain Gereon."

Gereon looked mildly embarrassed at his role of local promoter. "You probably want to get to business. Take a look at the documents in these tablets."

Percival and Galahad swiped through the first few.

"They're patrol reports from the last three months. My department keeps an eye on the border from here to the Peaceful Sea. It's a long border through a mountainous region."

"The area has a reputation for illegal crossings and smuggling," Galahad said.

Gereon blanched. "We do the best with what we have, sir."

Percival reassured the commander. "I think Galahad means that you have a difficult job with a border as porous as cheesecloth."

"We have occasional good luck on our patrols. A few weeks ago, we stopped smugglers transporting illegal coal."

"I remember the reports on the news chans in Camelot." Percival said. "Congratulations, Captain. Now, about our route?"

"You'll see a report by a detachment of the King's Regarders, which has a small base about a kilometer outside of town. The

Border Service tries to stay on our side of the frontier, but they have fewer, um, qualms about going further afield."

Percival tensed. The Regarders reported to Gawain, Mordred's brother, and they were Lothian partisans by and large, except for a few old-timers, such as Sir Bors.

"I'm not surprised," Galahad said. "Bors is a semi-retired Regarder, and he has a lot more freedom to enforce the king's environmental edicts than most ordinary officers."

Percival remembered his long-ago visit to Bors' farm and the story of his hunt for trolls selling illegal bush meat.

"Our people and the Regarders share information. We're hearing about increased banditry along the route you're planning to take to Aurelia. Some of the information helped us locate the coal smugglers, so we're pretty confident about it."

A map of the region was tacked to the conference room wall. Percival stood, went to it, and followed his planned route with his finger. "This is the main road to Aurelia. Are you saying we should avoid this route?"

"On the contrary, you should stick to it. There are two or three other routes, but they're not used much, and you'd be vulnerable. But the war has cut into the number of travelers, and it hasn't really picked up since the war ended. Before the war, you could count on safety in numbers. Now, that strategy isn't as reliable."

"So the bandits are hungrier," Galahad said.

"Literally and figuratively," Gereon said. "The region between our border and cities like Aurelia is sparsely populated, and a lot of people live off the land. A few of them think pilgrims and other travelers are just another resource to exploit."

"What about local police forces?" Percival said.

Gereon chuckled. "I'd say that part of the Hot Lands is about as lawless as you'd find between here and the Aztec Republic, with the exception of Aurelia and a few other places on the coast."

"Cassanti?" Percival wondered about their destination.

Gereon shrugged. "I've heard the name, but I know almost nothing about that area. It's pretty far away, correct?"

Percival expected the journey to take several weeks. "So you're saying, Captain Gereon, that we're taking a big risk, that we're likely to run into trouble."

"I'm saying, respectfully, that I understand your need to start your journey after the delay at Sir Galahad's estate. But you might pause for a little while longer, to see if any more information turns up. Frankly, sir, your trip has been trumpeted everywhere. Bandits might even be waiting for you."

"Galahad?"

Galahad leaned back in his chair. "We're pretty good at taking care of ourselves, Captain. Bandits aren't known for fighting prowess."

Percival agreed, but he kept thinking about Penny, and why Galahad insisted on bringing her along. She was less of a liability than he'd feared. At their camps along the way, she'd shown that she didn't mind putting in a day's work, putting up tents, washing dishes, even filling in latrines. She apparently knew how lucky she'd been to have Galahad as a sponsor. But bandits might still see her as a target.

Percival was also concerned about the expedition's retainers, Roz Goodread and Ben Playa, both seniors at the Keep. Percival hired them to manage the animals and the gear. They'd had military training, and both knew how to handle swords and pistols, but neither had seen any action. He was uncertain about their performance in a fight.

He'd think about a delay.

After a knock on the door, the young guardsman announced the arrival of Professor Merlin Ambrosius. The elder came in stiffly, as if he'd injured himself. Nonetheless, he greeted Percival warmly. They'd shared a harrowing journey across a desert after escaping Lucana. Percival still felt pangs of guilt at his loss of the Viridian Grail in the canyon, but Merlin never showed or expressed anger over it.

"Merlin, you don't look well."

"I was fine until I got to my hotel last night. The bed had lumps the size of mountains. I'd have slept better on a bed of nails. I'm a hundred years old, for Gaia's sake. Is that coffee?"

Gereon poured Merlin a cup while Percival introduced the sage-scientist.

"Your colleagues at the Great Machine compound come down to Ash occasionally, Professor, but I don't see you down here very much," Gereon said.

"I'm not a terribly social person, and right now, I'd rather be in the bowels of Apparatus Montis. Percival, you heard about the incident with the questing beast in Camelot?"

"During our stop at Galahad's estate, yes."

"Arturus didn't blame me, but a lot of people on the street did. Ignoramuses. Don't they understand what I achieved? It's not my fault Morgause abused my work to go after Arturus."

"Was that what the investigation found?"

"I don't know. I left for Apparatus Montis as soon as I could. But that's what I think." Merlin sipped the coffee. "Delicious."

Galahad said, "How goes the research, Professor? I had to stop most of my inquiries because of the war."

"Your work on the False Grail, Galahad, has helped me tremendously. Despite the fact that it was only for show, it contained valuable clues. In fact, it led me to Cassanti. I think it was manufactured there."

"So you think Cassanti might be the location of another working Grail?"

Merlin nodded. "I'm more convinced of it every day. My colleagues and I at the Great Machine are peeling back the layers of time. Here's an example. We found a relatively recent document that claimed the Cassanti Grail was located 'in a castle floating on the sea.'"

"What do you suppose that could mean?" Percival said.

"Some kind of ship or boat, obviously. The castle part is what's puzzling." Merlin rubbed his chin in thought. "Some of the other clues we've turned up are more cryptic. One speaks of a woman encased in gold."

"Perhaps wearing some sort of costume or head dress?" Galahad suggested.

"Or it might be a statue or a painting. It's not clear." Merlin cleared his throat. "Here's another one: A cup overflowing with healing blood. What do you make of that?"

Percival had no idea. "Wine?"

"Your guess is as good as mine, gentlemen. Here's the strangest clue. It was in a travel diary written more than two centuries ago by a Perditon trader. He wrote, 'A question that must be spoken before the Grail can be touched.'" Merlin shrugged.

"What question?" Percival said.

"'Whom does the Grail serve?'"

"And the answer?"

"That is unclear, my dear Percival. But the diary is adamant that no one can handle the Grail unless they speak the question and the answer, whatever that is."

Percival folded his arms. "Are you sure these clues are reliable? You said the diary was two hundred years old."

"I can't be sure of anything, my boy. That's the nature of this kind of research. No Viridian has been to Cassanti since before the civil wars. No Viridian really cared about it that much until I started my research to fix the Great Machine."

"We're gambling on fragments," Percival said, "like picking up tiny shards of glass and hoping to reconstruct a chandelier."

Merlin refilled his coffee. "Believe it or not, this is the best evidence I've ever seen. We sent you and Sir Kevin looking for a Grail on far less evidence."

Percival was the only survivor of that expedition, which turned out to be a wild goose chase set in motion by Gawain and Morgause.

"Here, Percival and Galahad, I've put together my latest research on a tablet for you." Merlin removed it from a shoulderbag. "I'm anxious to get back to Apparatus Montis. I'm on a project to ensure that when Percival brings back the Grail, we can install it within a day."

Percival huffed. "You sound way too confident, Merlin. The chances I'll come back with nothing are pretty good."

"I disagree, my friend. I'm not a superstitious man, but I'm convinced you are meant to find it. It's just a matter of time and effort."

The young guardsman showed Merlin out after a quick good-bye. Percival and Galahad spent the next hour going over travel logistics with Gereon. Meeting up with Penny, Roz and Ben, they arranged a campsite at a park on the edge of town. The weather had dried out, and the next day promised warm sunshine. The discussed their options and the reports of bandits. Percival wanted them to know what they faced. Twenty-four hours later, the decision made, they crossed the Viridian border into the Hot Lands.

CHAPTER 9:
CAMELIARD TAKEN

A messenger met Dee and Guinevere at Joyous Gard after their failed attempt to recruit Lancelot to Arturus' cause. The messenger begged Guinevere to accompany him to Cameliard instead of returning to Camelot. Dee and the queen had only a few minutes to bathe, change and tell Marsdon that Lancelot was alive before the messenger, called Dustin, urged them to the public car.

"Start over, Dustin, from the beginning," Guinevere said.

Dee listened closely to the young man dressed in the casual livery of the Cameliard ruling family. Guinevere was head of the family.

"Two days ago, the ducal police reported a large military force massing at a checkpoint on the border with Lothia. The Lothians crossed the border within hours and headed for Cameliard City, my lady."

"How many knights and men-at-arms?"

"The police could only provide an estimate. They ran for their lives."

"How many knights, Dustin?" Guinevere's face, already pained by the encounter with Lancelot, was stretched taut with worry.

"At least a thousand, maybe more, not counting support troops and vehicles."

"You're sure they're Lothian?"

Dee couldn't imagine what else they might be.

"Yes, ma'am. Here's the photos." Dustin opened his com and swiped through a half-dozen pictures. The flags and armor design confirmed their origin: Mordred's duchy.

"Where are they now?"

Dustin swallowed. "In Cameliard City. And they've taken the citadel."

Guinevere was incredulous. "In less than 48 hours?"

"The city garrison was taken completely by surprise. They surrendered immediately. The household guard tried to organize a resistance, but the commander stopped the fighting as soon as she saw the overwhelming Lothian numbers. A few dozen men-at-arms and knights managed to escape."

"Do you know who's commanding the Lothians?"

"That's not clear, ma'am. Their communications are vague. They didn't bother asking for terms. They marched into the citadel as if they'd owned it."

"Who sent you?"

"The household guard commander. She escaped as well. I would've found you sooner, but I went to Camelot first, and your staff directed me to Joyous Gard. I drove as fast as I could."

Dee digested the news. Lothia had invaded Cameliard, something that hadn't happened since the civil wars. What did this mean for Mordred's ambitions on Camelot?

Guinevere peppered Dustin with more questions, but apart from the general circumstances, he knew few details. One piece of good news: The invaders hadn't touched the city or its residents.

The drive to Camelot's border with Cameliard took three hours. Using Guinevere's more powerful com reader, Dee tried to gather as much information as she could via the com links, but signals were weak or non-existent in the mountains. Guinevere told her not to send messages or make calls on the chance that Lothian intelligence was intercepting communications. Guinevere's com had special encryption features, but the lack of a signal plagued Dee's efforts.

The modern towers of Cameliard's commercial district came into view, with the ancient citadel off to the east. After the car rounded a curve, Dee spotted a group of men-at-arms arranged on either side of the road. A makeshift gate—a pole laid over a pair of recycling bins—blocked the car's way.

"Checkpoint," Dustin said.

"Efficiency." Guinevere said. "That's something you can always count on with Lothians."

Dustin slowed the car and rolled down the window. A man with the Lothian crest on his tunic and a single-shot pistol in his belt peered in the car. Another soldier approached the car's opposite side. Other watchful soldiers holding pila and wearing pistols and swords stationed themselves further away. An officer oversaw the action.

Dee's hands were sweating. Months ago, at the last checkpoint where she ran into trouble—with Guinevere at the Lucian border with Ontari:io—Lancelot nearly died in a skirmish. The Lucians wore different uniforms, but they were as arrogant and pompous-looking as the Lothians. The only other difference between the Lucians and the Lothians was that the latter were her countrymen, rebelling against Arturus and the Round Table. They were following the orders of higher authority, as soldiers are trained to do, but she wanted to ask them why they didn't disobey or desert. What they were doing was clearly illegal. She'd have to ask Percival to explain their behavior.

"Papers," the first soldier said.

Dee, Guinevere, and Dustin held out their com rings, which the soldier scanned. His eyes flicked to Guinevere, but he betrayed nothing.

"Stay put," the soldier said. He showed his com reader to the officer, a graying man in his 40s. The officer approached the public car's open window.

The officer flicked his eyes from the com screen to Guinevere and back. "My lady, this says you are Guinevere Cameliard. Is that accurate?"

"Of course, it is. Are you accusing me of carrying false papers?"

"You are the wife of King Arturus?"

"Yes, major. Get to the point."

The officer straightened, stepped a few paces back, and waved to a group of men-at-arms standing near a vehicle. Instantly, they climbed in and the vehicle moved into position in front of Dustin's car.

"You are expected, madam. The car ahead of you will escort you to the citadel in Cameliard City. Do not attempt to escape. My men are under strict orders to use deadly force without mercy. Understood?"

Dee heard Mordred's Lothian accent in the officer's voice.

"We don't need your threats." Guinevere looked away. "However, we will follow your instructions."

Dustin edged the car forward, and the escort led the visitors from Camelot into the outskirts of Cameliard.

Guinevere reached out to Dee's hand and squeezed it.

* * *

Cameliard's streets were empty. The Lothians broadcast a decree shortly after their takeover, Dustin said, forbidding anyone on the streets for three days. The people had no time to react. Dee saw bread in the windows of bakeries, crows pilfering noodles on a street cart, and a half-mown lawn in a park, the mowing bot lonely in its isolation on the grass. The public com channels were empty of the usual chatter. The Lothians had shuttered those as well.

"I've never seen my city like this before." Guinevere took in the quiet streets from her window. "The Lothians have completely locked it down."

The escort car approached the citadel gate, which opened, allowing the two cars to pass through without stopping. The escort crossed a small square to a portico and stopped. Dustin came to a stop a few meters back. Lothian men-at-arms scrambled out of the vehicle and took up positions around Guinevere's car. An officer motioned the trio out.

On the citadel's keep flew the Lothian flag. Underneath, the flag of Cameliard flew limply, as if cowed by the sudden change in fortune.

A tall, burly officer emerged from the portico door, following by two lower-ranking officers. The ranking officer held himself as if he was seeing an old friend.

"Welcome back to Cameliard, Your Majesty." The officer bowed slightly. "And to your servants."

Dee didn't like being called a servant. Marsdon had done that, too.

"This is Dee Rathkeale. And my driver, Dustin. Explain yourself, sir."

"I am Major General Johnson Yama, Chief of Staff, at your service." Yama bowed again. "If you'll permit, I am to escort you to the Great Hall."

"Who sent you? Is Mordred here?"

"I'm sorry, my lady. I've been instructed to withhold that information."

Dee nearly laughed. The general's strutting matter was almost comical. But she understood his seriousness. She, Guinevere, and Dustin were prisoners, in everything but name.

"If you'll follow me, please," Yama said.

Guinevere started forward, with Dee and Dustin following, but the two lower-ranking officers blocked Dee and Dustin's way. Guinevere stopped.

"These are my aides. I'm responsible for them. They accompany me, or I'm going nowhere."

Yama thought a moment, then nodded to the young officers. They stepped aside, and then followed the group to the hall.

The room was large, but dim, a shadow of the Great Audience Hall in Camelot's palace. Dee thought of her light tapestry, and she wondered if she'd ever switch on the tablets and projectors to begin work again. A week ago, she was in the middle of a monumental project in one of Camelot's most important public spaces. Now she was a prisoner of a rebel duke.

Despite his game of withholding his name, Dee knew Mordred waited for them in the hall, so his appearance didn't surprise her. Mordred, as always dressed in black, sat on the ceremonial throne of Cameliard. He slouched a little in the large chair, his chin cradled in the nook of his thumb and forefinger, appearing bored. In the language of courtly behavior, Mordred's posture showed he was not intimidated by the queen's appearance in her family's own domain. His presence unnerved Dee, and she fought the urge to wipe her sweaty hands on her traveling slacks. How her feelings had changed since she flirted with the idea of loving him! Walking behind Guinevere, she couldn't gauge the queen's reaction, but she walked purposefully, without hesitation, toward the Lothian duke.

Dee noticed few, if any guards, apart from Yama and his aides.

"My lord," Yama said. "Allow me to present Her Majesty, Guinevere, Queen of Viridiae."

Mordred straightened himself, but not enough to show that he respected Guinevere. "Your Majesty, so good to see you."

"Get off my throne."

"You don't waste time, do you, my lady?"

"Do I have to repeat myself? Get off my throne."

"I don't understand this 'my throne' business. You're queen of Viridiae, not the backwater of Cameliard."

"You understand as well as I do. When my father died, I was chosen as his heir. I hold the title of Duchess of Cameliard."

Mordred grinned. "Oh yes, I'd forgotten. You have a half-dozen titles. One loses track, after a while. Myself, I plan to add one to my name shortly."

"I'll fight you to my last breath before letting you take Cameliard."

"You misunderstand me. I don't want your title or your hapless little duchy. I'm happy to hand this rather uncomfortable seat"—Mordred shifted and winced—"back to you, just not now."

"You will once Arturus gets here. You're a traitor, and traitors still die in Viridiae."

Mordred laughed. "You've been out of touch the last few days, chasing down your girlfriend Lancelot."

Dee breathed in. Guinevere's visit to Joyous Gard was supposed to be secret. Obviously, it had leaked.

"Arturus," Mordred continued, "is still trying to pull his army together. He wants to fight me, but he's not that good a general. Meanwhile, I'm preparing good ground on which to destroy him."

"Where?"

Mordred wagged his finger. "Oh no, that's a secret."

"Damn it, Mordred," Guinevere hissed. "Why are you here? What do you want?"

"Why am I here? Two reasons. Sides of the same coin, you might say. Firstly, protecting my flank. You have a respectable militia here, despite its total unpreparedness for my visit. If I let you get organized, you could make trouble for me while I lay Arturus to waste."

"I'll find a way to make trouble for you, no matter what."

"Maybe. Maybe not. I'd really prefer that you join me. We've talked about this before."

Dee glanced at Guinevere, whose expression turned from fury to watchful, as if expecting a trick. In the days after the Lucian invasion, rumors swept through Camelot that Guinevere and Mordred plotted to depose Arturus. Nothing happened, but the king sent Guinevere home to Cameliard just before the disastrous battle of the River Colum. She did not return until after Mordred and Arturus' victory over the Lucians months later.

"I'm sincere, my lady," Mordred continued. "I've always thought we'd be stronger together. I don't need to remind you that your ancestor laid a claim to Camelot before Arturus the Great brought him to heel. The episode has pricked at your family's pride like a thorn. Now's your chance to claim your rights, while I claim mine. Once Arturus is out of the way, we could rule Viridiae as equals."

Guinevere shifted her weight from one foot to another. Was she actually considering Mordred's offer, Dee wondered? The great families constantly jostled for power. Today, the competition was subtle, a favor here, a bribe there. In the distant past, they fought with private armies. Arturus the Great, the first of the Arturii kings, brought that to a halt with his own military victory. He imposed a new constitution, which resulted in the Round Table, half-elected by the people, half-appointed by the monarch, himself elected by the Table's delegates. Would Guinevere overturn the progress of the last century by reviving an old family grudge?

"As equals?" Guinevere said.

"As co-rulers."

"You're a snake, Mordred."

The Lord of Lothia shrugged.

"There's no provision in the constitution for co-rulers. You want the power for yourself."

"I'm willing to approach the Round Table and request a change to the constitution."

"At the point of a sword."

"They'd be more than willing, if they saw you at my side."

Guinevere folded her arms. "And what would your mother think of this arrangement?"

Dee gulped. Morgause was a woman who would not be stopped.

"Mother suggested it," Mordred said. "She may not like you, my queen, but she'll set that aside for the larger goal: Seeing me on Viridiae's throne."

"And afterward, sending an assassin to cut my throat." Guinevere shook her head. "She hates me because I'm Arturus' wife and she is not. I'll not subject myself to her vindictiveness. Better to oppose you and have a chance of surviving."

Mordred gripped the arms of the Cameliardian throne tighter. "If I capture Arturus, I promise not to harm him. He'll go into a comfortable retirement."

"I'll die before I let you touch him. You may be his bastard by your bitch of a mother, but you're less than a tenth of him as a man."

Mordred's face flushed crimson. "I suggest you reconsider. The consequences of opposing me would be grave."

"Go to hell, Mordred."

"I don't think you understand. I need you, but I don't need your companions. I can use them, however, to persuade you."

With that, Mordred nodded, and the two young officers grabbed Dee and Dustin. Dee cried out. For an instant, she was back in Lancelot's forest, gripped by the troll. The man who held her now smelled better, but he was just as threatening. And Lancelot could not rescue them.

Dustin kept silent, but his eyes boiled over with fear. "My lady!"

General Yama reached for Guinevere's arm, but she had slid out her dagger and slashed his arm. He yelped in pain. Out of the corner of her eye, Dee saw Dustin wrench free and attack Yama.

Dee saw her chance. She stomped her heel on the instep of her captor, and she heard a crunch. He howled and let Dee go. An instant later, the second younger office plunged his sword into Dustin's back. Dee saw the blade exit his chest below the sternum. He was dead before he hit the floor.

The violence happened so fast that everyone reacted to protect themselves first. The half-second of chaos was all Dee needed. She pulled Guinevere toward the entrance to the hall, intent on escape, but the queen recovered herself and resisted.

"No, this way."

"My lady, we have to leave."

Yama, holding his bleeding arm, barked orders, and guards appeared from nowhere.

"I know this place. I grew up here. Follow me."

The women raced down a hall toward a huge cloth tapestry. Guinevere pushed it aside, and Dee thought of times when she would hide behind a curtain when playing hide-and-seek with Percival. In the dim light, Guinevere searched for something along the wall with her hands. She found it, and an instant later, they were in a pitch-black room.

Dee fumbled for her com. She could hear the guards shouting in frustration on the other side of the stone wall. She turned on her com's light, and she spotted the seam of a narrow door.

"This way, Dee."

"What about Dustin?"

"We can't help him. Come on."

Guinevere led Dee down a passageway. The noise of the guards faded. They failed to find the door.

"I used to play in these passageways. Mordred's people know nothing about them."

"Where are we going?"

"Don't be afraid."

Ahead, all Dee saw was dust, cobwebs, and sconces for torches. The passageway went on forever. They passed branches and cutoffs Dee thought would swallow a person whole. Eventually, a dim light resolved into the shape of a narrow metal door. Guinevere listened for a moment, undid the latch, and pushed. The bottom of the door screeched against the stone floor. Outside, Dee blinked in the harsh light.

"This is one of the old sally ports, used when the citadel still functioned as a fortress," Guinevere said.

Dee heard distant shouts. "We need a car or horses."

They had come out into a run-down neighborhood of old houses, two-story brick buildings, and streets without side-walks or curbs. The wall of the citadel loomed above them. A block down, Dee spied a man getting out of a car. Most cars were public, but a few people owned their own cars, usually public ones that had become surplus. Trying not to draw attention, Guinevere walked toward the man, Dee following. She looked about, hoping no Lothian soldier would suddenly appear.

"I'd like to borrow your car, sir," Guinevere said.

"Excuse me?" The man wore a relatively clean set of coveralls.

"I need your car."

"You're crazy. Do I know you?" The man stared at Guinevere, as if she were a friend he hadn't seen in a long time.

"We've never met. Look, I'll trade you." She removed her dagger, Yama's blood still on the blade.

The man raised his hands. "Hey, I don't want trouble. You can have the car, just leave me alone."

"No, I'm giving this to you. The jewels on the hilt are worth three of these cars." Guinevere turned the hilt of the dagger toward the man and thrust it in his hand. "What's the start code?"

Eyes wide at the rubies and emeralds, disbelieving his luck, the man blurted it out.

"Dee, inside."

Dee jumped into the passenger seat. The car started, and Guinevere backed out of the parking space. "Thank you, sir! Viridiae thanks you as well!"

Dee turned to see the man, his jaw nearly on his chest, the dagger's blade pointed outward.

"You just made him a rich man, my lady."

"Small price for saving a country."

CHAPTER 10:
POET'S VALLEY

Dee feared another Lothian checkpoint, but Guinevere steered the car down Cameliard's backstreets and onto a single-lane road leading into back country. Pastures dotted with cottages and low-profile farm buildings turned into woods and a forest with widely spaced trees interspersed with stumps. Guinevere brought the car to a halt.

"We'll have to walk the rest of the way."

"Where are we going?"

"The rally point."

Dee had no idea what Guinevere meant, except that the words suggested a meeting. Dee trusted Guinevere; she'd saved her life in the citadel, and she was on home ground.

They walked on a well-used trail toward a ridge. Dee still wore the riding boots borrowed from Lancelot at Joyous Gard, but they were scratched and muddy from the long day. Just as the sun touched the western hills, they came to the top of the ridge and looked down on a flat valley bordered by steep cliffs. Long, dark green tents surrounded flickering electric fires.

They descended a trail, Dee following Guinevere closely. She feared tripping and tumbling down the slope into the moonless darkness. They reached a point where the slope eased into the valley floor.

A male voice came out of the darkness. "Halt! State your name and the passphrase."

"Guinevere Cameliard. Freedom now. Freedom forever."

Dee heard a whisper.

"What about your companion?"

"Dee Rathkeale of Camelot," Guinevere said. "I'll vouch for her."

A minute passed, though it felt like an hour. A light shone through the purple twilight on the trail ahead, bouncing as someone carried it toward them. Dee squinted when it shined on her face, then Guinevere's.

"It's her," someone said. More lights came on, one shining on a woman in a military tunic and helmet. She went down on one knee in front of Guinevere.

"My lady. Major Eloise Gramm, Ducal Household Guard, at your service."

Guinevere encouraged Eloise to stand. She introduced Dee.

"We thought you were lost, my lady. We heard you'd been captured. We assumed Mordred would imprison you."

"It almost came to that, but we were lucky."

"I must apologize for my incompetence at the citadel, my lady." Eloise said. "Now that you're here safely, you'll have my resignation immediately."

"Don't be ridiculous, Major. A retreat to fight later when you're in a stronger position is the height of good judgment. You followed our contingency plans and brought the household guard here to Poet's Valley. I should promote you."

Eloise relaxed and bowed her head. "Thank you, my lady."

"I want to hear your report, but first, my friend and I would like to refresh ourselves."

Eloise and a squad of soldiers made their way to the camp. Guinevere's private tent was pitched in hopes of her arrival. A steward brought hot food and water.

Dee thought a simple stew had never tasted so good. "My lady, can you tell me what's happening?"

"You know that I'm Duchess of Cameliard, as well as Arturus' wife. We had contingency plans if Cameliard was ever attacked. If the citadel was overrun, the remaining forces in the city were ordered to scatter and then rally here in the Poet's Valley."

"Why is it called Poet's Valley?"

"You'll see in the morning, at sunrise."

"What happens now?"

"I'll discuss the situation with Major Gramm. Then we'll decide what to do."

Eloise came for Guinevere. Dee rose to accompany them, but the queen asked Dee to stay and rest. Guinevere reassured Dee with a generous smile, but Dee understood; Certain matters of state could not include her. Dee prepared her cot and lay down. She fell asleep within seconds.

She awoke to birdsong and murmuring voices. Guinevere's cot was empty, its blankets and pillow undisturbed. She had been gone all night. Dee dressed and asked a soldier the way to the latrine. The sun had just peeked over the rim of the valley, and Dee grasped why it had been given over to poets. Sunlight illuminated undulating waves of stone in the vertical cliffs, highlighting pastel colors of red, orange and brown. The vision filled Dee with awe, and only a gnawing hunger broke her gaze on the image.

When she returned to Guinevere's tent, the queen was brushing her hair.

"Let me help you with that, my lady." Dee wove Guinevere's long hair into a single braid that cascaded down her back.

"I've put some spare clothes on your cot," the queen said. "I thought you'd like something fresh."

Guinevere's clothes hung a little lose on Dee's figure, but she didn't complain. She suppressed her curiosity about the previous night's meeting with Guinevere's advisors. She'd learn soon enough the queen's next move.

"Dee, I have some news for you. I'm sending you home."

Over the past days, Dee had felt the same kind of camaraderie she'd experienced with the queen on the embassy to Ontari:io. They'd shared a mission and the danger. Guinevere's statement brought her back to reality. This situation was different.

"Things have reached a new phase," Guinevere said. "I have so many things on my mind, and I don't want to be responsible for you in a military and political crisis. You're safer in Camelot."

Dee had trouble believing the capital was safe. After all, wasn't

Mordred going to attack it? She said nothing, however, to contradict the queen. She had decided, and Dee saw no point in pushing back.

"Mordred has already moved most of his troops out of Cameliard City. He was telling the truth: He's not interested in conquering Cameliard. They are marching toward Camelot, and Arturus is going to block their way as far from the city as possible."

The worst was happening. Dee had hoped Mordred would change his mind and return to Lothia. He'd call off his rebellion and he would reconcile with Arturus. That hadn't happened. Civil war was days, maybe hours away.

"I'm sending a few men-at-arms with you to the border with Camelot at the same place where we ran into the Lothian checkpoint. They've already abandoned the position. I'll also give you a letter of transit. No one will bother you."

"Yes, my lady." Dee wanted to beg Guinevere to let her stay. She felt safer with her queen than away from her, and she wanted to offer whatever help she could, even if it was only to lay out clothes in the morning or write correspondence or anything to please her. But Dee knew nothing about making war, except that it caused suffering.

Dee gathered her few belongings, as well as some food and a glass bottle of water, placing them in a borrowed knapsack. Everything in her life was borrowed these days, from food to clothes to shoes. Maybe her time left on earth was borrowed as well.

Dee's escort detail arrived. Guinevere fought back her emotions, but Dee let her tears fall freely. Guinevere reached out to Dee and brought her close.

"Safe travels, my dear."

Dee cleared her throat. "The same to you, my lady."

"I'm getting tired of saying goodbye to the women I love. I expect to see you in Camelot."

"When?" Dee's hopes lifted.

"I can't say. My plans… It's best that you not know."

Dee nodded, but something did not sound right to her. The tone of Guinevere, gentle, factual, and somehow, conspiratorial.

"Pray to Gaia for me, Dee."

Guinevere handed Dee to the three soldiers, led by a corporal who reminded her of Kenric, Lina's 10-year-old brother. Dee tried not to look back at Guinevere's tent, but when she did, the queen was gone.

* * *

The Cameliardian troops left Dee at the border with a horse and enough food and water to last her and her horse several days. They also gave her a printed map that showed several towns along the road home. A horse and walking trail followed the edge of the paved road, but Dee saw few cars. At first, she traveled alone. She kept alert, wondering if trolls might accost her, but nothing happened. Within a few hours, the first town appeared, and she stopped for a meal.

With each leg of her journey, more people traveled with her, until she realized they were refugees, the earliest trickle of people who knew more conflict was coming. She spoke to a few. Most just wanted to leave the area. Everyone expected a clash between Arturus and Mordred, but on one could guess where the battle or battles might occur. All shared the same emotion: anxiety. They hoped to find safety somewhere else, anywhere else.

Dee found lodging the first two nights, but on the third night, in a relatively large town, she couldn't find anything due to the refugees. The Cameliardians had provided a small tent, and Dee joined a group of travelers in a park on the edge of town. She ate a cold supper of bread, preserved meat, and cheese. Her horse munched on oats. She slept little, fearing someone would raid the camp or steal her horse. As morning broke, she packed up quickly and continued her journey.

The nine towers of Camelot appeared on the fifth day. She breathed a sigh of relief, even as she encountered Viridian men-at-arms, knights on horseback, and military vehicles. The number of refugees had swollen, reminding Dee of the days before the sack of her city by the Lucians. She asked Gaia to keep Camelot safe, as well as Guinevere and her family and friends. She also prayed for an easy entry in the city.

She followed the main road into the suburbs, passing through one of the old neighborhoods that had sprouted outside the central city's main wall. People walked the sidewalks, and traffic clogged the streets. The shops were open, but customers ducked in and out of them as if avoiding a hard rain. What were they afraid of? Mordred, of course, and war. The sky was cloudy, but no rain threatened. The tension felt as if someone had pulled a rope tight and might let go at any time.

Dee passed through the outer wall gate called the Weeping Way without trouble, but the atmosphere was even more taut as she approached the palace. She was filthy and exhausted. She wanted a bath and a hot meal. The palace gate appeared before her, and she held out her hand with her com ring to show her identification data.

The guard studied her photo, his eyes flicking back and forth, reminding Dee of the Lothian guard on the checkpoint outside Cameliard.

"Please dismount, Ms Rathkeale. I've been instructed to conduct you to the palace."

"Is something wrong?"

The guard said nothing in response, and Dee wondered if she had broken some law, maybe a curfew. Maybe that's why people were flitting about like birds. Had Guinevere sent a message that she was coming? Had she accused her of something? Dee shook her head to dislodge her fears. It was probably routine.

She left her Cameliard horse with a groom, gathered her knapsack of belongings, and followed the guard into the palace. She'd hoped he might escort her to her room, but he avoided the flight of stairs that led to her tiny apartment. They rode an elevator to the top floor, and Dee realized she was going to the royal offices. She had no time to prepare herself.

The elevator doors opened. Arturus sat at his desk, his back turned to her.

Dee swallowed hard. What sort of trouble had she caused?

Arturus swiveled around, slowly and evenly. Dee was shocked by what she saw. Arturus had never appeared so ill. His skin hung loose on his face, the color of boiled oatmeal. His eyes still sparkled with intelligence, but how long would that last if his body was in such terrible shape? His hands gripped the arms of his chair, as if angry, but with no way to express it without losing his temper.

Dee curtsied. "Your Majesty, I apologize if you were expecting me. I've only just arrived after a long time on the road. I—"

"I'm not concerned with that, Ms Rathkeale. I only have a few minutes. No doubt, you're aware of the situation?"

Dee feared saying the wrong thing. Arturus' reign, maybe his survival as monarch, maybe even his life, was in mortal danger. Mordred was about to attack everything Arturus had been entrusted with. "Lord Mordred is in rebellion."

"For a time, I thought my wife and you were going over to his side."

Dee jaw dropped. "Your Majesty, that's impossible. Guinevere traveled to Joyous Gard to find Lancelot."

"I was told Lancelot disappeared into the forest. How did you find her?"

"I think she found us before we found her."

"But Guinevere wanted to be with her lover now, instead of here with me."

"No, sire!" Dee stopped herself from shouting. "She begged Lancelot to help you and Camelot. I was there. I heard every word."

The strain in the king's face didn't ease. "Where is my lovely wife?"

"I left her five days ago in a place called Poet's Valley, near Cameliard."

Arturus rubbed his chin. "I know the place. Beautiful, especially at sunrise. What were her circumstances?"

"I don't understand, sire."

"Her military disposition."

The question felt strange to Dee. He didn't ask after Guinevere's health, physical or emotional. "I'm not a soldier, Your Majesty, except to say that most of her household guard was with her. I also saw soldiers in other uniforms but with the Cameliard flag on their shoulders."

"Can you estimate their numbers?"

"Perhaps 500 or 600."

"How many knights?"

Dee thought of Guinevere's frantic questioning of Dustin, rest his soul. "Maybe a few dozen. I don't know. Sire, is something wrong? I feel as if—"

"A battle is coming. Mordred has crossed Camelot's border in force. I know that he wants Guinevere as an ally. He made an offer to her, did he not?"

A bead of sweat formed on Dee's temple. "Yes, sire. But she rejected it, firmly."

"You're sure?"

"Again, sire, I was there. I witnessed it. We ran for our lives. Guinevere saved my life. She has no interest in helping Mordred. I'm sure of it."

"But she certainly has her own interests. What did she say about them?"

The question threw Dee into confusion. Was this why Guinevere would not tell her what she planned to do? "I asked, but she didn't tell me. It's none of my business. I'm just an artist—"

"Working on Mordred's commission."

Dee didn't know how to answer. Was Arturus accusing her of something? She couldn't imagine it, but what should she say? She worked her jaw, but nothing came out.

Arturus dropped his eyes to his desk. "Forgive me, Ms Rathkeale. These days, I see enemies everywhere, even if they are longtime friends. Guinevere has said nothing to me since she left for Joyous Gard. I don't understand her sometimes. One day, she is the pillar I rely on for support. The next day, the pillar seems to crumble. Did she say anything else?"

"Only that she would be there for you."

"At the coming battle?"

"I don't know, sire."

Arturus sighed. "Thank you, Dee. You've been very helpful." He called the guard, and he ordered him to escort Dee to her room.

Arturus had frightened Dee. She imagined him calling her a traitor, and a guard dragging her to a prison cell. It didn't happen, but the fear of it was enough to shatter her sense of safety within the palace. How long before Arturus changed his mind and decided she was a threat?

Dee felt better after she showered and put on her own clothes. She boiled water for tea and found some crackers. The food and drink revived her spirits.

A new worry wormed its way into her consciousness. The mural project had survived the Lucian War. Would it survive the coming battle between Arturus and Mordred, especially if Arturus won and saw the work as the project of a traitor? She decided to check on it.

Dee poked her head into the corridor. No guards were in sight. As quietly as she could, she made her way to the Great Audience Hall. She passed a few guards, but none spoke to her. Inside the hall, the curtains hiding the partially completed work were untouched. All of her equipment—the tablets, the projectors, the notes—were as she left them. Prior to Guinevere's invitation to accompany her to Joyous Gard, Dee thought she had many weeks, even months to finish. Now, time was as precious as water in a desert. Dee started her tablets and the projectors and began to work.

CHAPTER 11: A RATTLER STRIKES

Percival presented his letters of transit at the Viridian border post. A pair of sleepy guards greeted him from a modest guard shack. A half-finished breastworks, built for a Lucian attack from the Hot Lands, which never came, marked the southern-most frontier of Viridiae. The territory beyond was technically under the influence of the city-state of Aurelia, more than 500 kilometers away on the Peaceful Sea, but neither of the guards had ever seen an Aurelian official. Percival had heard the area called the Wastes, but the ponderosa pine and thin, green under-brush didn't fit the metaphor.

The guards recommended the party refill its canteens before moving on.

Within a day, the moniker for the landscape made more sense. The dirt road descended into a narrow valley with a flat floor that trapped the heat of the day. They came to a tiny settlement called Reek, which had a sweetwater well, a corral with a single, swayback horse, the remains of a car, and a proprietor who claimed to own fifteen cats, though Percival saw none. Gala-had asked about reports of troll or bandit activity, and the old woman shrugged. Percival wondered if she knew something but wouldn't tell. It would be easy to frighten a lonely elder at a run-down station into silence.

The expedition made camp for the night.

The next morning dawned bright and cool. Sipping the morn-ing's first coffee, Percival felt good about the journey so far. The six travelers were becoming a tight-knit group, even with the interruption at Galahad's home. In front of Galahad's tent, Roz put Penny's long brown hair into braids. She and Penny chatted away as if they'd been friends for years. Percival wondered if Penny had ever enjoyed a true friend while avoiding the predators in Perditon. Ben showed promise with his war blade as he sparred with Percival. The cadet asked Percival about advanced training, and Percival promised to write a letter of recommendation. Roz was a rougher kind of warrior, more interested in doing the work of soldiery than studying it, but Percival believed she'd command her own unit sooner rather than later.

The clear blue sky promised heat. Galahad suggested traveling at night, but the expedition's route eventually took it to the coast of the Peaceful Sea, where Percival expected cooler conditions. Studying his printed map—the com system faded as they got further from Viridiae—he saw two or three places where an ambush was possible, if Gereon's warnings had any substance. Galahad noted that they were looking at the map with military eyes. Who knows what a greedy bandit or hungry troll might do or where they might strike in desperation?

Wearing a wide-brimmed straw hat he'd purchased in Reek, Percival found a stark beauty in the landscape, which was not much different than the desert he, Arturus, and Merlin traversed after their escape from Lucana. Despite the heat and the sweat, Percival enjoyed watching small seed-eating birds tussle in the dust. A huge snow-capped mountain loomed to the southeast, but the expedition's route took them west, away from the peak.

That evening, Percival was on watch. His head lay on his saddle, transformed into a pillow, but he was wide awake. Crickets filled the night with raspy sound. He marveled at the number of stars flowing in the stream of the Milky Way. Bright Venus led a crescent moon behind a line of mountains. The electric fire was turned low to conserve the battery, but it shed enough light to show three tents: one for Percival and Ben, one for Galahad and Penny, and one for Roz with extra space used for storage.

The attack came around midnight. The touch of a blade on Percival's neck announced the bandits' arrival.

"Move and I'll slice your neck open."

The voice belonged to a man, perhaps thirty years old. Percival moved his eyes upward, and the orange glow of the fire illuminated a bearded face framed by stringy hair. The knight tensed in readiness, but he reflected on the fact that he'd faced far worse dangers already in his young life. Percival attended to his ears, and he heard, rather than saw three, possibly four other strangers on the camp's perimeter.

"Get up, mister," the bandit said. "Wake the others."

"You're making a mistake, sir," Percival said.

"Stop talking. We've been watching you all day. We won't hurt you if you cooperate."

"I can't very well wake them up if you have a sword on my neck."

The bandit leader stepped back, keeping his sword pointed at Percival's belly. The knight's blade was hidden under his blanket on the ground. Looking at the bandit, with his worn trousers, dirty shirt and vest, and rusted weapon, he wondered if he'd need his war blade. Before going on watch, though, he'd put on his light body armor as a precaution.

"Galahad." Percival spoke firmly and calmly. "We have guests."

Galahad had likely heard the quiet commotion, because he came out of the tent fully dressed, including his boots. He either expected trouble, or sensed it coming. Percival also called on Ben and Roz, but he did not call Penny's name.

"There's a kid in one of the tents," the leader said. "Bring her out."

"She's none of your concern, sir."

The bandit leader pulled out his single-shot pistol from his belt and pointed it at Percival's head. "That's for me to decide."

Galahad called Penny's name, relieving Percival of the need to obey a criminal. She lifted the flap and stood in front of the tent. Her face had an expression of calm determination. Life on the streets of Perditon had prepared her for moments like this. Did she already have a plan for escape?

"Not quite as pretty as I would like, but she'll do," the bandit leader said.

"What's that supposed to mean?" Galahad's voice rose.

"You her daddy?"

"I'm her guardian."

"You're a terrible guardian." The leader laughed at his own joke. "I've got a gun pointed at her."

One of the other bandits whispered in the leader's ear. Percival confirmed his count of four men, all relatively young. There might be more out in the darkness, possibly their women, but they'd likely be caring for horses or the gang's gear.

"If you're going to steal our stuff, you might as well tell us your name," Percival said.

"Why?"

"So we can spread it far and wide after you let us go."

The leader grunted. "You can call me Rattler, because I strike when you least expect it."

"Are you kidding me?" Ben snickered.

With a hard look, Percival quieted Ben. He didn't want to give Rattler an excuse for lashing out.

Rattler lifted the point of his sword to Ben's eye. "Would you like to be the first one I bite tonight?"

Ben shook his head.

Rattler barked at one of his men. While Percival and the others in the expedition stood and watched, the bandits rifled through their belongings. One of them started putting the panniers back on one of the expedition horses. With his foot, Rattler moved Percival's blanket and saw the sword. He regarded Percival with new interest.

"Where are you headed?"

"Cassanti." Percival didn't see a reason to lie.

"You're after the Grail, aren't you?"

Percival caught Galahad's glance. "We are, Mr Rattler. What do you know of it?"

"Only that it's a myth that people around here like to talk about. It's good bait for fools."

Could he be right, Percival thought? Was the Cassanti Grail

just a story told to lure victims of banditry south of Viridiae's border? Percival didn't believe it. He had more faith in Merlin's research than that.

"We're going to find it, whatever you say, Mr Rattler."

"What's your name, if you don't mind my asking."

Percival introduced himself, then Galahad. He mentioned the first names of the others, but nothing more.

"Gaia's blood," Rattler said, mouth gaping, "real Viridian knights. Not something you see around here often. Pretty poor examples, if you ask me."

"I take it you're of the higher quality of outlaws in these parts?" Galahad said.

"Who's holding the gun on you, Sir Galahad?" Rattle said. "That argues for a certain competence on my part and incompetence on yours, don't you think?"

One of Rattler's men reported that they had everything they could carry or sell: food, tablets, canteens, and the horses.

"One last item." Rattler grabbed Penny by the arm and dragged her toward him. "I need help with chores. You'll do nicely."

Penny struggled, but Galahad spoke to her. "Penny, he'll hurt you if you fight. Don't worry. I'll come for you."

Penny stared at Galahad, but she relaxed, as if she'd heard a hoped-for message.

"Oh, really, Sir Best-Dressed?" Rattler flicked the tip of his sword on Galahad's pricey riding cape. "Not until after I've explained my expectations to her."

The remark drew laughter from his fellows. The implication frightened Penny, who struggled again against Rattler's grip until Galahad eased her down from her anxiety with a "Don't worry, my dear."

Percival willed himself to stay cool and calm. The opportunity he expected might come at any moment.

Another of the bandits reported no one else in the immediate area.

"Okay, Percival Rathkeale, my friends and I are going to walk away. If you make even the smallest move in our direction, or we spot you following us, I'll cut her throat." He winked at Penny. "Understood?"

Rattler called for his companions to follow. He pulled Penny by the wrist, but she didn't scream or cry. Instead, she kept her eyes on Galahad. As if on a signal, she started to struggle one more time against Rattler's pull until he stopped and turned. Penny opened her mouth and bit hard on Rattler's bare forearm. Rattle screamed in pain and rage. Percival thought he saw her tear a mouthful of skin. Galahad was on him, pummeling his face with a fist. Rattler released Penny, who ran off into the night.

In that instant when every bandit froze, Percival reached for the grip of his blade and swung it in a practiced arc. The nearest bandit lost his arm at the elbow. Blood escaped him in sheets. Percival turned again in a wide arc, like a dancer in the king's ballet, and he faced another bandit with a pistol. His hesitation was all Percival needed. He lunged forward, sinking his weapon into the bandit's belly. The hapless robber fell with his hand over his belly to keep his intestines from spilling onto the sand.

Percival scanned the scene. He saw no other enemies.

"Sir Percival!" Ben was on his knees next to Galahad. Rattler lay on his back, eyes open, the hilt of Galahad's dagger dangling under the dead man's chin. But Galahad gasped. Somehow, Rattler's sword had found Galahad's side, just below the last rib. Roz had a corner of a blanket pressed on the wound to staunch the bleeding.

"Gaia, I've fucked up." Even in the dim light of the electric fire, Galahad's face was pale. He winced in pain when he grabbed Percival's arm. "Find Penny. Please!"

Percival ran in the direction he last saw the girl. Calling out her name, he soon found her, crouched behind a boulder. Her mouth was bloody from the bite on Rattler's arm. Percival brought her back to camp. She ran to her guardian. That was the only time Percival saw her cry like a child half her age.

Percival sent Ben to search for the stolen gear and horses. He returned a short time later with almost everything. The fight had frightened off the remaining bandits, though Percival worried they might return. Just how loyal were bandits to each other? Would they try to avenge Rattler's death? Percival didn't want to find out.

Galahad was badly wounded. He needed a doctor. The bleeding lessened, but Percival couldn't be sure his friend hadn't suffered an internal injury. They had a tendency to hide until too late. The travelers talked over the situation, even as Galahad grew weaker. Percival couldn't risk another attack. He couldn't take Galahad all the way to Aurelia. That was a death sentence. He had no choice. The group had to turn back, at least to Ash and a doctor.

Percival had no qualms about his decision. Galahad's life depended on him. Ben and Roz agreed, but they were disappointed. As far as Percival was concerned, Penny did not have a say in the matter. If, Gaia forbid, Galahad died, he could not take a child to a strange city he himself had never visited. Despite all the rational, good reasons for turning back, Percival cursed himself for the bad luck. Was this another lost chance to find and bring back the Grail to Camelot? Failure seemed to follow him everywhere, and he had no idea what to do about it.

CHAPTER 12: TWO DECISIONS FOR DEE

Getting back to the light tapestry in the Great Audience Hall relieved some of Dee's tension, but not all. Maybe it was the constant cloud of Mordred's rebellion. Or maybe it was guilt at abandoning Percival. Whatever the cause of her anxiety, Dee determined to catch up on lost time. While she focused on the tapestry's major figures, color scheme, and key animations, Lina handled the smaller figures, settings, and landscapes. After a week of 16-hour days, barely eating or resting, the project was mostly complete.

Despite the progress, Dee struggled with major figures that would carry most of the story. She couldn't find the exact expressions, sweep of gestures, or even some color mixes. As the floating laser projectors buzzed overhead, the final arrangement of the composition eluded her.

"Why can't I see the climax of the story, Lina?" Dee asked the question in desperation.

"You will, eventually," Lina said. "Maybe you're suffering from a form of writers block."

"That makes no sense."

"Sure it does. I have a writer friend who describes it as a plague of indecision. It's really a loss of confidence."

"I don't have that problem when it comes to painting." Dee swiped through her tablet, only half-believing her own words.

"The well goes dry sometimes. It always fills back up."

Dee appreciated Lina's suggestions. She had soaked up enough of her approach and technique that Dee could give her important tasks without too much oversight. Dee even considered recommending Lina for a few commission offers that had come her way. Dee no longer had time to accept them.

Late one night, Dee sent Lina home. She wanted time to mediate on her trouble in front of the sprawling canvas of wall. She practiced a breathing exercise Ganieda taught that emptied the mind of all distractions. Just as she entered a calm state, someone cleared their throat.

"Lina, I told you to go home."

A young male voice responded. One of Arturus' pages said the king wished to see her immediately. Dee sighed, frustrated that she was always at the royals' beck and call. Without voicing her annoyance, she gathered her wrap and tablets, and followed the boy to the king's offices.

Alone at his desk, Arturus hunched over a glowing tablet. The low lights and darkness of evening made his office feel like a cave. The glow from the tablet deepened his constant pallor.

"How can I be of service, Your Majesty?" The words came out with more impatience that she expected. She was tired from the long day.

"Ms Rathkeale... Dee, thank you for coming." He gestured toward a chair.

Arturus' courtesy with Dee was tinged with disappointment. Had she displeased him?

"Dee, I knew you were working late, and I thought you'd want to hear some news before it hits the news chans."

In a flash, all kinds of frightening fantasies flew through Dee's mind. Her mother had died. Guinevere was captured by Mordred and killed. Would Arturus be the one to tell her that Percival had died?

"Percival has returned to the border town of Ash with the expedition. Galahad was badly wounded in a fight with bandits." Arturus gave a brief account of the skirmish.

Dee held her breath. Bandits had been killed, but no one in the expedition had died. "I'm sorry to hear about Galahad, Majesty. How is he doing?"

"They ran into a Regarder patrol near a town called Reek. The patrol brought Galahad in. Percival's just arrived at the hospital and he sent me this report."

"Is Percival…"

"He's well. So are the others in the expedition."

This was a major crisis, Dee thought. She was happy that everyone survived, but Arturus had staked his kingship on the success of the Grail expedition. He needed to show progress if he was to hold the country together against Mordred.

"Has the expedition failed, sire?"

Arturus folded his hands on the desk. "That's part of the reason I called you here, Dee."

"Sire?"

"You probably remember that I appointed Galahad to accompany Percival when you declined to go with your brother."

"Yes, my lord." Dee swallowed, dreading Arturus' next words.

"Galahad's wound is very serious. His convalescence will take several weeks, maybe months."

Dee's breathes came faster.

"The expedition is largely intact, apart from Galahad. His page Penny will stay with him, no doubt. But Percival needs a partner. He has two good retainers, but they aren't what he needs. Dee, the fact is, he needs you by his side."

A flicker of anger rose within Dee's breast. Had Percival taken advantage of Galahad's loss to get what he really wanted, which was Dee? "Did he ask for me, sire?"

"No, he has not. In fact, he's already offered to return to the journey with, um" —He glanced at the tablet— "Ben and Roz, the retainers. They're ready and willing, he says."

Dee was confused. "I don't understand, sire. If he didn't ask for me, what's the problem?"

"I got to know Percival very well while we were in Lucanus. I don't think you realize how he depends on you. You're his twin, of course, but the connection goes even deeper. Without someone to support him, he's crippled by self-doubt. His chances of success at finding the Grail have fallen dramatically with Galahad's loss. His odds would improve dramatically if you joined him."

"So you're ordering me to go with Percival." Dee clenched her teeth. This wasn't what she wanted. She wanted to finish the light tapestry!

"I can't order you go. Well, I could, I suppose. I'm the King of Viridiae after all. But I'd much rather you went by choice. Volunteering tends to make a difference in a person's level of enthusiasm for a task."

Dee couldn't return the king's expectant gaze. All around her were symbols of the Viridian state: faded flags, busts of ancient, pre-unification kings, artifacts from the Dark Years after the Dissolution, when the world fell apart. Dee felt pressed down by the history and the responsibility it represented. *For Gaia's sake,* she thought, *I just want to make art!*

"My lord, you're asking a lot of me. I have a major commission to complete, and if I leave Camelot now, I don't know when I'll ever finish it."

"It can wait. Finding the Grail is more important."

"Are you sure, Majesty?" Dee knew she was overstepping her bounds, but she was angry. "We've been chasing the Grail for so long. How do we know it's not an illusion?"

"I won't allow myself to believe that. If I did, I would be giving up, and that's not why the Round Table put me here. They told me to care for our beautiful kingdom and pass it intact to our children. I intend to do that. And right now, I need your help."

"You're arguing survival. So am I, my lord. What is life without beauty? Just as you have a purpose, so do I."

"We both carry a burden. But if the Great Machine finally fails, and Viridiae vanishes, then what purpose will your art serve, except to fascinate some distant descendant of Merlin as an artifact of a lost world?"

Dee could not persuade Arturus, but she needed to speak her mind. At least he'd listened without judgment.

"This is a big decision, sire. I need to think about it."

"Of course. Tomorrow?"

Dee nodded, but with little enthusiasm.

* * *

Dee could not sleep. Arturus' words echoed in her mind all night. The king expected a decision from her quickly, and no matter how she tried to let go of the day's cares, she could not put the thought of joining Percival's expedition out of her mind. The next morning, after some breakfast, she willed herself to focus on her creative logjam. It was the only way to get her body to move.

In the Great Audience Hall, Ganieda waited for her with coffee already brewing in the pot. Dee hadn't seen her mentor for several weeks, though they'd exchanged a few texts and calls. Dee regretted that she hadn't found time to visit, but the press of business was too great. Ganieda forgave her with a hug and a warm mug. The elder asked Dee about the tapestry's progress.

"Terrible. I've hit a wall."

Ganieda studied the nearly finished work. "Dee, your work is stunning. It's going to excite the entire country."

In rapid fire sentences, Dee complained about practically everything related to the painting. Nothing measured up to what she originally wanted. She couldn't put into light and color what she saw in her mind. "Sometimes I want to scrap it and start over."

"That would be a mistake of monstrous proportions," Ganieda said. "For an artist so young, this is an achievement you should be proud of."

"Don't worry, I won't wreck it. I'm just frustrated, that's all."

"Part of being an artist is accepting that you'll never be perfect."

Dee was not in the mood for one of Ganieda's lectures, but she was glad of her presence. "How is life in your world?"

Ganieda sighed. "Could be better. It's Morgause. I've received information from members of the Society of Theurgists in Lothia. There's evidence she's toying with the dark forces again."

"To help Mordred, I suppose."

"Mordred has lost all control of himself. Before the war, he was resentful, but he knew his duty and served Arturus well. Since the war, he's become obsessed with his grievances to the exclusion of everything else. No doubt his mother is fanning the flames. I'm convinced his rebellion is really her doing."

Just as Dee responded that Mordred had written to her, Lina came in as if she hoped Dee wouldn't notice. Lina nodded her morning greeting, but she said nothing as she scurried to her tablets and notes.

Ganieda noticed Lina, and her expression grew concerned. She kept her attention on Dee. "What did Mordred have to say?"

"Here, read for yourself." Dee swiped through her com to the letter and handed the device to Ganieda.

My dear Dee,

I'm writing to apologize for the incident at Cameliard City. I didn't mean for you to get caught up in the politics of the moment. I also regret the death of Guinevere's servant, Dustin. It was an accident.

You must understand that I have a right to claim what belongs to me. I know you have a little influence with Guinevere. I ask that you plead my case with her. I still have feelings for you, and when I take what is mine, I will reward you beyond anything Arturus could give you.

If you do not see things my way, I can't answer for the consequences.

Mordred

"Not exactly a romantic, is he?" Ganieda said.

"As if threats would bring me to his side," Dee said. "I'm tempted to show it to Arturus. He'd probably label it treasonous."

"I think Mordred has already provided plenty of evidence for that."

"But what could Morgause do to make things worse?"

"I'm not entirely sure. My sources are reporting rumors, but

I think there's substance to them. Mordred is gaining strength each day. The populace is losing faith in Arturus. And now this news about Galahad. It's a bad time for Viridiae."

"Do you think Morgause had something to do with the attack on Percival's expedition?"

"It's not outside the realm of possibility, but I don't have any evidence."

What was that thing Arturus said last night. Dee wondered? The Regarders had intercepted the expedition and taken Galahad to Ash? Did they just happen to be in the area? Don't the Regarders report to Gawain, Mordred's brother? Dee's suspicions rose.

Lina dropped a tablet. She was crying.

"Lina!" Dee rushed over. "What's wrong?"

"It's my brother, Kenric."

Dee picked up Lina's tablet while Ganieda guided her to a chair.

"He's sick, isn't he?" Dee said.

"He had a seizure in the middle of the night. My parents took him to the hospital. He's unconscious. There was nothing I could do. My parents are there, so I came to work."

"Poor child," Ganieda said. "How can we help?"

Dee flashed to the conversation with Lina about Kenric's disease and Dee's unique mutation. Lina would not look at Dee, but the message was clear. Dee had the key to saving Kenric's life. Dee cursed her own life. She felt overwhelmed and out of control with every passing minute. Her dream of completing the commission in the Great Audience Hall was slipping away. Too much was getting in the way. A few hours ago, her king had asked her to sacrifice her calling as an artist to help Percival find something that might not even exist. Now, unspoken but loud as a bell, fate had offered another choice to Dee. Should she risk her life to save a child's future?

Ganieda noticed Dee's distress. "Everything will be alright, my dear. You'll do the right thing."

Dee wasn't sure she wanted to do the right thing.

CHAPTER 13:
KENRIC IS DYING

Lina's hands trembled when holding the tablet with the composition software. The embarrassment of dropping it broke the dam of her emotion. She spilled all her fears to Dee and Ganieda about her brother's prognosis, but she couldn't bring herself to remind Dee about donating her blood factor to save Kenric. To tell the truth, Lina was intimidated by Dee, an accomplished artist who had a close relationship with the king and queen. Lina was only an assistant. Who was she to ask Dee for literally a portion of her blood? On the other hand, as the two older women listened to Lina's fears, Dee seemed to know what needed to be done without saying it out loud. It was in her expression and compassionate manner.

Dee told Lina to go to the hospital to be with her brother.

In the hospital room, Lina's parents sat next to the unconscious Kenric. Monitors beeped. Daylight filtered through the window coverings. Mother's eyes were red with crying, but she maintained as much composure as she could muster. Father's face was torn with worry.

A few hours later, Dee knocked on the hospital room door. Her appearance thrilled Lina, who rose to hug her.

"How is Ken doing?" Dee said.

Lina pursed her lips, scared to say anything that might break down her self-control again.

"I want to talk to the doctor," Dee said.

Lina looked at Dee, full of hope. Had Dee decided to help? She led her to a nurse's station, where the sage-physician, a middle-aged man wearing a lab coat, studied his com.

He sat them down in a waiting area. "Lina and her parents told me about you some time ago, Ms Rathkeale. We hoped Ken's condition wouldn't get so bad that we'd have to bring up the possibility of harvesting the proteins he needs. I took the liberty of checking the literature and speaking with a researcher. The evidence is clear. You're part of a very small population with the mutation that could help Kenric. We're not even sure if there's another person alive in Viridiae with your blood's qualities."

"What about the procedure?" Dee said. "I've heard it's dangerous."

"There are risks. We have to inject a drug that ramps up your production of the protein. Its side effects are unpredictable."

Dee covered her face with her hands, as if hiding could change the circumstances.

The doctor seemed to understand her anxiety. "The risks are manageable. We'd take every precaution."

Lina said, "This is the best hospital in the country, Dee."

A sage-nurse called the doctor away.

Dee pulled out her com. The contact name was "Mother," and Lina didn't feel comfortable listening in. She left Dee alone. However, she couldn't help hearing fragments of the conversation.

"… little boy… Lina's brother… they think it will work… talked with Percival? He told you he's fine with it?… when it's over." Sighing, Dee closed the connection.

There was a commotion outside of Ken's room. Lina ran over just as a nurse wheeled a tray into the room. Another nurse prevented Lina from going inside, but she could hear the doctor giving orders. Lina could no longer keep the tears from streaming down her face. She thought of Percival. Would he have been here, to keep her company? She thought so. She'd heard he had come back over the border after a fight with bandits. He wasn't hurt, but Galahad was in surgery. She wanted to call Percival, but he had enough on his mind, and she had her own family to worry about.

The hospital room grew silent, and Lina's father came out. They embraced each other, and she relaxed in his warmth, but anxiety saturated the air like a pall.

Dee said, "What just happened, Lina?"

"Ken's heart fluttered. It was frightening, but he's stable now. Dee, please, are you going to help him?"

Dee squeezed Lina's hand. "Yes, I have to try."

Relief flooded Lina, and she lost all control, falling into Dee's arms.

The next hours passed like a blur. The sage-physician took Dee to an adjacent room. Lina helped her into a hospital gown. Because Dee had no family nearby, they allowed Lina to stay with her while the doctor and a team of nurses prepped her. An intravenous drip sent the protein-enhancement drug into her system, as well as a sedative to keep her calm. Her blood flowed through another tube into a plastic bag. Lina's hands sweat with fear as she watched her friend fall unconscious. Lina was afraid not only for Dee, but for Kenric. What if the treatment didn't work?

An hour into the procedure, the activity around Dee increased. A nurse ushered Lina out of the room. She asked for information, but the nurse said nothing. Lina found herself alone in the waiting area. She put her head down.

Lina woke up, startled by her father, Rueben. Morning sunlight streamed through a window. Lina followed him to Kenric's room. Isra, his mother, and Dee, wearing a hospital robe and slippers, stood over Kenric. He was awake, but groggy, and everyone was smiling. His doctor listened to his chest.

"The procedure worked, Lina," Dee said. "The doctors said I came through fine."

Lina breathed out. Not only was Dee okay, Ken was looking better.

"Is he cured?" Dee said.

"There's no cure for Ken's disease," the doctor said. "But your donated blood factor is long-lasting and completely compatible with his system. It won't be rejected. You've added years to Ken's life. And there's new research on a way to synthesize the factor. Ken probably won't need a second procedure in the future."

Lina embraced Dee again. She looked tired and pale, with dark circles under eyes, but she smiled.

"Thank you, Dee."

Dee nodded. "One big problem solved. Now on to the next one."

CHAPTER 14: AURELIA ON THE PEACEFUL SEA

Aurelia, the legendary city on the Peaceful Sea, stood on a peninsula across an inlet. Percival and Dee took in the astounding prospect from the headland opposite the city. The tops of the city's towers glowed above, reaching to the heavens like a prayer, even as their bases were rooted firmly to the earth. The tall, thin structures glittered with red and orange and hints of green, as if made of fine crystal, reflecting and refracting the setting sun. The brother and sister had heard stories of the city-state. They'd seen photos on the Viridian com network. But nothing prepared them for its jewel-like quality.

They sat on a blanket eating a dinner of cheese, bread, and bottled ale. Roz and Ben, Percival's retainers, shared their meal. When Percival departed Ash again, this time with Dee on his team, they learned Galahad would recover. The second attempt to reach Aurelia had been uneventful.

"I've wondered so many times in the past few weeks whether we'd ever see the city. I can't believe it's real," Percival said. "Thanks again, Dee, for coming with us."

"Ganieda asked me to imagine how I'd feel if I didn't go. Guilt and disgust with myself was the answer. I couldn't ignore that."

"But you were giving up so much."

"Lina can keep the work on the light tapestry going. I can always finish it when I get home."

"When we were in Ash, and I got your note you were coming, I felt as if everything would be alright. We'd find the Grail, come home, and I could be with Lina. That was an amazing thing you did for her brother."

"You keep saying that. All I did was give him a blood protein."

"No one else could've saved his life. You deserve as much praise as any Round Table knight."

"Maybe that was why I ran out of creative juice, just as I was getting close to finishing Mordred's commission. I knew unconsciously I had other business to take care of."

"Mordred." Percival said the word as if it described vermin. "His rebellion won't end peacefully. Part of me wishes I'd stayed behind to fight beside Arturus. But he's right; I need to be here, about to visit a city that's more dream than reality."

Finishing up their meal, they led the horses down the path that led to a bridge. Percival made notes in his tablet while Dee sketched the sparkling metropolis. Percival had lost communications with Viridiae weeks ago, but he kept daily notes, hoping to send them to Merlin through the Viridian embassy in Aurelia. In return, Percival hoped Merlin would send him the latest clues about the Last Grail.

A stiff wind, carrying the thick green smell of the sea, wrestled with his blood-red hair. All four showed their passports at the entrance to a soaring bridge that crossed the inlet. In Percival's mind, the rust-colored structure flew across the strait, arcing gently like a dancer. Though it was as solid as rock beneath his feet, he tread as he might when he entered a temple to Gaia, with reverence. Below him, wind ships passed into and out of a broad bay.

Inside the city, each step revealed something outside his experience. For one thing, he had never seen so many people packed into one space. They appeared to walk faster than everyone he'd known, but they managed to avoid collisions as they studied their coms and tablets. More than 100,000 people lived in Camelot, but most lived outside the walled city in suburbs and semi-rural outskirts. That number must live on this Aurelian street alone, he thought, nestled in the towers that turned the streets into canyons. The feeling was at once claustrophobic and comforting. You were never by yourself, although if Percival lived here, he'd miss the solitude he could find in the People's Preserve outside of Camelot and the forests around his mother's cottage.

The constant buzz of vehicles and voices compared only to the crowded three-day festivals of summer and winter solstices at home. Food carts sent familiar smells of cooking fish and vegetables, but with a spicy edge Percival couldn't name. The windows of shops displayed clothing fit for royalty, but everyone on the streets and sidewalks seemed to be wearing them. He evaluated his own clothes, and the clothing of his companions, average by Viridian standards, but poor in comparison to Aurelia's. Could all of these Aurelians be so wealthy? The six horses in Percival's caravan were six more than he'd spied for several blocks, and this observation made him uneasy. His caravan stood out in more ways than one, and that couldn't be a good thing. There was little he could do about the problem.

He focused on his mission, and the address for the Viridian embassy given him by Merlin. Percival and Dee studied the street markers, but they couldn't orient themselves. Dee noticed a large man in a blue uniform making notes on a tablet. He wore a cap and a sidearm, which made Percival think of his sword, tucked away on a pack horse's back.

Percival approached him slowly. All police tended to be skittish, in his opinion. "Officer, we're new to Aurelia. Can you point the way to the Viridian embassy?" Percival showed him the address on his com. His battered device looked about ten years out of date, compared to the officer's.

Instead of looking at Percival's com, the officer stared at his clothes. "You're with them?" He glanced at Dee and the two retainers.

"Yes, sir. We're from Viridiae. We need to speak to local representatives of our government."

The officer wrinkled his nose. "Smelling like that?"

"Like what?"

"Horse manure. All of you disconnected smell like horse manure, or urine."

"Disconnected?"

"Are you deaf? Off the grid, homeless, vagrant."

Percival wasn't sure what to make of the description.

"Go to the public Camp Town. That's where new immigrants go. There's showers there and a laundry. And for Gaia's sake, clean up after your horses."

Two of Percival's animals had the bad timing to drop manure.

Percival didn't like the affront to his pride. Yes, they'd been on the road for weeks, and they'd taken care to clean their clothes and themselves and care for their animals. He knew he'd need to make an impression on local people if he was to gain their cooperation for finding the Last Grail. But he didn't need to take insults.

"Is this the way you treat visitors? I'm a knight of Arturus' Round Table, I—" He stopped himself. He didn't need to get into a fight so soon.

"Really? So you run around on horseback pointing swords at each other? If I catch you doing that here, you'll do a week in jail, guaranteed."

"I'm a warrior, and I'm on an important mission. You—"

"Yeah, we got missions too. They're next to Camp Town. A half-dozen full of derelicts like you."

Dee interrupted, pulling Percival away. "We're sorry, officer. Like my brother said, we're new here. We don't know the rules. Where is Camp Town?"

"This guy's your brother? Camp Town is down that street, two kilometers or so. Look for the signs."

Dee thanked the officer and directed Ben and Roz to follow her and Percival.

"That was really stupid, Perce."

"All I did was ask for directions. He didn't need to insult me."

"I guess they don't like strangers. Maybe they don't like Viridians in particular. Seems odd, but it doesn't matter. It's getting dark. We need to find Camp Town."

By the time they reached the neighborhood, darkness had fallen, but the street lights were far brighter than Camelot's lamps. The buildings were older, dingier, not a tenth as tall as the radiant towers. The people matched the rundown streetscape, their clothing worn, colors faded, and they walked as if they carried heavy burdens. Percival could see why the police officer thought he belonged here, and not among the elites.

A thought struck him. He was part of Camelot's elite, though the people around him didn't like to use the word, preferring to style themselves as proletarian, like the shopkeepers who sold them groceries or ale. It was an accepted fiction. In Aurelia, Percival had no such status, fictional or real. He was as lowly as the elderly man he saw sweeping the sidewalk of grime.

Eventually, they came across a paved lot occupied by tents and a few shacks. Dee spotted two horses, and Percival relaxed. Seeing the familiar animals lowered his anxiety, like seeing a friend. It also meant fodder for his animals; the expedition was running low. Percival asked who was in charge, and he was directed to a shack taking up a corner nearest the street. A man with a head covered in stubble sat in the doorway.

"You own this lot, sir?"

"I manage it." His voice rasped. "Who wants to know?"

"My name is Percival Rathkeale, This is my sister, Dee. These are my retainers, Roz and Ben."

"Retainers?"

"Servants."

"Rich enough for servants, and you've wandered in with horses, looking like something the cat dragged in? Go away."

Percival stood his ground. "We can pay. What's your rate?"

"Can't you read?" The man pointed at the sign.

Outside of the man's name—Poddle—Percival could not make out the words. He looked at Dee, who shrugged. "We've just arrived from Viridiae. Our script is different. I can't read yours."

"Your accent's so thick, I can barely understand what you're saying," Poddle said. "We don't get many people from that far north. Where in Viridiae?"

"Camelot." Percival said the word with pride.

"Is it still standing? We heard those cocksucking Lucians destroyed it."

"We took it back. We're rebuilding it. Please, how much for a space? We're very tired."

"100 bits."

"What?" Dee said. "That's outrageous."

Percival relied on Merlin to help him plan for expenses. Merlin's information on local prices was either long out-of-date or completely wrong. "What can we get for 10 bits?"

Poddle laughed, then coughed. He sounded sick. "You're funny, Rathkeale. I can give you a corner by the manure pile for 50 bits."

"Forty bits and a three-meter by three-meter spot."

Poddle grunted and nodded.

Percival thought he'd made a good deal. "Will you take Viridian shillings? I also have Lucian dinarii."

Poddle looked at Percival's coins as if they were worthless stones. "Are you insane? Are you setting me up to be robbed? I only accept virtual coinage in Aurelian bits. If you can't pay in bits, go away."

Percival was crestfallen.

"Unless…" Poddle looked at Percival sideways. "You let me exchange the currency for you."

"Careful, Perce. This shark is prowling for victims."

"I'm a businessman, miss. Do you think this crowd is making me rich?" He swept a hand across the lot, half-used by families whose children looked as if they hadn't eaten in days. "I get a hundred immigrants like you a week, mostly from the desert, and no one ever has more than a penny to their name. I have to supplement my income one way or another. Money changing pays the electric bill."

Percival had heard enough. "What are your terms?"

"Fifteen percent of the transaction."

"Why don't you just take a liter of our blood?" Dee said.

Poddle sneered. "Because that's harder to sell, my dear. No one wants a foreigner's plasma."

For an instant, Percival wanted to tell Poddle about Dee's unique biology, but he kept quiet. Revealing too much information might put her and the expedition in danger. He handed over the currency to Poddle, as well as information for an account Merlin had set up at a Viridian bank that operated in Aurelia. Poddle changed the money, and Percival moved the bits to Poddle's account. He suddenly felt much poorer than he'd expected.

"Show us the site, please, Mr Poddle."

Poddle led the four Viridians to a site further away from the manure pile than Percival expected. "I've decided I like you people. You know how to do business. You deserve more than sleeping near shit."

"Percival, he wants something from us."

"Suspicious girl, aren't you, miss? Take what I offer as a gift."

Roz and Dee unloaded the animals, then got started raising the four-person tent on a small wooden platform that took up most of the nine-square meter site. Percival and Ben took the horses to the covered paddock. The night's rent included a small amount of feed for the animals, and Ben set to work brushing down the horses.

"If you don't mind my asking, sir," said Ben as he cleared the brush, "tell me again why we're here?"

"I want to talk to the Viridian embassy. We need to know more about the conditions to the south in Cassanti. Merlin thinks the Grail is there. And I want to catch up on news from home. We haven't heard a thing in weeks, and the Aurelians don't seem to care much what happens in Camelot."

"I told my family we were headed to Aurelia. They might have sent a message."

Percival patted Ben's shoulder. "We won't forget to ask."

After the animals were put to bed, Percival and the others sat on camp chairs eating a simple stew made of dried peas, carrots, potatoes, and a half-chicken Roz traded for a fresh egg. Though Roz was known as a champion wrestler at The Keep, she'd taken up the role of cook, because she made the best meals.

As they sat around the electric fire sipping Nihon tea, Poddle approached.

"Is all well?" Poddle said. "It's my time to head home."

Dee said, "We're fine, thank you, Mr Poddle, We have a whole pot of tea. Would you care to join us?" She gestured to an empty camp stool. Percival stood by the tent, listening.

Poddle grinned, though the rest of his face was askew, as if he rarely got invitations. "Well, if it's not too much trouble."

"Of course not." Dee poured the hot, earthy liquid into a tin cup. "Tell us about yourself."

Poddle shrugged. "There's not much to tell. Born and raised just a few kilometers away. Family moved to Camp Town when I was just a tyke. It was a lot nicer then. Lived here ever since."

"How long have you owned this business?" Dee said.

"As I said before, I manage it. I don't own it. The owner lives in one of the downtown high-rises." Poddle gestured toward downtown. The movement had no precision, suggesting a lack of respect for his boss. "I see him once a month when he comes for his money."

"I lived my whole life in a cottage in a forest," Dee said, "before I met the king of Viridiae. He invited my brother Percival and I to live in Camelot."

"You know the king himself? His name is, um…"

"Arturus, the third in his line." Dee sipped her tea. "Roz here has lived in a hundred places."

"My dad was in the military. We were always moving around. Sometimes I thought my home was on the back of a horse."

"This is Ben, best horseman here."

Ben touched his cap.

Percival found another stool and sat beside Poddle. "Have you traveled at all, Mr Poddle?"

"Please, you can just call me Poddle. The answer is no. I've always been a homebody. I've always wanted to visit Viridiae, though. I've heard that you have soldiers on horseback that use swords and armor. Is that really true?"

"Percival is a knight," Ben said. "He fought against the Lucians. He was captured and escaped, along with the king. I hope to be a knight someday."

Poddle's jaw dropped. "I always thought the stories about Viridian knights were bullshit. I guess not. Aurelians and the Lucians don't get along that well, but then no one like the Lucians. They don't bother us much, I guess. I've never heard of a war between us." He scratched his head, as if trying to remember something.

Percival cleared his throat. "I try to keep fighting to a minimum these days, unless it's to defend myself or someone in danger."

"Do you still use a sword?"

"I carry my war blade. I feel practically naked without it."

Poddle rubbed his chin. "Any chance I could see it?"

Percival nodded and rummaged in a pack. He removed the long blade, tight in its tooled scabbard, and handed it to Poddle. He cradled it as if it were a baby and he didn't know how to hold it.

"You're welcome to remove it, if you like."

Percival could tell Poddle had never held a long sword before. He seemed in awe. He returned the blade to the scabbard, and handed it back to Percival. "Thank you, Sir Percival. Uh, did I say that right?"

"You did," Percival said, "but Percival is fine."

The four Viridians and their Aurelian guest stared into the electric fire for a moment.

"If you don't mind my asking," Poddle said, "what are your plans?"

"I need to find the Viridian embassy. We have to check in, to see if anything's changed about our mission."

"Your mission?"

Percival hesitated.

"Oh, it's not a state secret, Perce," Dee said. "We're trying to find the Last Grail, so Merlin, our best scientist, can fix the Great Machine and restore the health of our climate."

Poddle looked skeptical. "The Last... We'll, it seems like a, uh, a worthy quest."

"If we don't find it," Ben said, "the climate will deteriorate to the point where Viridiae might die, not to mention the planet. We have to find it."

"Mmmm." Poddle nodded. "Not something you hear every day, but I'll take your word for it."

"Poddle," Dee said, "do you know where the Viridian embassy is?"

"Not offhand."

Percival removed his com and showed the screen to Poddle. "I have an address. None of us can read the street signs. Does it make sense to you?"

Poddle nodded. "Yes, actually. It does." He scanned the four faces, all watching expectantly. "I could take you there. It's on the edge of downtown, near the waterfront."

"That would be excellent, Mr Poddle," Percival said. "First thing in the morning?"

Poddle allowed a laugh, tinged with a nervousness. "I'm not sure what I've volunteered for, but I'll be here."

CHAPTER 15: A NEW COMMISSION

The building housing the Viridian embassy in Aurelia disappointed Dee. She expected a graceful, sensitive structure that resembled Camelot with its nine towers. She didn't think it would be as large, or as packed with history, but she thought it would be more than a suite of rooms on the fourth floor in an office building aesthetically identical to its neighbors. Viridiae was a special country, with special people she missed after weeks on strange roads and unfamiliar towns. The embassy deserved more than sharing an address with a law firm, two dentists, and a government agency that apparently eradicated vermin from the sewers.

That's how Poddle translated the incomprehensible characters in the glass-cased directory. He'd proven to be a capable guide, showing up at the eighth hour freshly shaven and dressed in clothing resembling the better day wear of most downtown Aurelians. Dee and her brother put on their best clothes, but they felt drab and unfashionable. She wanted to make a good impression on the ambassador.

Leaving Ben and Roz to tend to the camp and the animals, Dee and Percival followed Poddle, making enough twists and turns through Aurelia's back streets to confuse a practiced taxi driver. By the ninth hour, they stood in the building lobby. Percival invited Poddle along to the embassy office, just in case they needed more translating.

The suite itself proved to be tight, but cheery, with reproductions of classic Viridian paintings on the walls of the waiting room and pamphlets urging Aurelians to visit Viridian sights. The pamphlets' colors had that faded look of printed materials left out too long.

"Excuse me," Percival said to the young receptionist, who wore a style of business jacket Dee had noticed on other young Aurelian women. "I'm Percival Rathkeale and this is my sister Dee Rathkeale. I was wondering if Ambassador Grenwick was available."

"Do you have an appointment?"

"No, I'm sorry we don't. Our expedition only arrived last night."

"Sir Percival, as I live and breathe!"

One of the tallest men Dee had ever seen rounded a corner and beamed a dentist's dream of straight white teeth. He was dressed as an Aurelian businessman, sporting a frilled shirt and neck piece, but his accented speech marked him as pure Viridian.

"Let me shake your hand, sir, as well as that of the great artist, Dindrane Rathkeale."

Dee thought her wrist would break if the man shook it any harder.

"We're sorry to drop in like this, Mister..."

"Apologies! I'm Walter Grenwick, current ambassador to Aurelia. We've been anticipating your arrival. His Majesty and Merlin have been pestering us for weeks about you." Grenwick looked about his visitors, as if he had lost something. "We heard about your trouble at the border, but your expedition is smaller than I understood. I see just you and Dindrane."

"We left our retainers in Camp Town, at a private camping spot run by Mr Poddle." Percival gestured toward the proprietor.

Poddle rose and extended his hand. "Pleased to be of service, sir."

Grenwick's expression had a note of disdain. "Why Camp Town, Sir Percival?"

"We had barely crossed the bridge when a policeman took one look at us and shooed us toward that neighborhood."

Grenwick shook his head. "Aurelians have a deserved reputation as prideful, which comes across as snobbishness. If you don't make the right first impression, they decide you don't belong, and send you away like a lame dog. No offense, Mr Poddle."

"None taken, sir." Poddle grinned, though Dee thought it was insincere. And she wondered how Grenwick had survived in a diplomatic post that depended on soft-pedaling your criticism of the local culture.

"Do you have some time to discuss our plans, Ambassador?" Percival said.

"Of course! My office is available. Follow me."

"Mr Poddle, would you wait here for us?"

Poddle's grin turned sour as he resumed his seat in the waiting area.

Grenwick's office was roomy, with a desk flanked by two large flags, one of Viridiae, the other of King Arturus. The ambassador gestured toward a sitting area with a sofa, chairs, and a low table.

"Miss Rathkeale, I must ask you something before we get to business. I've been admiring your work from afar for years. How goes the project in the Great Audience Hall?"

"I don't actually know, Ambassador. I left a very capable artist in charge of continuing the work while I'm on the expedition. I assume she's making progress. Have you heard anything?"

Grenwick's face darkened. "Nothing, I'm afraid. Please, Miss Rathkeale—May I call you Dindrane? Dee then—it would please me and do the embassy honor if you'd consider loaning one of your tapestries to us in the near future. I'd put it in the waiting area. I enjoy showcasing Viridian artists, but few travel here, and even fewer show their work."

Dee suppressed her pleasure, and surprise. One of her works hanging in an embassy? "Happy to do so, Mr Ambassador. When I return to Camelot, I'll send something to you."

Grenwick beamed. "You must be very proud of your sister, Percival. All of Viridiae loves her."

Dee detected a slight rolling of eyes on the part of her brother.

A tone sounded on Grenwick's desk. He picked up his com and his face lit up. "Dee, I took the liberty of letting my wife Trudy know you were here. She's a fan as well. Do you have a moment to speak to her?"

"Of, cour—"

Percival said, "I was hoping we could speak about the next leg of the expedition—"

Grenwick glanced at the door. "Ah! Darling, come in, please!"

A plump woman in a flowery dress extended both hands toward Dee. Trudy Grenwick wore a hat that added half-again as much height to her pumpkin-like frame. The neon colors of her dress were so bright, Dee squinted. Her hat mirrored the colors with ribbons and bird feathers.

"Miss Rathkeale, you are even more beautiful in person than in your photographs. A brilliant artist and beauty fit for royalty. You'll be as popular in this city as the Aurelian Eagles!"

Dee furrowed her brow, not understanding the term.

"Our championship gridball team," Grenwick said.

"Thank you, um, Trudy?"

"As soon as I heard you'd arrived, I contacted all of my friends in the arts community and we've already put one together."

"I'm sorry?" Dee said.

"A welcoming party! Do you know how many famous and talented Viridian artists come to visit us? None! I'm not going to miss this opportunity, and neither should you. Aurelians love visual art. And they pay good money for quality work. You could become rich very quickly if you play your cards right."

Dee hesitated, "Well, normally I'd love to attend, but my brother and I are on an important journey to find the Grail, and —"

"Sir, I'd really like to see what kind of transporta—"

The ambassador blew a sound of dismissal from his nose. "Oh, it's all been arranged, Percival. I've chartered a ship for your trip south. Much faster and safer than an overland trip."

Dee wasn't sure she liked the idea of a trip by sea. She had prepared herself for a long hike along the coast to Cassanti.

That's what they'd planned. However, Percival's nod signaled his acceptance of Grenwick's plan. Percival had experience with sea voyages. He'd sailed aboard the *Dolphin* to Koda with Lancelot, Bors, and Galahad.

"The ship won't be ready until tomorrow, so we have time to prepare for tonight. I'm going to loan Percival some good Aurelian clothes so you'll fit right in. Trudy, will you do the honors with Dee?"

"I'd be delighted." Trudy clapped her hands. "I can't wait!"

"Come along then," Grenwick said.

He ushered Dee and Percival out of his office and led them to the waiting room. The ambassador nearly tore the grubby knapsack from Percival's back and gave it to Poddle, who received it with a surprised look. Percival shrugged and promised to let Poddle know where to find them.

* * *

Dee stepped out of the private car in front of a high-rise whose top floor reached into the star-filled night. She wore a dark green sleeveless dress made of a fabric that felt like silk but wasn't. Despite Trudy's short stature, her closet was stuffed with business and evening clothes and shoes for every taste and body shape, explaining that women often arrived from other countries or cities with nothing appropriate for an Aurelian social event. Dee wasn't one for heavy makeup, but she succumbed to Trudy's entreaties for at least some enhancement of her gray-green eyes and wide mouth. It was expected, she said, and now was not the time to come up short of expectations.

They rode a private elevator to the 158th floor. The door opened to a foyer and a set of double-doors the height of two men. One of the doors swung open, and a young man in a tuxedo and white gloves showed them down a hallway to a room full of milling people, primarily Aurelians, by the look of their clothes and hair. A few turned to look at the new arrivals.

"Ah, my dearest, you've brought the guest of honor!" Grenwick bent down to kiss his wife's cheeks. He reached out his hands to Dee. "So radiant! Better than any artist could imagine!"

Dee hoped the diffuse lights would hide her feeling of unreality. She'd attended several formal and semi-formal events at the palace in Camelot, but they didn't compare in opulence to this party's venue or the people. Did everyone in Aurelia dress this way for an evening out? She grinned and nodded to dozens of faces, some friendly and smiling, others wary and skeptical. After a moment, she noticed something odd about a few of the faces. One appeared to belong to a tiger, with whiskers and amber eyes. Another resembled a bird, with a long, beak-like nose and skin stained to iridescent shades of blue-green. She had to keep from staring.

Grenwick eased through the crowd toward a window and group of tables. Dee didn't know a soul, apart from the Grenwicks, and she relaxed when she spotted Percival, outfitted in a dark business suit. On his shoulder, he wore an enameled pin in the form of Viridiae's flag. Dee sat next to him, while Grenwick waved over servers, who brought Napene wine and canapes. Dee recognized salmon, strawberries, and avocado, but not much else.

A man caught Grenwick's attention, and they fell into a discussion. The man's face was colored to resemble an orca. When he smiled, he had the orca's pointed teeth.

"You've noticed it, too," Percival said, half-whispering to Dee in the din of conversation.

"It reminds me of the Ontarii and their clan facial stripes. This is different, though. Do you know what it is?"

Percival shrugged.

"It's DNA modification," Trudy said.

"What?" The comment reminded Dee of her own genome's differences from ordinary humans, but hers was handed down from the time before the Dissolution, when the world fell apart. "They've modified their genetic code?"

"Very popular in wealthy Aurelian society."

"How do they do it?"

"A harmless virus inserts specially designed strands of DNA into skin cells to produce an effect resembling an animal's coloration or plumage, in the case of birds."

"Why would anyone do that?" Dee found herself growing upset. "Humanity tried this a thousand years ago, and we're still suffering the effects. Just look at trolls."

"Calm down, Dee." Trudy patted her hand. "I agree with you, but we're in another country, another culture. We have to respect our hosts, in spite of their shortsightedness."

In Trudy's words, Dee could hear her teacher Ganieda's voice. She preached tolerance as well, almost to a fault. Dee had a flash of loneliness for the old woman's advice and company. She missed Camelot more with each passing hour.

Grenwick approached her. "Would you mind very much joining this gentleman and myself? He's our host and he'd like to introduce you to other guests."

Dee calmed herself and followed the two men into an adjoining room. She startled when she spied three of her light tapestries on one wall. They were among the pieces she had shown at her first gallery show in Camelot before the Lucian war, when she met Lord Mordred. Soon after, he commissioned her work in the Great Audience Hall. In the room at the top of an Aurelian skyscraper, the gathering of 10 or 15 people started to applaud.

Grenwick spoke up. "Ladies and gentlemen, I see that you've already recognized our guest of honor. Perhaps you feel that you already know Ms Dindrane Rathkeale after enjoying her stunning tapestries. She's only in Aurelia for a very short time, but she graciously agreed to join us this evening. I am so proud of our nation's artists, who are world-renowned for their creativity and daring. Let me introduce you formally to Ms Rathkeale."

Dee froze. Was she expected to speak? No one told her. She had nothing prepared and didn't know any of these people. What was she supposed to say?

Trudy came to her rescue. She whispered in Dee's ear.

"Thank you so much, Mr Ambassador." Dee's heart pumped hard. "I'm so excited to be in one of the most beautiful cities on the Peaceful Sea." Trudy turned away slightly, but kept whispering. "I won't keep you all from enjoying each other's company. I'm happy to answer any questions you may have about my work."

The crowd applauded again.

"You're good at this." Percival held a glass of wine.

"I'm terrified. If Trudy hadn't given me the words, like I was a puppet, I would've vomited."

"You're good, just the same."

Grenwick introduced Dee to each guest one at a time, a process she found much less intimidating than speaking to a group. She fell back on her experience with chatting up courtiers at Arturus' court and art lovers at gallery shows, though she couldn't remember meeting any Aurelians in Camelot. She wasn't even sure they had an embassy.

She accepted the praise and endured the questions, knowing that most buyers and admirers had no idea why they liked something, only that it was pretty or fit in that spot on the living room wall where nothing else worked, so to say. She had met only a few true connoisseurs, one of them Mordred, who could talk with her about her technique or artistic philosophy.

A woman of about 50 came up to her during a moment when Dee found herself alone. She wore a three-quarter sleeved, floor length dress over her lanky frame. Her round face, with black eyes and small mouth, resembled an owl's, and Dee briefly wondered if she had taken the cosmetic DNA treatment. If she did, the effect was subtle.

"These gatherings are often exhausting, don't you think?" she said, her voice a low rasp.

"I agree, but it's part of being a public person, at least in the art world."

"My name is Chek, Andrea Chek."

Dee touched hands with the woman. "Pleased to meet you."

"Did you not study with Ganieda Ambrosius?"

Dee thrilled to hear the familiar name. "I did. Do you know her?"

"I met her once, when I was about your age. We've corresponded over the years, and I've purchased some of her work. She's a brilliant teacher."

"I owe a lot to her. She's the one who nurtured me, believed in me."

"She has an eye for talent. You're one of her most important finds."

Dee felt her ears go hot. Chek was different from the other guests.

"I don't mean to embarrass. Let me explain. I'm the tapestries curator of the Aurelian Museum of Art. We're the most important museum in the city, if you don't mind my saying."

"I'm flattered by your praise. You know, I've only been painting in the light tapestry medium for a few years. I feel like I've barely mastered the basics."

The crowd began to thin out, and the two women sat at a table.

"Many artists say it's impossible to master anything. They are always learning, always discovering new methods. I tried to make a career in sculpture, but I found I was better at uncovering beautiful and important work, or encouraging it, rather than making it."

Dee relaxed. Here was someone like Ganieda, or even Mordred, with whom she could discuss her passion. "Encouraging it?"

"One of my jobs is commissioning work." She cited several well-known artists from the Hot Lands, Lucanus, and Viridiae, even one from far off Nihon. "My board of directors believes collecting and showing isn't enough. We have to push artists to new accomplishments."

Dee's mouth went dry. Was Chek offering something? "I'm taking a break from creating, apart from some sketching here and there. King Arturus wanted me to accompany my brother on a mission to find the Grail, so we can repair the Great Machine in Viridiae's care."

"A noble thing, but I fear your skills might atrophy after months on the road. That would be an equal tragedy."

"I don't know what you mean."

"Let me ask you something. Do you have a project or an idea, an artistic idea, that you've always wanted to pursue?"

Dee thought a moment. Her mural in the Great Audience Hall was her biggest project, though she had to leave it behind to join the expedition. But she hadn't thought much about a future, large project.

"I see." Chek appeared disappointed, then brightened. "Do you know the story of Aurelia? How it was founded?"

Dee shook her head.

"The city was founded before the Dissolution. Virtually all the records from that time are lost, but there are hints. Some say it was founded by an ancient empire as a military outpost. I happen to like the idea that it was founded by a traveling monk who attracted followers to his message of peace and understanding. Neither are probably true, but the second story has an inspirational quality, don't you agree?"

Dee nodded.

"It also has a quality of light, of a dawning, somehow. An artist who works with light could do something with this story."

Dee's heart beat faster.

"Let me be blunt. My board has authorized me to offer you a commission to create a monumental light tapestry depicting the founding of Aurelia by this traveling monk."

Her hands sweaty, Dee didn't know what to think. By what reasoning did this person think she had the talent to pull off something like she described? She barely felt capable of finishing the mural in Camelot, and now she was offered a commission at least as hard, maybe harder, because Chek clearly knew what she wanted.

"What do you think, Dee?"

"I'm, well, I don't know what to say. I'm not sure..."

"Yes, I know this is a big job, maybe your biggest. We wouldn't offer it to you if we didn't think you were up to it. And let me assure you that you will be well paid."

"Okay." Dee wasn't sure if it was polite to ask how much. "How much?"

"Fifty thousand bits when you sign the contract. Fifty thousand upon completion. We will provide accommodations for you near the museum at no cost while you're working."

Dee looked around for Percival. He had no head for business, but she wanted him near. She felt as if she was entering another universe. "I don't have any equipment. I left it all in Camelot."

"Our budget provides for the best projectors, software, and tablets. We can also provide assistants, if you need them."

It was the chance of a lifetime. Dee understood that much. What would Ganieda say? Was she ready for such a huge task? "It sounds very interesting, Andrea. Um, if you don't mind my asking, how much is 100,000 bits in Viridian currency?"

"Let me check today's exchange rate." Chek touched her com, and made the calculation. She showed it to Dee.

Dee used every fiber of her being to keep herself from fainting. She'd never seen so much money in her life. It reminded her that proud Viridiae was relatively poor, compared to Aurelia. Money was not the only way to measure value in a culture, but you couldn't ignore the power of numbers like these.

"I realize this is a major decision, Dee. I don't expect an answer now."

Out of the corner of her eye, Percival approached, and she sighed in relief.

"Dee, I want to show you something."

"Please think about it, Ms Rathkeale, won't you?" Chek said. She grinned confidently.

"Who's that? Think about what?" Percival said.

Dee wasn't ready to talk about what she'd just heard. "It's nothing. What do you need, Percival?"

"I want you to look down there."

They stood at a window, the sunset illuminating the towers in golden colors.

Percival pointed down, his eyes alight. "Do you see the harbor and the piers? I know we're hundreds of meters up, but do you see that ship on the far pier?"

At this height, it resembled a sliver of wood floating on a pond.

"It's the *Dolphin*, my old ship! Well, I was never really part of the crew, but I feel like I was. We're sailing on the *Dolphin*!"

Percival's excitement pleased Dee, but her mind was already weighing her new choice: Continue on the expedition with her brother, or achieve something that would send her career in a direction she never imagined.

CHAPTER 16: THE DOLPHIN DEPARTS

Dee and Percival returned to Camp Town late in the evening after stopping at the ambassador's residence to change back into their Viridian clothes. Poddle picked them up in a public car, but by the time they found Ben and Roz still awake by the electric fire, they were in a heated argument.

"You never wanted to come on the expedition," Percival said.

"That may have been true once, but I changed my mind," Dee said.

"It was only when Arturus basically ordered you that you came."

"Bullshit. I came of my own free will."

Dee sympathized with her brother. He'd been given a chance to redeem himself for his mistakes during the Lucian war, and he wanted to do a service for Viridiae and Arturus. He wanted her support. Sometimes Percival could be overbearing, taking his role as a leader of the expedition too seriously, but all-in-all, they had gotten along over the past weeks. But who would've thought that the most important museum in Aurelia would offer her a job that could set her up for life?

"I've been to the museum once," Poddle said. "They have a free day once a month. I've never been so confused in my life."

"Why?' Dee said.

"Some of it was interesting. I liked the older stuff, because I could recognize things and what was happening. But the newer stuff?" Poddle shrugged. "Hard to believe someone actually paid for it."

Dee didn't argue. She could've advised Poddle to simply enjoy the colors or the shapes or the subtle animations. The advice was an easy out. Though she had never visited the Aurelian Museum of Art, she'd seen plenty of head-scratching work at Camelot's big museum, the Royal Academy. She thought its money had been wasted on more than one artist.

There was no accounting for taste, however. An opportunity was an opportunity. A leader in the Aurelian art world believed in Dee's work. Dee had the self-doubt that plagued every artist, writer, and musician. She had frozen plenty of times in front of a blank canvas. Saying no, however, to Andrea Chek would be a huge mistake, and not just because of the money and prestige. It sealed her identity.

"I need you, Dee," Percival said. "All the time we were growing up, we were partners. We did everything together. Sometimes I think the reason I failed on the other expeditions was because you weren't there to keep me from doing something stupid or to tell me that I was doing the right thing."

"Ben and Roz will help you."

The two retainers shrank away. They wanted no part of the argument.

"They aren't you, Dee. No one knows me like you do, not even our mother."

"You can handle the expedition on your own," Dee said. "You aren't the same Percival who left on his first expedition two years ago. You're more confident, seasoned, mature. I'm not sure how much I'm helping you."

"You are. I'm just not explaining it very well." Percival face was filled with desperation.

No, he was explaining it clearly, Dee thought. She gave him perspective and kept him on course. But that wasn't enough of a reason to give up on her dreams. As the days and weeks wore on after their departure from Ash, Dee grew less and less confident about prospects to resume her old life. Ganieda and her mother had told her many times that you couldn't go backwards, only forward. How would things be different in Camelot in weeks or months? The ambassador had shared the latest political news with Dee and Percival. Tensions were rising between Arturus and Mordred. Many people feared a civil war. Even the Aurelians were taking notice. Their government debated whether to send an expeditionary force north to make sure hostilities didn't spill over in their territory.

"Percival, my support for you will never change. I love you. Even if you fail—and I know you won't—we'll always be sister and brother. We shared our mother's womb. It's impossible for me not to love you!"

Percival rubbed his hands, as if all his confidence had vanished. "You've decided to stay then."

"No, I haven't." Dee was sincere. "I'm just imagining things if I did. I know you'll succeed, with or without me."

"I wish I had your confidence."

"Don't be so sure. I don't really know what to do. Aurelia is an amazing place. Tonight, I met a lot of gallery owners and other artists. They welcomed me with open arms. I love Camelot, but it seems like a small town with blinders compared to Aurelia. I could spread my wings here."

Percival huffed, and the sound was full of cynicism. "You always fall back on cliches when you're trying to convince yourself to do something you don't really want to do."

"And you fall into whining whenever you don't get your way."

The acrimony had poisoned the conversation. Percival disappeared into a tent to escape the spat.

Poddle stood in the shadows. "I hate it when families argue. I had an argument with my parents. They wanted me to go to college. I wanted to go to work. I did what I wanted, and we rarely spoke after that. We couldn't see outside our little worlds."

Dee sat on a camp chair and stared into the fire. "Did you make up with them?"

"They died before I could work up the nerve. Don't make my mistake."

That was the crux of it. Which was the mistake? Going for what she wanted? Or continuing to follow Percival? She had no idea.

* * *

Percival woke up early to the street sounds of cruising cars and cooing pigeons. Sleep eluded him for hours after his argument with Dee, but the day's plan overcame his smoldering hurt and disappointment. She had betrayed him to even think of abandoning his expedition for money and prestige, though he understood what the job could mean for her career. Of course, he wanted her to pursue her dreams, just not now.

He woke up Ben and told him to start packing. The four of them were due at the *Dolphin* in a few hours. Poddle promised to help again as impromptu guide. He wanted something more than their rent money, but Percival had too much on his mind to puzzle it out.

Roz returned from the communal faucet with water for oatmeal and tea. Dee emerged from her tent looking as if she'd barely slept. She gave her personal knapsack with her clothes and personal belongings to Ben for loading. Percival wanted to say something to his sister, but no words formed in his mind. His anger had dissipated, but he could barely look at her, for fear of his wound of last night reopening. He just wanted to get to the ship and get underway.

The four said little to each beyond polite morning greetings. Ben and Roz stole glances at each other, uncertain whether the siblings might reconcile or not. Poddle brought some pastries from a bakery next door to the camp ground. Percival eyed the sugar-covered cake, but didn't take one. Neither did Dee. Ben and Roz dug in.

"So everyone is cheery this morning," Poddle said. "The weather people say it'll be a fine day."

Poddle's attempt to break the frosty atmosphere failed, but Percival directed everyone to check their gear one last time. Poddle had slung a small backpack over his shoulder. It appeared half-full, though Percival couldn't tell what was inside. Perhaps it was his lunch.

"Thanks, Poddle," Percival said, as they made their way to the waterfront, "for helping us navigate Aurelia."

"My pleasure, Percival. I actually have a request."

Percival thought of the coins in his purse. "Oh, yes. I was meaning to give you something for your help. What would be fair?"

Poddle looked at his shoes. "That's not what I had in mind. I'd like to go with you. To Cassanti."

Percival took in Poddle's expression, a mix of longing and timidity.

"I know this is sudden, but I've thought it over."

"I'm not sure I have room for you, Poddle." Percival's equivocation took in Dee's expected decision to stay, but Percival didn't feel comfortable simply offering the empty spot to Poddle. "Grenwick booked passage for four people and our animals."

"I understand, but I have a little money saved up. I can pay my own way. I've been useful to you, and you might need more help."

"How do you know?"

Poddle shrugged. "You're strangers to the Hot Lands. Anything could happen."

"Have you been to Cassanti?"

"No."

"Do you know anyone or have relatives there?"

"No." Poddle breathed out, and stared ahead, as if he didn't want to meet Percival's gaze.

Percival was uncertain how to respond. If Poddle could pay his own way, Percival couldn't prevent him from buying a ticket and accompanying him to Cassanti, though what might happen after arrival was another thing altogether.

Percival said, "Why do you want to come with us?"

"I'm going to be 40 years old soon. I have no wife, no children. My parents are dead. I hate my job. I'm bored as hell. I like the fact that you know what you want and where you're going. Maybe I can find some of that by going with you."

"We don't really know what we'll find. It may seem like we're on solid ground, but all we have is rumors and unconfirmed facts. Merlin probably knows less than what he's letting on. He's as much salesman as scientist. It might even be dangerous for you."

"I'm not worried," Poddle said. "Honestly, I just need to get out of Aurelia before I go crazy. Call it cabin fever."

After descending a series of steep grades, the hills flattened out to a man-made strand, leading to piers and wharves that stretched up and down the shore for two or three kilometers. Closer to the water, the air grew humid and tasted of salt and decay. Bits of garbage floated on the smooth surface. Warehouses, low-profile office buildings, restaurants, and chandlers occupied the piers. Between them, a forest of masts pierced the blue sky. The narrow strait lay to the west; Percival could see the tops of the great bridge's towers behind a hill. To the north and east was a large bay with the far shore obscured by haze. Grenwick had given Percival a number for the pier where he'd find his ship. Poddle led the group directly to it. Percival's excitement grew when he saw the familiar transom of the *Dolphin*. He recognized the figure at the gangway.

"Michael!"

Captain Michael Libb looked up from a tablet and a broad smile filled his face. He reached out his hand to Percival, then pulled the younger man into a bear hug. "Sir Percival, my old shipmate!"

Percival took in the *Dolphin*'s Old Man, who looked as if he'd gained a few more gray hairs and a few kilos. "This is my sister, Dee."

Michael touched his cap. "Pleased to meet you, miss."

"And Ben, Roz, and a local friend, Poddle."

"Well, then, I'm anxious to chat with you all, but you have your horses and gear to stow. The slings for the animals are ready, and so are your cabins. Ambassador Grenwick said at least three were going to Cassanti. I see five."

Percival was about to explain when he saw Grenwick approaching, along with a woman he recognized from the party. He didn't know her name. Dee was already speaking to them.

"Ambassador. Andrea, it's nice to see you again," Dee said.

"We've come to see you and your brother off," Grenwick said. "At least most of you."

Dee had told Percival the woman's name, Andrea Chek, but he didn't make the connection until that moment. This was the woman who'd disrupted his plans. He couldn't resist his feelings of resentment. She was about to steal Dee away with what amounted to a bribe. But he couldn't stay angry at Dee. She was her own person, and she could run her life as she pleased. He had no idea how he would fill the gap she left behind.

"Is everything in order, Percival?"

"Yes, ambassador."

"Wonderful!"

Behind the group, the horses clambered over a cargo gangway through a hatch in the side of the vessel. Slings would hold the animals in place during the voyage. Ben and Roz would be in charge of keeping the horses healthy.

"Dee," Chek said. "I know things are happening quickly, but I came because I need a decision from you. Will you accept the commission?"

Percival wished he could leave and help Ben and Roz. He didn't want to hear that Dee would stay. It would be humiliating for her to accept in front of him, almost abandoning him to whatever he might find in Cassanti. But he couldn't leave either, for fear of hurting his sister. He wanted to be there for her. He planned to say the right words of congratulations, wish her luck, kiss her goodbye, and board the *Dolphin*. He braced himself.

Dee said, "Andrea, I'm so flattered by your offer, I still don't know what to say, except thank you. But I must turn it down."

Andrea's face fell, as if her offers were rarely, if ever, refused. "May I ask why?"

Percival's heart leaped.

"I'm a Viridian, Andrea. My people need me. But it's really more my brother. He's my only family, besides our mother. He wants me to help him, and I always have. I can't say no to that. I'm sorry."

Grenwick's face also blanched. Had Dee committed some diplomatic *faux pas*? "Is there nothing that can persuade you, Miss Rathkeale?"

"Don't misunderstand me, ambassador. This project is beyond my wildest dreams. I would love to raise Viridiae's stature among the Aurelians. But I have something more important to work on right now."

"Perhaps... Perhaps..." Grenwick was at a loss for words, another rarity for a diplomat. "Is there a chance you would take up the commission when you return to Aurelia? You'll only be gone a few weeks, correct, Percival? You're coming back here on your way home?"

"We'd planned to stop in Aurelia on the way home, assuming nothing detoured us."

"Then it's settled," Grenwick said, relieved. "Dee can take up the work at the museum in a few weeks. What do you think, Andrea?"

The museum curator narrowed her eyes. "I'll have to speak to my board. There are other candidates, but you were always at the top of their wish list. When you suddenly turned up, they sweetened the package to entice you. I'm almost certain they'll hold off, if you're certain you'll be back, Dee."

"I'm as certain as I can be, Andrea. Of course, I'd be happy to take the job then."

Grenwick clapped his hands. "Oh, excellent! A win-win, as the ancient saying goes. We won't take any more of your time, Percival. I have so much to do, news releases, com interviews, dispatches to home. By the way, I've informed Camelot of your arrival and imminent departure. The king and queen send their best wishes."

Grenwick practically bounced on the pier deck as he and Chek departed.

Percival regarded his sister. He'd never loved her so much as he did in that moment. "Thanks, Dee. Really."

"This had better be fun. I just gave up a hundred-thousand-bit gig for a boat trip."

Percival wanted to hug and kiss her, but he held back. Even in an emotional moment like this, he had to play the steady, even-tempered leader. He vowed he'd find some way to thank her more than with a word or two.

Percival spent the next hour directing the stowage of the expedition's gear and checking on the horses. Everyone worked at speed to meet Captain Libb's request to leave on the tide. Poddle, too, pitched in.

When everything was ready, Libb ordered his crew to prepare for departure. Poddle eyed Percival, but waited patiently. Percival made his decision.

"Thanks for all your help, Poddle. You've made our stay a lot easier."

"My pleasure." Poddle's hand ran along the edge of the ship's rail nervously. "I suppose I'll be off then."

"You're welcome to join the expedition, Poddle. With any luck, we'll bring you home in a few weeks."

Poddle beamed. "Thank you, Percival. Thank you very much."

The *Dolphin*'s crew stowed the gangway and threw off the bow and stern lines. A tug pulled the ship away from its slip, and Percival felt the breeze brush away his red hair.

CHAPTER 17: A PLAGUE AT SEA

On their second day at sea, Ben came to Percival complaining of illness. Most of the dozen passengers on the *Dolphin*, including Percival's expedition, suffered through seasickness in varying degrees. Percival adjusted without any discomfort. Dee had some queasiness, but it only lasted a day. Ben, though, was sick with a dry cough and a fever. Percival sent him back to his bunk. With no doctor on board, Captain Libb served as the ship's medical officer. He had a basic medical kit, first-aid supplies, common medicines, and a tablet full of medical texts, but not much else. He measured Ben's fever at 38.3 Celsius. The diagnosis was influenza. The prescription was rest.

Otherwise, the voyage proceeded as Percival hoped. They had departed Aurelia's waterfront at the beginning of the good season for weather, and the Peaceful Sea had greeted them with fresh breezes and a sky full of fair-weather clouds. The breeze was strong enough to take the tops off the waves. Percival took in lungfuls of clean sea air, leavened with the cries of the ever-present gulls. He strolled the 60-meter deck and surprised himself with how well he remembered all but the most obscure names for the hundreds of lines that made up *Dolphin*'s standing and running rigging. He asked Libb's permission to climb to the head of the foremast, and Libb agreed, provided one of his crew accompanied him for safety.

At the masthead, Percival had an unobstructed view of the western horizon. The sea stretched on forever, and he felt the ancient temptation to forget all that lay behind him and sail as far west as he could, touching Nihon and the continent beyond. A dozen meters above the pitching deck, a quest to find an old gadget to fix a broken contraption seemed trivial, compared to the possibilities at the edge of the world. His responsibilities weighed on him like dirty weather, and he wished he could shrug them off. Even if the world warmed itself to destruction and fell apart in a new Dissolution, he'd find a way to survive on an ocean as wide as the universe.

That would mean he'd lose Lina. Even though he hadn't seen her or talked to her in a dozen weeks, the fire still burned, if not quite as hot. Among the messages Grenwick had agreed to pass on was a note from Percival to Lina. He loved her, and he would do everything he could to see her, once he'd collected the Grail. He prayed she loved him, and that she would wait for him. He had no way of knowing whether she even remembered who he was, now that she was probably buried in work and surrounded by the excitement of the palace.

Percival shielded his eyes against the sun, and glanced at the deck, 15 meters below. Dee waved to him. Her mouth moved, as if calling to him, but he couldn't hear a word. With the *Dolphin*'s crew member leading him like a guardian angel, he made his way down the shrouds.

"I thought you'd never come down," Dee said, exasperated.

"I almost didn't," Percival said. "I'd forgotten how amazing it is up there."

"Ben's getting worse. You should take a look."

Ben was soaked in sweat, his black hair pasted to his forehead and neck, despite the chill air coming through a small window. Dee did her best to comfort him with a damp cloth.

"How are you doing, Ben?" Percival said.

"I've been better, sir."

"We're here for you. We'll take good care of you. Who else is going to help me with the horses?"

"Roz is good with them."

"We need two good assistants. I can't afford you to be sick. Did you get the messages from your parents? I asked the ambassador to relay them to you."

"Yes, sir. They're doing fine. They said they missed me."

Percival patted Ben's shoulder. He felt the fever's heat. "Once we find the Grail, we'll take the fastest way home, I promise."

Libb came in with a bottle of tablets and fresh water. "These should bring down his fever, and we need to keep him hydrated." Libb gestured for Percival to follow him into the passageway.

Libb brought his tablet out from a pouch. "I found a portable device for analyzing blood in the medical stores. I put a drop of Ben's blood into the device. It's not the flu."

"What is it, then?"

"It's definitely a virus, but the device keeps saying 'Inconclusive' when I ask for an identification. We have to sequence the virus's DNA to identify it, but there's no way I can do that on *Dolphin*. You'd need a hospital or a research lab."

"What do we do now? Go back to port?" Percival chafed at the potential for another delay, but he didn't have a choice.

"I wouldn't recommend that just now."

"What?"

"I kind of had to leave in a hurry. It was pure luck that Grenwick found a spot for you and your people on *Dolphin*. I was going to shove off an hour before he contacted me. I decided to wait for you. I knew your money was good."

"I'm not following you."

"Let's just say the Aurelian tax collectors are inflexible when it comes to late dock fees and bad credit. Grenwick's cash didn't pay for everything."

"You're broke and you had one foot in jail."

Libb flushed. "That's an unkind way to put it. I was going to pay everything I owed. Just not right now."

"It doesn't matter at this point," Percival said. "Where do we find a doctor?"

"I've ordered a course for Luna Bay. That's the nearest port other than Aurelia, and they don't care about late Aurelian dockage fees."

Percival could no nothing more. He was only one passenger

among 12. He gave Ben the news.

* * *

Ben died just after midnight. Libb could do nothing to stop it, and Luna Bay was still a half-day away. Percival had a bad headache, but he pushed it aside to bring Dee and Roz together to talk it over.

"How did this happen?" Roz's voice quivered. She and Ben had become good friends. She got along well with everybody. Percival remembered her friendship with Penny.

"Libb doesn't know. He thinks it was some kind of exotic virus, but he's not a doctor."

"What do we do, sir?"

"What does Libb think?" Dee said.

"He wants to continue south. He has the other passengers to think about. And he has an interest in keeping a low profile. He owes several people money, not just the government in Aurelia. He might lose his ship if the authorities think there's illness aboard."

"But that's the truth."

Percival snapped at Dee. "Which is why he wants to stay as far away from the coast as possible."

He immediately felt sorry, and he apologized to Dee. His head was hurting like hell and he wanted to turn in. Dawn was only a few hours away.

"You don't look good, Perce," Dee said. "Are you feeling okay?"

Percival had to stay strong. "I'm fine. I just need some sleep." He glanced at Ben's cabin, where the young man's body lay, a blanket over his face. Libb couldn't leave it there for long, and he couldn't keep Ben's death a secret. The news would travel on *Dolphin* like wildfire. "We'll discuss it more in the morning."

Percival slipped into the cabin he shared with Dee, next door to Ben's. Roz shared Ben's cabin, but she decided to spend the rest of the night with the horses. Dee went to the galley to see if there was any hot water for tea. As Percival changed into a nightshirt, a wave of heat washed over him, and he started to cough. It was a dry, wracking cough that produced no phlegm. He lay down in his bunk, and his body shivered, as he had dived into an icy river and returned to weather worthy of an Arctic blizzard. Sweat dripped into his eyes, and the cough kept him from sleeping.

Dee returned with a cup. "Gaia in Heaven, you're sick. You'd better drink this. I put some lemon in it. It'll soothe the cough." She put her hand on his forehead. "I'd better get Libb."

The captain took Percival's temperature and pricked Percival's forefinger for a blood sample, placing it on a thin slip of paper before inserting it into his analyzer. "Same result as Ben's, Percival. Inconclusive." Libb's attitude was grave.

"You'll have to take me to Luna Bay."

Libb didn't answer.

"You have to get Percival help, Captain," Dee said. "I demand it."

Libb waited a moment before responding. "I've already ordered the course change, but the weather is turning, and the welcome may not be what you expect."

Dee tended to Percival as best she could. She dabbed his forehead with a damp cloth, and forced him to drink tea with honey and lemon. As the first slivers of light signaled dawn, she could no longer keep her eyes open. She lay in her bunk and fell asleep.

Percival watched the comings and goings of Dee, Libb, and Roz, who had given up her bed with the horses for a mat outside of Percival's door. Disembodied whispers surrounded him, like ghosts. Was Ben trying to say something to him? That was impossible. He was dead. An overhead lamp threw pale light on the cabin. More visitors came. Arturus gave him orders to ride hard and come back quickly with the Grail. Guinevere smiled, but the expression hid more than it revealed. Merlin shoved a sheaf of papers and a pile of tablets at him, saying these would help him find the Grail. Mordred loomed over everyone like a threatening raptor. Percival's father, Sir Adnan de Grosse, laughed like a madman, while his mother Eleanor sobbed hard for the loss of her son.

When Percival's mind cleared, he called for Dee. She came in a second later.

"Percival, you're awake!" Dee's face was consumed with worry.

"How long have I been asleep?"

"It's almost sundown."

"How many hours?"

"Thirteen, maybe fourteen."

"Good Gaia. Are we in port?"

"Take these." Dee handed him tablets and a cup of water. "No, we're not. We're still at sea. The land is over the horizon."

"What is Libb doing?"

"Percival, three more people are ill with whatever Ben had."

Percival didn't know what to think. "I need to talk to Libb." He tried to get out of bed, but his head felt like someone had pounded it with a sledgehammer. He coughed, and his chest hurt as if knives had sliced it open.

"Percival, we don't know if you're going to live or die. You have to rest."

"I need to know what's going on." He forced himself to sit up and wrap himself in the blanket. With Dee following, he made his way to the deck. The setting sun, still burning bright, almost blinded him. He nearly fainted.

Libb rushed over. "Percival, you should be in bed."

"That's what I keep telling him," Dee said. "But he's even more pig-headed when he's sick."

"How is Roz?"

"She's fine. She's grooming the horses."

"What about Poddle?"

Dee looked at Libb. "We haven't seen him. I don't remember him at breakfast or lunch."

Percival descended the companionway to the cabins. Poddle occupied a hastily arranged bunk on the floor of a closet for cleaning and toilet supplies. Percival, with Dee and Libb behind him, opened the door and turned on the light.

A large figure with his back to Percival lay in the bunk breathing like an asthmatic. Percival touched his shoulder, and the figure turned its head. The harsh light from the bare overhead bulb cast shadows over his pinkish eyes and nose, covering an angry, drooling mouth. A curse escaped Libb's lips, and Dee backed away. Percival reached for his sword, non-existent on his hip.

"Poddle..." Percival forced himself to keep from running.

Hearing the name, the creature that might have been Poddle relaxed, as if the name were a calming spell. "Percival, is that you? I thought you were sick."

Percival wasn't sure how to tell Poddle what he looked like. "You're... not doing well either."

"I've been feeling crappy since I came aboard."

Like a switch, Poddle's mood changed, as if two beings, one human, the other inhuman, struggled for control. For the moment, the inhuman had the advantage, and it swung its legs out of a fetal position. Percival and the others backed out of the closet.

"Dee, find Roz. Have her get me my sword and pistol. Libb, you'd better find a weapon."

The creature relaxed again, and its features transformed from a snarling imp to Poddle's own placid, regular features."I feel like I'm dying."

"You're not dead yet."

Poddle held out his hands, and then noticed them, like a baby exploring his own limbs for the first time. "What's happening to me, Percival? I felt sick, and I went to bed. That's all I remember. Wait, Ben was sick too."

"Ben is dead."

Poddle's distorted face twisted further. "Am I going to..."

"Not if I can help it, Poddle. But you have to keep control. You have to fight whatever is trying to take over your body. Do you understand?"

"What? No. I feel woozy. And itchy, like I haven't had a bath in a week."

In the dim passageway lights, Poddle's skin was gray and scaly, like a troll's. He got out of his bunk, forcing Percival out of the tiny cabin. Poddle walked strangely, as if something had happened to his bones and joints, and he had trouble keeping his balance.

"Percival, I'm scared. Something's happening to me."

Percival swallowed. Where was Roz with his weapons? "Poddle, has anything like this happened to you before?"

"No, of course not." Poddle's breathing grew labored.

Percival's mind raced through the possibilities. Poddle started to resemble the questing beasts he'd seen on Koda, long-necked, small-headed, with tails ending in a paddle-like structure. Poddle didn't have a tail, but it made Percival wonder. The virus, the one that made Ben sick, was odd. Libb's equipment couldn't identify it. It wasn't in its database, assuming it was updated regularly.

Steps distracted Percival. Dee and Roz came up. Percival took the pistol and unsheathed his sword. He needed to get out on deck in the open if he was to fight with it.

Poddle looked at him, puzzled. He was losing his battle with the creature inside him. His features twisted into something resembling a lizard with horns. Poddle stepped forward. "Are you going to shoot me?"

Percival back up a step. Poddle matched his move. A wave of weakness flowed through every muscle of Percival's, and he was afraid he might faint. He was just as sick as Poddle, but the virus had attacked the Aurelian differently. How was that possible?

"Roz, go on deck, but stay clear."

Roz leaped up the companionway into the sunlight.

"Dee, what do you know about your DNA mutations?"

Poddle twitched his head, listening. A hissing sound came from his throat.

"Why are you asking now?"

"How did the ancient scientists make the change to a person's genome?"

Dee's eyes widened. "A virus. It inserted the genes, but they were meant for cosmetic changes mostly, like fur or feathers."

"What if the virus was still around? What if it attacks people, like any virus. Some get sick, some die, and some change."

"I don't know, Percival. Do you think that's what happened to Poddle?"

"How the hell should I know? But I can't think of any other reason why he looks and acts the way he does right now. Merlin once told me that humans share a huge amount of DNA with other living things, from bacteria to birds. What if the virus usually just sickens or kills a victim? But what if sometimes it does what it was designed to do. It turns on some genes and turns off others, but at random. The result is..." He nodded at Poddle.

While Percival's imagination went manic, Poddle's metamorphosis solidified, like water freezing into ice. The creature who was Poddle stepped toward Percival and Dee, awkward, yet determined. It wanted something, and Percival didn't like its gleaming eye and sharp teeth.

"Dee, up on deck. Stay with Roz."

"What about you?"

"I'll follow. Just stay clear."

The thing that was currently not Poddle followed Percival up the companionway to the main deck. The creature wobbled on unsteady legs. It hissed at Percival.

Libb, behind the creature, raised his pistol.

"No, wait!" Percival barked. "Poddle is still in there."

The creature grasped a belaying pin to steady itself, then it took another step toward Percival. He raised his sword, prepared to strike. He didn't feel threatened by the creature, despite its frightening moves. Maybe it was as afraid of him. He was holding a deadly weapon in his hand, after all. He put the sword on the deck. "Poddle, go back to your bunk. We won't harm you. We'll try to help you."

The creature raised its head a little, as if listening carefully. Had its hearing been damaged in its transformation? It blinked, then dropped to its knees. It cried out, and Percival thought he heard Poddle's voice in the wail. Then it pitched forward onto the deck.

The creature barely breathed, and Percival watched its skin begin to blister, then boil. Poddle was dying.

"Help me, Dee, Libb! Let's get him below."

Percival touched his arm, but a chunk of charred, dead skin came off in his hand.

While the creature whimpered, Libb brought over a tarp. Together, Percival and Dee rolled Poddle onto the tarp, which they used like a litter to taken Poddle below to his bunk. The creature groaned and hissed by turns while dark blood and yellowish fluid from burst boils stained the tarp.

The creature opened its eyes, and Percival saw Poddle again, barely conscious, but aware of his surroundings. His mouth opened in a silent scream.

"Poddle," Dee said, "drink some water. You're badly burned. It must've been the sunlight. We'll make bandages and wrap you up."

Poddle tried to sip, but he was so weak, he could only manage a swallow. "I made a mistake, didn't I, Percival?"

"No, you didn't."

"I should've stay home. I wasn't meant for adventuring."

Percival thought the disease might have hit him anyway. "You're going to be fine, Poddle. It'll hurt for a while, but you'll heal and we'll find the Grail together."

"No, I'm not going to make it. I know it. I don't understand, but it doesn't matter. It wasn't meant to be."

Poddle closed his eyes, and his breathe escaped his chest in a death rattle.

Percival sat in a chair next to Poddle's bunk. Two companions lay dead in less than a day. How close had he come to his own death and another failure? Others sick, maybe Dee and Libb shortly. What if he had stuck to his original plan and walked to Cassanti? Maybe the same thing, sickness and death. Had the disease come aboard with him? With Libb? Maybe it was dormant for months or years in Poddle's body until the right conditions came along. He'd likely never know. Percival held his head in his hands, half-crazy with guilt, feeling that he had been here before, first after returning from the Koda expedition, then after losing the Viridian Grail in the canyon. And then there was Galahad's injury. He was always failing, never succeeding.

Dee stood at the doorway, a cloth and washbasin with water in her hand, now unneeded. Percival couldn't look at her. He'd dragged her away from a promising artistic career to sail on a ship of death. Why even go to Cassanti?

Nauseous and weak from his own bout with the mysterious sickness, Percival returned to his bunk, leaving Dee and Libb to deal with Poddle's body. Percival could hardly stand. He wondered if he'd wind up like Poddle, distorted by burns, looking like a coal-black tumor had taken over his entire body.

Percival slept until morning. Still weak, but feeling better, he climbed up the companionway to the deck and another bright morning. Next to the bulwark were two long bundles. They were Poddle and Ben's bodies, wrapped for burial.

Percival joined Libb on the quarterdeck. A crew member came up to Libb holding a yellow flag. Libb nodded, and the crew member headed for the quarterdeck.

"What is that?" Percival said.

"It's a warning. I'm telling other ships we have a disease on board. They're to stay away."

The crew member ran the flag up a line. It flapped without enthusiasm in the light breeze. Percival saw himself in the flag, sad, lonely, and weak. He wanted nothing more than to go home.

CHAPTER 18:
CEREMONY AT
CASSANTI

Percival pulled himself together enough to say a few words over the bodies of Ben and Poddle before they were dropped over the side. Percival watched the bodies sink until they disappeared into the green-blue water, almost wishing he could join them. Libb had no way to refrigerate the corpses, which made a sea burial mandatory, because no port would allow him to touch their facilities while he flew the yellow flag of disease. Under maritime law, he couldn't take it down for a minimum of two weeks after the last case of disease was diagnosed. If they sailed back to Aurelia, they'd be anchored off the city for many days, enduring the scrutiny of city health officials, the com chans, and Libb's enemies. It might be weeks or months before Percival could mount another attempt at reaching Cassanti.

"What do we do, Dee?" Still recovering from his brush with the virus, Percival felt he lacked the strength for any kind of decision.

"Go on. What else can we do? Merlin still needs the Grail to fix the Great Machine. I want to finish my mural. You need to return to Lina."

Dee was right, of course. She was always right, whether it was arguing as preschoolers over the proper rules of jump-rope or hopscotch, or in affairs of the heart. Despite the fact they were twins, she always seemed to have more knowledge and experience to draw on. Compared to her, Percival's expertise at life was as limited as a creek compared to an ocean.

He spoke to Libb, and the captain agreed to continue to Cassanti. By the time they arrived, his self-imposed quarantine would be close to ending. Maybe they could salvage something from the voyage. By the time they reached Cassanti Bay where its namesake city lay, more than half the passengers and crew had suffered the illness. Only two died, Ben and Poddle. Dee and Libb never showed symptoms. Now that all the passengers and crew had recovered, Libb lowered the plague flag.

Finding no sheltered anchorage outside the bay, Libb guided *Dolphin* inside at the flood tide, just before sunset. Libb's chart showed a deep channel all the way to the anchorage, but his chart was old and he'd never visited Cassanti. Once a principal city before the Dissolution, when the world fell apart, few people lived there, according to Libb's almanac. Several of the crew recounted rumors of strange rituals and a sick leader, which fit with Merlin's research.

Percival suggested using the *Dolphin*'s secret fossil-fueled engine to reconnoiter, but Libb had no fuel. When the wind died to a whisper, he ordered the jolly boat lowered to the water. With powerful electric lamps showing the way, the boat and its crew of six towed *Dolphin* toward the city. They slow-marched past bluffs illuminated blood orange by the setting sun. In the silence, interrupted by the lapping of water on the *Dolphin*'s hull and the call of a seaman throwing the lead to check the depth, Percival prayed he was getting closer to his goal.

In the fading light, *Dolphin* rounded a point, and a broad harbor appeared. Aurelia's harbor was at least as large, but there the comparison ended. Where Aurelia's harbor teemed with boats at all hours and lights illuminated every inch of shoreline, only a few dim lamps marked houses or streets on the far shore of the bay. A long, low, almost black shape interrupted the staccato of lights where the shore met the water, but the growing darkness masked details.

Libb ordered the jolly boat back to *Dolphin*. He let it float behind the ship, should he need it again. He called for sail. In a moment, *Dolphin* was underway again, the light wind allowing him to cross the bay.

"There's a wharf below that hill." Libb pointed to a peak in the distance. "I hope the docking fees are low."

Dolphin approached the wharf, and even in the darkness, with a half-moon throwing lemonade-colored light on the scene, Percival could tell the wharf was decrepit, with pilings askew and missing planks. Libb identified the least battered section of the wharf, and he ordered two crew members ferried over to a ladder secured to one of the pilings. The ladder held when the mariner stepped on its rungs. Using the jolly boat as a tug, the crew managed to secure *Dolphin* to a pair of bollards.

"I'm going to have a look around," Percival said.

"I'd wait until morning, if I were you," Libb said. "You could fall through a hole in that deck."

"We'll take power torches." Dee handed Percival one. "We've come all this way. I don't see much point in waiting."

"I should come, too," Roz said.

"No, someone needs to stay behind and care for the animals."

"Well, then, wait a moment, sir. You've forgotten something." When Roz returned from below, she held Percival's sword and single-shot pistols. "Just in case."

Percival thought a moment. "Thanks, but I don't want the locals to think I'm unfriendly." Percival and Dee climbed the ladder to the deck. *Dolphin*'s three masts disappeared behind them in the darkness.

* * *

The hollow thud of Percival's boots on the wooden planks gave way to the solid tap of hard rubber on concrete. His self-doubt yielded to excitement. With Dee beside him, a new confidence formed in his mind. This time, he'd find the Grail and his self-respect.

Apart from their torches, few lights guided their way on the paved walk that paralleled the shore, but the sound of chanting drew them forward. After a few dozen meters, they saw a procession of a hundred or so, led by people with their own electric torches. A few held paper lamps at the end of poles, illuminated by candles. They wore dark, ordinary clothing of working people. Masks covered their faces or just their eyes, making it impossible to tell their ages. By their gait, some were elderly, though he saw no young children. Skirts and pants indicated their gender, assuming the styles of Cassanti followed the common fashion. The procession moved at a solemn pace, resembling a funeral, but the singing had none of the low, mournful tones of a funeral dirge. Nor did it sound like an exuberant celebration. Percival and Dee had stumbled onto a festival, but what it celebrated, neither he nor Dee could guess. They fell into the train at its tail end.

The procession made its way along the shoreline, with the saltwater bay on one side and multi-story buildings on the other. Piers jutted into the water with boats and ships of various sizes attached like jewels on a woman's hand. One of the marchers handed Percival and Dee masks.

"They must be traditional for this festival or whatever it is," Dee said. "Anonymity must be important. Or the disappearance of the individual into the group."

Percival couldn't judge the anthropological meaning of the mask. It made observing the scene harder, but he agreed it was better for himself and Dee to follow local custom. Despite his sudden tunnel vision, there was no mistaking the looming shape ahead on the water side of the avenue. The same protracted shape with few lights attracted his attention when *Dolphin* entered the bay. From this angle, it resembled one of Aurelia's towers laid down on its side by a giant. Flat on top, the shape tapered on its vertical sides toward the water. It stretched at least 300 meters against its own tumbledown wharf, except for a pair of illuminated bridges from the shore to gaping holes in its side. The procession turned onto one of these bridges, and the recital of hundreds of footfalls identified the construction as metal. The portion of the artificial light that played on the sides of the huge structure revealed streaks of black rust. The procession entered the portal, and Percival stepped onto a metal floor.

"What is this place?" Dee whispered.

Percival scanned the ceiling and the walls, noting girders and beams, all pockmarked by rust. Light from the portable lamps played on the surfaces. One of the holes in the ceiling revealed a glimpse of the moon. An insight hit Percival. "I think it's what's left of an old ship."

"That's not possible. No one builds ships this big."

"Maybe before the Dissolution. There were ships that aircraft could fly from out on the ocean. Maybe this is one of those."

"How could it still be here, a thousand years later? Wouldn't it sink or rust into nothing?"

Percival shrugged. His idea was crazy, but everything about Cassanti was unfamiliar, from the procession to this structure sitting on the water, or perhaps on the bottom in the shallows. It reminded him of a religious shrine. Viridiae was dotted with small shrines to Gaia, like the one he'd visited when they departed Camelot, but none could hold more than a few dozen people. He couldn't imagine what god the people of Cassanti worshiped aboard the hulk of a steel-hulled ship stuck in the mud of a bay a thousand kilometers from anywhere, if that's what it was.

The chanting stopped, leaving behind a murmur of voices. The rectangular room was enormous, bigger than the Great Audience Hall. On one end. a tall curtain separated a raised dais from the rest of the space. The people in his procession edged forward until it was absorbed by a larger crowd. The voices and the echoes of shuffling feet indicated thousands of people, all waiting for something. He took Dee's hand.

"What's wrong, Perce?"

"I've never been in a crowd like this, under a roof anyway. It's making me a little nervous. I don't want to lose track of you."

"But it's exciting, don't you think?"

Percival nodded. Though he had no idea what was happening,

he could sense the tension. The audience was waiting for something to begin.

A musical chord sounded, low in octave, but with highlights in a higher pitch. The echoes reverberated for three seconds until the chord sounded again, and then a third time. The sounds of shoes scuffing metal and the murmurs of reverent voices led Percival to stand on his toes to see better. The crowd parted to make a lane between the raised dais and a door on the opposite end of the room.

A brace of trumpets blared, filling the room with sound almost to the point of pain. The echoes clotted the air, and Percival imagined demons or spirits driven from the space. When the horns stopped, the atmosphere took minutes to fall back into silence, which was interrupted again by the rhythmic pounding of a dozen or more drums. The trumpets, accompanied by reed instruments and bagpipes, filled the air again, but with less volume, so that Percival could make out a tune. After a few beats, a chorus joined the song, but the voices came from the door opposite the dais. No one in the crowd made noise, though all eyes were on the door.

Two spotlights shone on the door. Percival's heart beat faster. The noise prevented anyone from speaking. Hearing the words would be impossible, unless you yelled in someone's ear. Dee squeezed her brother's hand in reassurance, and he squeezed back in kind. They were witnessing a ritual that no Viridian had seen in hundreds of years. Merlin had never mentioned anything like this.

The music changed, as if one song ended and another began, but seamlessly. Hooded figures, dressed in red robes, emerged from the door, which was twice as tall as a man. On their shoulders, they carried a platform, also draped in red. On the platform, resting on two holders, was a long, thin object, as if arranged to point toward the dais. Percival recognized it as a javelin, because its head was a simple steel point, and its tail tapered to a point of wood almost as sharp. Though he no longer carried a javelin, he knew the weapon intimately. Even from meters away, he could see that it was ceremonial, decorated with abstract carvings and whorls of chromatic tones from salmon to scarlet with highlights of gold.

The bearers took slow steps toward the dais, and as if rehearsed, the entire crowd turned to the opposite end of the lane. The curtains were drawn apart, and a masked figure, clad in silver and gold, sat on a chair, reminding Percival of Arturus' throne in the Great Audience Hall. The figure stared straight ahead, waiting for the arrival of the javelin. The meaning of the ritual escaped Percival, but he was enthralled by the combination of solemnity and other-world atmosphere. Whoever designed the ritual intended to take the viewer out of his or her ordinary experience.

The music's key changed. Another platform emerged, its bearers draped in shades of yellow, as was the platform itself. The object they carried shone bright light, as if they carried a sliver of the noonday sun. Percival, Dee, and many others in the crowd shaded their eyes, but many didn't, as if they didn't want to block any of the flare's power.

A third platform appeared, this time with an orange theme. The platform displayed two objects, a cup of gold at least a meter in height with a broad, shallow mouth, almost a bowl. Next to it was a decanter, almost as tall as the cup, in clear glass, with a neck and mouth resembling the neck of a swan. Percival strained to see the tiny portion of liquid at the decanter's bottom, which sloshed a little, revealing another shade of red. Percival thought it might be wine, but it seemed more viscous.

The bearers of all three platforms climbed three steps to the dais. They set the platforms down, the javelin to the figure's left, the sun-like lamp to its right, and the decanter at its feet. The music ended, and silence filled the space. From the crowd came a shout, more like an order, and the crowd dropped to its knees. All the congregants bowed their heads. Percival and Dee followed suit, though both strained to see what was happening ahead of them. A single drum, its bass notes thrumming like a low, slow heartbeat, and another platform came from the door. Instead of a platform borne on shoulders, it was on a small cart, pulled by two men, dressed in golden costumes with masks similar to the masks worn by Percival, Dee and the other participants. On the platform was a square object draped with yellow gold cloth embroidered in silver and red gold. Percival had no way to tell the meaning of this part of the ritual. Why a cart and not a platform carried on shoulders? Percival could hear whispers that could only be prayers.

As the cart passed, individuals rose to their feet and the lane between the door and the dais disappeared as the crowd followed the cart toward the dais. The two large men drawing the cart stopped. With the kind of reverence reserved for objects of great age and power, they lifted the cloth-covered box. By their movements, the box and its golden cover appeared heavy and awkward. They climbed steps to the dais, and lowered it to a small raised portion in front of the figure. At this, all of the remaining congregants still kneeling rose to their feet.

The figure raised its hands and looked up, as if in supplication to a spirit in the night above. Lowering its arms, and sweeping them across the crowd in an imitation of an embrace, a voice spoke.

"My people, on this night, of all nights of the year, we mark who we are."

The voice was female, and it rang out clear as a bell, despite the heavy mask on her face.

"We are protectors of the Grail," the crowd responded.

Percival's heart stopped. Merlin was right. The Last Grail was here. He'd practically stumbled over it by accident. He squeezed Dee's hand again. Her eyes were full of wonder at their discovery.

"Why do we protect the Grail?"

"Because it is the Grail," the crowd responded.

Percival moved his lips, as if he knew the ritual.

The priestess—that's how Percival came to think of her—touched the javelin. "On this night, of all nights of the year, I warn all who wish us harm, that I will destroy them."

"They are the enemies of the earth."

The priestess gestured toward the light on the platform. "On this night, of all nights of the year, I welcome those who would bring us friendship and knowledge, the only true gifts."

"The Grail restores us."

Approaching the cup and decanter, the priestess poured out the small amount of liquid into the cup. Grasping the cup with both hands, she put it to her lips, and drank all of it. "On this night, of all nights, I drink the blood of renewal."

"The Grail gives us life."

Percival, Dee, and the entire crowd edged closer to the cloth-covered box.

"We are protectors of the Grail," the priestess intoned. "We defend it with our lives, because it restores the earth and gives us life. We await the One Who Comes, because he, or she, will heal the world. Behold the Grail, the instrument of healing."

The priestess gestured to the two men in gold. As the electric lights dimmed, leaving only a few candles to push away the dark, they took the four corners of the cloth and lifted it.

Percival drew in a breath, echoed by Dee's stifled cry. A crystal-line ball, bejeweled and glowing, floated in the center of a glass box. It thrummed in a strange rhythm, which Percival knew. He'd felt that rhythm when he saw the Viridian Grail in Lucana, stolen from the Viridian Great Machine.

This device, the key to making the Great Machine function again, was different. Perhaps it was the darkness, the ritual, or the awe of the people surrounding the dais. The Viridian Grail in its mount at the Lucana Academy of Science pulsed with light, and seemed to hum with energy. The Last Grail, floating in its case, throbbed like a beating heart. Percival soaked in its light and warmth. It gave him energy and vigor. It was exciting and humbling at the same time. He had failed so often in his past Grail quests. Was he worthy of even looking upon his country's, perhaps the planet's, last hope of survival?

The figure in gold glanced about. "Are there any strangers here?"

Percival heard the question, but he was transfixed by the orb of the Grail. The geometric patterns engraved on its surface, and the abstract representations of humans and animals that glowed with the essence of life, hypnotized him. Dee brought him back. "Perce, pay attention."

"I ask again, are there strangers among us?"

"I am a stranger." Percival was suddenly aware of thousands of pairs of eyes on him. "My name is Percival Rathkeale. I am from Viridiae, in the north. This is my sister, Dindrane Rathkeale."

"Percival of Viridiae, why are you here?" The woman's voice was quieter, gentler, resembling the tone of Eleanor, his mother when she would wish him good night as child. But the voice also had a quality of expectation.

"I seek the Grail."

The priestess regarded Percival, working her jaw as if surprised. He could see almost nothing of her body, except for glimpses of the skin of her hands, her full lips, and the color of her eyes, which were a deep brown.

"Percival of Viridiae, will you then ask the question?"

Percival's mouth opened, but nothing came out. Her question about a question tickled his memory, but nothing came to mind. Merlin had said something about a question, one of the thousands of dim facts and half-rumors about the Last Grail. But Percival's mind was awash with sensations, as if the now-silent drums and wail of instruments and chorus still flowed up his veins and down bones, turning his mind into a confused mush. He turned to Dee, but she was as perplexed as he was.

"Percival of Viridiae, you say you seek the Grail. Then you must know the question."

Percival shook his head. "I'm sorry, but I don't know it."

With a hint of disappointment, the priestess said, "Dindrane Rathkeale, you also seek the Grail. What is the question?"

Dee glanced at the floor and said nothing.

The robed priestess let out a slow breath. Percival could feel her dejection. "Then you have failed the world."

CHAPTER 19: CERERIS AND THE GRAIL

Dee watched the cart with the Grail, re-covered with the cloth of embroidered gold, disappear into the door from whence it came. The priestess departed, and the masked crowd dispersed in silence, leaving the twins alone. A handful of artificial lights kept total darkness at bay.

"Perce, what do we do now?" Dee whispered, still awed by the reverential atmosphere. "Should we go back to the *Dolphin*?"

Her brother stood before the dais, mute. His expression resembled the one of loss after Ben and Poddle's deaths.

"Perce, talk to me. I'm sorry if I screwed up. I didn't think I'd be asked anything."

"It's not your fault," he said. "It's mine. Merlin told me about the Grail question, but it seemed so weird at the time. I didn't put much stock in it, so I forgot about it."

"Don't blame yourself."

"This ritual. The parade. The music. It was like a drug. I forgot everything Merlin said."

Dee felt as if her mind had been hijacked as well. She took Percival's hand and they sat on the steps that led to the dais. "It doesn't matter. We've found the Last Grail. We've halfway to the finish."

Percival looked at Dee, asking soundlessly to say more.

"We just have to find a way to get it home."

The swishing sound of fabric drawn across a smooth surface interrupted Dee's thoughts. Accompanying the swish was a reciprocating hiss, like a piston.

"I'd hoped you'd still be here." The priestess stood by, her robe draped on the metal floor behind her. "I wanted to extend my welcome on behalf of the Chancery of the Grail."

Dee nudged Percival.

Percival said, "Thank you very much, Madame…"

"You may call me Cereris. My title is High Cleric. I am the caretaker and deacon of the Chancery. You said your names a moment ago. Please don't take this the wrong way, but can you prove your identities?"

"I have signed letters from Arturus III and other documents. They are on the ship that brought us here."

Cereris inclined her head. "I would like to see them. For now, may I offer my hospitality? Will you join me for a late supper?"

"We don't mean to trouble you," Dee said.

"No trouble at all. Please follow me."

Dee grinned enthusiastically at Percival, as if to say, *All is not lost.*

Cereris led them down a corridor to a long, broad space with a low ceiling. A carpet muffled the echoes of their footsteps. Dividers split the room into discrete spaces, though the entire room itself wasn't meant as a living space, in Dee's opinion. It reminded her of a communal eating space, like the cafeteria at Camelot University, though there was no sign of long tables, benches, or food service equipment. Cereris invited them toward a sitting area with upholstered chairs.

Cereris unclasped the golden cloak and draped it over a dress form. Underneath the cloak, Cereris was surrounded by armor, but not the kind that knights wore into battle. It resembled the lighter, translucent training armor, hugging her form, but strong and rigid. The hissing sound came from her joints. The armor reached up to the priestess's neck, and when she took off her ceremonial mask, the armor extended over her head, leaving her face uncovered. Dee resisted a comparison with an insect's shell, if it weren't for the tunic and loose pants that softened its edges.

A steward brought a plate of sliced bread, preserved meats,

and fresh vegetables. He placed a carafe of wine and glasses on a side table.

Cereris reached for bread and a slice of meat. "I see you have a thousand questions. Don't be afraid to ask. I'm not embarrassed."

Percival cleared his throat. "Your covering, ma'am. Please explain, if you will."

"It was designed by an Aurelian robotics engineer. I suffer from a wasting disease."

Cereris' face was middle-aged, and without her golden, partially obscuring mask, she appeared older and gaunt, as if she didn't eat enough to maintain her weight.

Dee said, "I'm sorry, Cereris. It must be difficult."

"I'm grateful that Aurelian technology has advanced as much as it has. The exoskeleton gives me movement I wouldn't normally enjoy. Before I was fitted five years ago, I could barely walk. I wasn't sure if I could perform my duties as the Chancery Deacon. I'm blessed with a dedicated, supportive congregation, who raised the money to fund my treatment. They also purchased my exoskeleton."

"Your illness is…" Dee tried to think of way to ask that wasn't embarrassing. "What is it called?"

Cereris pronounced the multi-syllabic name. "It's incurable and terminal. No, no pity, please. It's not a secret, and I've come to terms with it."

"With all the help you've received, I'm sure you have many more years ahead of you," Dee said.

"Not as many as I would like."

"I know someone else who suffers from this disease," Dee said. "He's a little boy, the brother of a dear friend."

"A tragedy for anyone, but especially for a child."

"Oh, Kenric is doing better these days." Dee wanted to lighten the mood. "He was healthy and strong when we left Camelot."

"Interesting," Cereris said. "Tell me about his treatment."

"It involved a rare blood protein."

"Indeed. I'm glad it worked for him. Was it manufactured? Artificial, I mean?"

Dee squirmed in the chair. An internal voice told her to be careful. "There was a donor."

"Was the donor a relative?"

"No."

Cereris observed Dee's discomfort. "I apologize if I'm prying, but you must understand my interest. I've no desire to die. My disease is progressing rapidly and I've researched every known treatment. I've not heard of this one. May I ask who the donor was? I wish to contact them. Perhaps the person could help me."

Dee glanced at Percival. His eyes flicked toward Cereris. He wanted Dee to tell her.

"I was the donor, ma'am."

"I see." Cereris' eyes widened. She raised herself in her chair. "You are a lifesaver, Ms Rathkeale."

Dee felt as if she had fallen into a trap, but this was different than the situation with Kenric. Cereris was a perfect stranger with power over her and Percival. She had the Grail; Dee had the protein that might save her life.

The tension of an unspoken request hung in the air. Cereris' obligations as a hostess trumped her self-interest for the moment. She changed the subject.

"Percival, tell me about your journey here."

Dee breathed out. Perhaps Cereris had decided against asking for Dee's blood, in a manner of speaking.

Percival related the basics of the trip from Viridiae, though he softened the core truth of the quest, to take the Grail back to Viridiae to repair the Great Machine. Dee thought the move was smart. There was no way to tell how Cereris might react.

"So you've come to take the Grail away from us." Without betraying a hint of emotion, Cereris lifted a slice of carrot with thin fingers. Tiny puffs of air signaled the mechanics of her integument.

"Ma'am, we have great respect for your people and traditions." Dee recovered from her uneasiness and flashed to Guinevere's diplomatic mission to the Ontarii. She'd try what she'd learned about diplomacy and negotiation on Cereris. "May I suggest an accommodation? You're an important leader here. I could bring a proposal for a relationship between Viridiae and Cassanti that could benefit everyone."

"There's no need, Ms Rathkeale."

Dee stole a glance at Percival.

"You may have the Grail, with my blessing."

Percival's jaw opened. He expected resistance, even a fight. "We're grateful beyond words, ma'am. But won't your congregation—"

"They will be happy as well. Overjoyed, even."

"I don't understand, Cereris." Though it was wise to keep questions to a minimum with a stranger, for fear of offending, Dee thought Cereris' attitude was odd.

"Our Cult of the Grail is unlike any other faith. Even before the Dissolution, when the world fell apart, the people of Cassanti understood the importance of the Great Machines. When Joseph Arimathea designed the 12 machines to manage the world's climate after the Warming, he needed engineers to build them." Cereris poured herself wine.

"Arimathea built the machines here?" Percival said.

"Components were built all over the world and assembled at the 12 sites. The Grail component was constructed here in Cassanti. It was so important to Arimathea's project that he lived next to the factory for twenty years. The site of his old home is a shrine to us."

"His house still exists?"

"No, but there's a marker, very old."

"If the factory was here, then it also made spare parts," Dee said.

"Indeed, Ms Rathkeale."

Cereris sipped the wine. Despite the sophistication of the exoskeleton, Dee perceived clumsiness, as if the priestess hadn't mastered fine movements, or the suit was not capable of them. She said she was dying; perhaps the suit couldn't adjust to the deterioration of her body.

"Most people don't know that the Great Machines weren't terribly reliable in their first few decades. Arimathea was a brilliant designer, but the complexity of managing the global climate was beyond any single human being's capabilities. Virtually all the early models of the Grail failed in their first thirty years of use."

"But most of the machines are still operating today, a thousand years later," Percival said.

"A testament to the perseverance of Arimathea and his successors. There's an ancient word that described mechanical or software problems in new systems. The word was 'bugs.'"

Percival turned to Dee. "I've heard Merlin use that word."

"Merlin?" Cereris said.

"Merlin Ambrosius, Viridiae's leading scientist, an advisor to King Arturus. He's our expert on the Viridian Great Machine and the Grail."

"Well, after about 50 years of operation, Arimathea's engineers, as they said, 'squashed the bugs,' and the machines needed little intervention."

"Until recently," Percival said. "The device in Lucanus failed. The Lucians stole the Viridian Grail to fix it. Apparently, they didn't know about Cassanti."

"Or didn't believe the rumors," Dee said.

"What happened to the Viridian device?" Cereris said.

"It was lost," Percival said.

Dee felt for her brother, but it wasn't necessary to recount the destruction of the Viridian Grail on his return from Lucana.

"This worries me," Cereris said. "The Grail you saw in our ceremony is the last fully-operational Grail. All were made here in Cassanti. There are no others, and there aren't enough parts to build a new one."

"Couldn't you make more? Isn't the factory still here?"

Ceresis smiled grimly. "I'm sure your teachers explained what happened after the Dissolution. The Old Civilization disappeared, or rather dissolved, piece by piece. The factory fell into disrepair. The engineers died and their knowledge didn't survive the centuries. The world forgot how to maintain its technology.

The Old Civilization left remnants behind, some of which still work, such as the Great Machines, but no one knows how to build one."

One of the remnants of Old Civilization technology coursed through Dee's blood as artificially modified DNA.

"Merlin is trying to learn how the Great Machines work," Percival said. "He understands the importance of the Grail component. Perhaps he could build a new one."

"He sounds like a brilliant man, perhaps on the order of Joseph Arimathea himself. I wish him luck."

Percival fidgeted with the arm of his chair. As Cereris reached for another sliver of vegetable, Dee tapped her foot to get his attention. She mouthed, *What next?*

Percival cleared his throat. "Madame Cereris, we thank you for your hospitality. We would like to collect the Grail and be on our way. A ship is waiting for us in the bay."

Cereris grinned, but it seemed pained. "I understand, Sir Percival, but that is impossible."

Percival looked alarmed. "Why not?"

"Because you did not ask the Grail question. We are quite strict about matters of ceremony. We've been protecting the Grail for a millennium. I'm not going to just give it to you as if it were, I don't know, a hand-me-down."

Dee sighed. "When is the next opportunity to ask the question, Cereris?"

"About this time next year."

"A year?" Percival said. "We can't wait that long."

"Perce! Be respectful."

"I appreciate the urgency of your mission, Sir Percival. The climate won't wait for your Merlin to complete the repairs, but I would face a revolt by my congregation if I didn't follow our sacred traditions."

Percival's face fell at the setback.

"Is there anything we can do?" Dee said. "Perhaps schedule a special ceremony? Appeal to the congregation?"

Cereris studied Dee for a long moment. "Let me think on it."

CHAPTER 20: AN ATTEMPT AT THEFT

Sleep evaded Dee that night aboard *Dolphin*. She was certain Cereris would ask for a donation of her rare blood protein. The donation was hazardous enough in a Camelot hospital with the best-trained doctors and nurses, latest equipment, and advanced medicines. She'd yet to see Cassanti's facilities, but judging by the look of the city in the morning light, they would probably not match up. Much of it was half-wrecked buildings on hills above a thin strip of one and two-story structures hugging the shore. Not exactly the nine towers of Dee's home.

Her country, however, maybe the whole world, needed the Grail and a functioning Great Machine. Like every other Viridian, she'd watched the land deteriorate. Wheat wouldn't grow. Trees wouldn't bear fruit, at least not as much. Summers were hotter, winters wetter. Could the Great Machine, even if it worked well again after Merlin installed the Last Grail, reverse the decline? No one really knew.

As she thought about the high priestess who lived in a giant metal box, she found Percival and Michael Libb hunched over a device. Dee had only seen one up close once or twice during the war. People called them "flying eyes," because the army and police used it to watch—some said spy—on enemy formations or the local populations. "What are you going to use that for, Perce?"

"I want to know more about that church or whatever it is. I also want to see where the Grail might be hidden."

"I don't know if hidden is the right word. Cereris was pretty open with us about her attitude toward the Grail."

"She didn't show us where she put it after the ceremony."

"Why should she? Religious objects brought out once a year are usually put in a special place, like a chamber, or a vault."

"Why didn't she show it to us, if it was alright for us to take it?"

"Perce, you're being paranoid."

Percival pulled Dee aside. "Look, I haven't come all this way to wait a year. She's giving it to us. Why can't we take it now?"

"This is no time to be impatient, Percival."

"She said it herself: The climate can't wait. I need to take the Grail back to Camelot. Now."

"Don't you see? She wants to negotiate."

"You're being naive, Dee. What she really wants is your blood."

Dee found it hard to argue the point.

"You took the risk for Kenric willingly. But that was in Camelot. It's too much of a risk here. I'd never forgive myself if something happened to you because of a botched operation."

"So you're going to steal the Grail from Cereris."

Percival's attention returned to the flying eyes. "I'll do what I have to do."

"And what's that for?" Dee pointed to the gadget.

"It'll help us see the enemy before she sees us."

Dee snarled at her brother. "The enemy? Is that how you see Cereris? I think she's trying to be helpful. It's natural to want something in return for potentially angering the people who clothe and feed her."

"All I know is that I'm not handing you over to her to be bled like some kind of sacrificial animal. Now please let me get back to work."

Dee didn't want to risk her health, but she didn't like Percival's paternalistic attitude toward her. Normally, he didn't interfere with her autonomy. Why was he behaving differently now? He was worried. He might have to trade the potential for Dee to lose her life in order to retrieve the Grail, and that was an impossible choice for him. Was it a possible choice for her? She tried not to think about it.

"Do you have any idea what you're getting into? They might have weapons or guards we haven't seen."

"I'll take the chance."

* * *

Dee watched her brother, Libb, Roz, and a couple of adventurous mariners load the flying eyes, some climbing gear, and light weapons into the jolly boat.

"I'm going, too," Dee said.

"I wish you wouldn't." Percival adjusted his fighting armor. "If I'm hurt, Gaia forbid, you'll have to take the Grail to Merlin."

"What do you get out of this, Michael?"

Libb shrugged. "Trying to be helpful? Good story to tell in a bar?"

"I think all sailors have a drop of pirate's blood," Dee said. "This is a mistake. Cereris said we could have the Grail. Why can't we wait a while and try to negotiate for it?"

But Percival had made up his mind to take the Grail, though he caved in to Dee's persistence about going along. At dusk, after she climbed into the boat, they pushed off from the *Dolphin*. Dee grabbed an oar, and after a few minutes of instruction, they rowed silently toward the half-sunk hulk.

The bay had only a small swell, and the current carried them toward the strange temple. The cloudy night proved perfect cover. Light from the widely spaced streetlamps along the shoreline reflected off the water. They heard no sound, not even voices from the shore. Cassanti did not fit the cliché of the raucous port town.

The jolly boat bumped the rust-caked wall of the steel box. The top of the box loomed above them, perhaps seven meters, or about two stories. The tablet controller glowing on his lap, Libb launched the flying eyes, letting it peek over the edge above them. The infrared cameras showed a nearly flat surface, pockmarked here and there with a few holes.

The flying eyes trailed a strong, knotted line, and it dropped a grappling hook on the deck. Percival carefully pulled until the hook snagged. The flying eyes showed that the hook had fallen into one of the holes and grasped something inside. Percival put all his weight on the line, and it held. With slow, steady movements, he shimmied up the line, clutched the edge of the deck, and pulled himself over. He trailed his own line, and brought up the end of a Jacob's ladder, which he secured on the end of a thick pipe. Over the next few minutes, nearly everyone climbed the ladder to the deck. They left Roz and one *Dolphin* crew member behind to care for the jolly boat and fend off intruders, if necessary.

"What do we do now, Percival?" Dee said.

"Look for a way in."

"And then what?"

"Find the Grail and take it."

"This is your plan?"

Percival didn't answer. He had developed a kind of blindness. Had he decided that he was smarter than the Cassantians, and that he could actually get away with this? In the near pitch darkness, with the way lit only by glow from Libb's tablet and Percival's electric torch, Dee feared falling into an invisible hole, figuratively and literally.

They came upon stairs that led down. Dee heard faint sounds like murmurs at a distance, as if the passageways funneled sound from a distance place. Air flowed upward, lifting hairs off her tightly wound and pinned braids. Drawing his single-shot pistol, Percival led the way.

The trio descended two flights of stairs to another deck. A rising stink suggested fetid water. The murmurs were louder, but still distant through a passageway with a dim, diffuse light at the far end.

"This seems a likely route," Percival said.

"To what?" Dee said.

"We'll find out. Libb, can you send the flying eyes ahead?"

The *Dolphin*'s captain moved a joystick attached to his tablet, and the flying eyes flew down the corridor, sounding like a bumblebee.

Dee grabbed Percival's arm. "This is stupid. We're burglarizing someone's home."

"You don't have to be here." Percival glanced up the flights of stairs.

Dee could not abandon her brother. She followed him. He tread carefully down the passage a few meters behind the flying eyes, which sent images back in infrared.

They made a number of turns down the pitch-dark passage. Puddles of water dotted the deck. Streaks of rust stained the walls. An oily smell made the humid air dense. Dee caught glimpses of what might have been doors or cabinets, and occasionally writing, but she didn't recognize the script. Everything looked as if it had sat in place for centuries, with rainwater from above and seawater from the bay slowly dissolving everything.

And then, with no warning, they stepped into the space they'd visited the night before. It appeared larger, perhaps because there were fewer people. The dozen or so people present gathered at a niche on the opposite wall. The place reminded Dee of the temple to Gaia just inside Camelot's walls. It had a small chapel off the nave for more intimate ceremonies. Had they happened on a ceremony in progress? Libb steered the flying eyes into the upper corners of the open space to discover what was going on.

"Welcome back."

The familiar voice startled Dee. Percival froze. Libb straightened, letting his hands rest at his sides, one holding the tablet.

Cereris stood in her exoskeleton, backlit by the light from a corridor, the one that led to her quarters. She was flanked by two masked men, tall and muscled, each holding a stabbing sword.

"Bring down the drone."

Libb glanced at Percival, who nodded. The buzzing flying eyes dropped from the ceiling, landing at the captain's feet.

One of the guards picked it up and handed it to Cereris. She examined it for a moment, turning it over, her eyes lingering on the lenses. She handed it to the second guard, who dropped it and crushed it with his booted foot.

"Rude to spy on a new friend," Cereris said. "Don't you Viridians have any manners?"

"I told you, Percival," Dee whispered.

Percival remained stone-faced.

"I forgive you, my Viridian friends. No harm, no foul. We have no secrets here." Cereris moved toward the niche on the wall, followed by her guards. "I'll show you want you came for."

Dee and Percival looked at each other. Dee shrugged. Libb looked heartbroken over the loss of his flying eyes.

At the niche, a handful of supplicants in robes similar to the guards made room for the high priestess. The exoskeleton exhaled puffs of air as Cereris knelt on one of three prie dieus. In front of her, illuminated by overhead lamps, was the Grail, covered by its golden embroidered cloth. Dee's breath came faster. Even covered, the device had a presence. It touched her senses, as if reaching out from underneath the heavy textile. She didn't know how it worked or how it fit into the Great Machine, but she understood why it was so important. Without it, the Great Machine was like a human body without a heart.

"I've cared for the Grail all my adult life." Cereris sighed. "I'm the 130th high priestess of the Grail, and it seems I will be the last."

Dee wasn't sure whether to feel sad for Cereris or happy for Viridiae. Cereris' loss was Camelot's gain.

"But all of us, over the centuries, have worked for this moment. In a year's time, I will be glad to hand it over to you, Percival. I'm sure you and your Merlin will use it for its intended purpose."

After a long silence, Percival spoke. "I came tonight to take it now."

"I'm afraid that's out of the question. My duty—"

"My duty, ma'am, is to my lord king Arturus and to my country. A year may be too late. I expect the journey back to Camelot will take many weeks, perhaps months. That much delay is unacceptable to me. You say that the Grail already belongs to us. Why keep it longer than necessary?"

Even though a mask partially obscured Cereris's face, Dee could discern her scorn. "The instructions handed down to me from the first Clerics of the Grail do not account for arrogance, therefore I will have to ignore yours, Percival Rathkeale."

Percival stiffened. Dee was secretly sympathetic to Cereris, but she said nothing.

"It doesn't matter, Cereris. I'm taking the Grail with me." Percival put his hand on his sword hilt.

Cereris guards mirrored Percival's move. The group of supplicants backed away. Libb sucked in a breath. Cereris didn't move.

"I don't want to take the Grail by force," Percival said, "but I'll do what I have to in order to protect my country. You are preventing me from retrieving what belongs to Viridiae. You've said as much."

"Well argued, Percival. You should've been a lawyer." Cereris paused, then spoke to her acolytes. "Leave us, please. I would like to speak to our friends in private."

As the attendants departed, Percival relaxed, letting go of his sword.

"Let's discuss a trade," Cereris said.

Dee said, "You want my blood protein for the Grail."

"I am still bound by my sacred laws, but religions, like laws, are full of loopholes. I'll find a way to explain it to my people."

"No," Percival said. "The procedure could kill my sister. I won't allow it. Her death is unnecessary."

"I'll decide that, Perce."

Percival faced Dee. "You're always so stubborn. You never take no for an answer. You're bound and determined to do something stupid."

"Like steal the Grail?"

"That's not—"

"You always manage to find the worst times to pick a fight, Percival. I'm not going to die. I trust Cereris. She's treated us well. You're the one bound and determined to behave like a Lucian, just taking things without any concern for others."

Even in the dim light, Dee could see her brother's face go crimson under his flaming red hair.

"Libb, talk some sense into her."

The captain raised his hands. "I'm not getting involved, but it's her life, not yours."

Percival appeared ready to stamp his foot in frustration.

Dee had made her decision. The risk was worth it. "Cleric Cereris, I am at your disposal."

CHAPTER 21: THE ROAD TO AURELIA

As a woman who managed a private forest and properties in a remote province of Viridiae, Percival's mother, Eleanor, developed a keen eye for bargains and swindles. She taught her son everything she knew, and although Percival had no interest in business as a life's work, he knew a cheat when he saw it. Initially, over the days that followed his abortive attempt to steal the Grail, he thought the bargain he and Dee had struck with Cereris was fair. Despite his misgivings, Dee was a willing partner, and Cereris followed through on her promise to hand over the Grail by putting carpenters to work on a sturdy crate to hold the device for transport.

Seeing Cassanti in full daylight raised the first doubts. The town hadn't enjoyed anything resembling prosperity since the Dissolution. No wonder it was mostly a blank spot in Merlin's research. Half the buildings were empty shells overlooking the rust-caked Chancery. Most of the piers and wharves were as poorly maintained as the wharf where *Dolphin* lay. The town might not survive after he took the away the Grail, its only attraction.

The doubts intensified when they visited the medical facility where the blood protein procedure would take place. Though clean with earnest staff, the clinic trailed Camelot by at least a century, as far as Percival was concerned. The lead doctor let slip that he had never performed a protein extraction before, and he had to scrounge the equipment. Percival was unconvinced that he'd had any formal training at all, though he'd heard of the procedure at a conference in Aurelia. Cereris had few doubts; this was her only chance of surviving another year.

If Dee had private reservations, she showed no sign of backing out. On the scheduled day, the same day workmen loaded the crate with the Grail into *Dolphin*'s hold under Libb's supervision, Percival accompanied Dee to the clinic. He sat in a corner of the operating room while the lead doctor and his assistants inserted the intravenous needle and attached the filtering mechanism. In order to get enough of the protein, the procedure required Dee's blood be filtered twice. It put a strain on her heart, spleen, kidneys, practically every organ. Highly perishable, the protein had to be injected into Cereris immediately. Fortunately for the high priestess, Dee's blood type matched hers exactly.

The procedure took a full eight hours. In the afternoon, Libb sent a message saying all was secure aboard *Dolphin*, and he could sail with the midnight tide. When the procedure was complete, Percival wanted nothing more than to get Dee out of the clinic and aboard the ship. He didn't care whether Cereris was helped or even cured. Dee was exhausted, and when the ambulance brought them to the wharf, he and Roz carried her to her bunk on a makeshift stretcher.

Just before *Dolphin* cast off, a messenger arrived from Cereris. In a note written in Common Script, she expressed her gratitude to Dee for saving her life. She also offered a gift, which was a leather-bound, elaborately decorated book of about 200 pages. Cereris described it as a technical manual for the Grail.

Dee slept through the night, Percival and Roz taking turns keeping watch in the bunk below her. He barely slept, dreaming of the time when they had fought and killed their father, Sir Adnan de Grosse, in the Range of Needles. When Dee awoke, *Dolphin* was on the Peaceful Sea sailing north, out of sight of land, and Dee was ravenously hungry. Percival felt the weight of Camelot's nine towers lift from his shoulders. The procedure hadn't harmed his sister, and the ship's cook complained in a good-natured way that Dee would consume all of his stores.

On their second day of the voyage, Dee sat on a hatch cover, wrapped in a blanket and watching dolphins shadow their namesake ship. The sun hid behind clouds floating on the edge of the horizon.

"How are you feeling?" Percival said.

"Still tired. What do you make of the book from Cereris?"

"It's full of engineering-style drawings of the Grail. There's circuit diagrams and what I think are step-by-step instructions. I don't recognize more than a few words. I hope Merlin can read it."

Dee stared at the horizon, lost in thought.

"What is it? What are you thinking about?"

"What if you and me just took off, Perce?"

"I don't understand."

"Put Roz off at a Viridian port, maybe Grey Harbor, and send her to Camelot with the Grail."

Why was Dee asking this now? She had never hinted at this kind of thing before. "Are you okay, Dee?"

"I can see why going to sea is so appealing. You told me about it after your first voyage on *Dolphin*, but I didn't really get it until now. It would be so easy to just drop what you're doing, sign up as *Dolphin* crew, and go, well, anywhere. No responsibilities, no one to answer to, except maybe the captain and your shipmates."

Every once in a while, Dee reminded Percival that she was his twin, if not in body, then in mind. How often had he fantasized about similar things?

Percival said, "It's fun to think about, but we'd be abandoning our friends and family, not to mention the king and the rest of the country. I wouldn't want to carry that with me forever."

Dee fell into a long silence. The deck moved in a slow rhythm. Near the forecastle, where the crew bunked, someone started singing, the tempo matching the deck's movement.

I dreamed a dream the other night.
Lowlands, Lowlands, away, my John.
My love she came dressed all in white.
My Lowlands away.

I dreamed my love came in my sleep.
Lowlands, Lowlands, away, my John.
Her cheeks were wet, her eyes did weep.
My Lowlands away.

She made no sound. No word she said.
Lowlands, Lowlands, away, my John.
And then I knew my love was dead.
My Lowlands away.

Dee's mood made Percival nervous. She wasn't usually so darkly contemplative.

"Perce?"

"Yes?"

"What would you do if I died?"

What a morbid thing to ask, he wanted to say. Instead, he focused on her mood, not just her words. What was she really talking about? "Are you sick, Dee? Did something go wrong with the procedure in Cassanti?"

"I don't know, Perce. I dreamed last night that Lina was finishing the light tapestry in the Great Audience Hall. She was crying. I tried to ask her why, but she didn't hear me. I couldn't see the portion she was working on, but I had a feeling it was about me."

Percival shook his head, as if wanting to be rid of her words from his ears. He didn't believe that dreams had meaning beyond the experience itself. They weren't secret messages from some other world. But the story gave him chills, even as the warm breeze off the Hot Lands drew sweat from his brow.

"You're recovering from a difficult time. The doctor said you wouldn't be yourself for several days. That's what's happening to you, Dee. Just your body trying to heal."

Dee smiled and put her hand on his. She hadn't done that since they were children.

* * *

The following day, around noon, one of the crew called out "Sail, ho! Dead ahead!" The vessel was square-rigged, meant for crossing the deep ocean. Libb signaled the ship, asking if its captain would come aboard *Dolphin* for a gam. The other vessel accepted, and Libb asked Cook to prepare a dinner for everyone. With the light winds, it took more than an hour for the vessels to draw together, and by the time they did, the winds fell to near calm, making a social visit easy. *Dolphin* sent over two dozen large cinnamon rolls via the jolly boat, while the *Sagittarius* contributed a pot of stew to the dinner.

The master of the *Sagittarius* was a middle-aged woman with short hair named Becu, and she loved to tell stories. There was the Viridian lord who mistook her for a restaurant server until she poured hot soup on his groin. Her ship outraced a Lucian war galley after its captain called *Sagittarius* a "wallowing pig too fat to pull itself out of the mud." In Aurelia, she stuck a knife into a handsy banker who suggested a way to pay off her debts with a certain kind of favor. "He got too close," she said, "and my knife slipped." The judge, however, was not sympathetic, and she spent a year in prison for her act of self-defense.

Percival got the sense that Becu embellished her stories, adding details or dialog that hadn't actually happened. But it made for good entertainment. Dee laughed at the tales, soaking up the energy of good fellowship. It brought a little color back to her pale visage.

"The Aurelians are sticklers for laws and regulations," Libb declared. "You can't spit in the water without getting swarmed by cops."

Becu sipped from her glass of Napene wine. "You've got a reputation on the Aurelian waterfront, Captain Libb."

"Really?" Libb grinned, happy to know he had a measure of fame.

"That was my last port of call, and the first thing the customs officer asked—after taking his fee, of course—was if I'd seen you in my travels."

"What did you say?"

"The truth, that the last time I saw you, the *Dolphin* was heading north. I didn't know where you were going, but I heard later it was Koda."

Libb glanced at Percival, who shrugged. "I was transporting a Viridian expedition to the island to find the Grail."

"Another one?" Becu laughed. "I'd thought Merlin would've given up that silliness by this point. It's a waste of time, in my opinion. So what if the Great Machines are breaking down? Were they ever working in the first place? A thousand years is a long time. Maybe it was all just a story to keep people like Merlin Ambrosius employed."

Percival kept his composure. He'd learned a long time ago that some people couldn't be convinced of the truth of a thing, even when the facts were overwhelming.

"Anyhow, Michael, you say you are bound for Aurelia?"

"Indeed. I plan to drop off my passengers and head out the same day."

Becu drummed her fingers on the table. "I'd rethink that, if I were you."

"Oh?"

"Rumor is you're so far behind on your debts, half of Aurelia's lawyers will be waiting for you on the dock."

"The rumors are exaggerated, but..."

"Just saying that showing up now might be bad for your digestion." Becu patted her ample stomach. "Prison food is terrible, you know."

"I'll think on it, Becu. Thanks for the tip."

Dee said, "Have you heard any news from home, I mean, Camelot, Captain Becu?"

"Don't you get the news feeds?"

"Yes, but, you can't always trust them."

"Mmm. Do you follow politics much?"

"I'm interested." Dee inclined her head to her brother. "We both are."

Becu paused. "Things are, well, unsettled. Before I stopped at

Aurelia, I picked up cargo in Grey Harbor. Everyone was nervous as cats. The whole country is like a cocked pistol. I probably shouldn't say more. I can't take sides."

Ambassador Grenwick had hinted at trouble back home, but Percival hadn't thought much about it. How would it affect him and his expedition so far away from the machinations at court? Now that he was on his way home with the Grail, whatever was going on in Viridiae might matter more.

Downing another glass of wine, Becu said her goodbyes. Percival and Dee retired to their cabins, but Libb stayed up, directing his crew to set a northerly course. After catching a few hours sleep, Percival ran into Libb in the galley refilling his coffee cup. The captain offered a perfunctory greeting and slipped out. Percival could tell Libb was tired, but he also had a reticence Percival couldn't explain away.

That evening at dinner, Libb made an announcement. "Percival, I'm sorry, but I won't be able to take you to Aurelia."

"Becu's warning," Dee said.

"If *Dolphin* were seized, and I was arrested for bad debts, I'd be ruined. My crew would be out of work, and business is marginal right now. I'm an honest man, but I don't have the cash to satisfy otherwise fat creditors."

Percival didn't blame Libb for fearing the loss of his livelihood. "What happens now?"

"I'm going to let you off at a town called Port Morris." Libb showed its location on a tablet. "It's a day's sail from our position. Friendly port with people who ask few questions. You'll be able to pass through without notice. There's a secondary coastal road that will take you north to Aurelia. Not a lot of traffic, so I'm told. Maybe you can catch another ship to Grey Harbor or Bell's Ham."

"You're abandoning us," Dee said, irritated.

"That's not fair. There's a chance you might get caught up in my affairs. I think I'm being generous."

Percival gave a look to Dee that asked for patience. She still hadn't recovered from the medical procedure in Cassanti, and even appeared worse today than yesterday, though it could've been the effects of drinks and a late night.

"We'll be fine, Michael," Percival said. "You've been the best kind of friend."

The following morning, with the help of the jolly boat, *Dolphin* eased up to the Port Morris public dock, which charged no fees for brief stops. Two hours later, all the expedition horses and gear, including the unmarked crate carrying the Last Grail, was ashore. Dee did as much as she could to help, but she had no energy, and her color grew worse. Leaving Dee and Roz at a shoreside park, Percival sold Ben's horse and most of his personal belongings to a second-hand trader, hoping to give the cash, the com, and his identity documents to the dead cadet's parents. Percival returned with extra food and supplies. All three watched the departing *Dolphin* pass under a massive haystack rock, which marked the entrance to the harbor.

"I'm really worried, sir." Roz spoke to Percival privately while Dee napped under a tree. "She has no appetite, and she took only a few sips of water. She refuses to see a doctor. She says she's just tired."

Percival touched Roz's arm. "I'm worried, too. But all we can do is head home." He wanted to add "and hope she gets better," but it seemed too much to ask for.

Port Morris harbor and town lay beneath high bluffs, and the climb to the road recommended by Libb took several hours. Dee kept up for the first two kilometers, but gradually fell behind. Whenever Roz joined her and offered a hand, Dee shook her head. She also refused to ride her horse. She wasn't going to burden anyone, she said. When the spur road to the town finally flattened out and joined Libb's recommended road, Dee collapsed into a heap. Percival brought her a flask of water.

"I'm sorry, Perce. I don't know why I'm so tired."

"You're still recovering. Maybe we should've stayed in Port Morris so you can rest. A few days won't matter to Merlin."

"Let's stop here for the night."

The sun was already less than an hour from touching the rim

of the Peaceful Sea, so Percival and Roz set up the two tents, although with Ben gone, Percival would sleep alone. A few other travelers were scattered around, apparently taking the same road. Percival introduced himself—without revealing anything about his mission—and learned that the road was relatively safe from bandits and police. The trip to Aurelia would take about two weeks.

In the morning, Dee said she felt a little better, and she was ready to travel. Percival didn't believe her. She was as pale as he'd ever seen her, and her breaths were noticeable, as if her lungs weren't working properly. He insisted she ride while he and Roz walked. Dee didn't argue.

The days on the dusty track grew monotonous. Despite the clump of travelers at the campsite, the trio from Viridiae saw few others. That suited Percival fine, because he'd rather not meet any trouble. He could handle anything, he was certain, and he picked Roz because she was skilled with a sword and pistol. But he almost wished someone would approach his group, if only to break the steady landscape of flat earth, dirt trail, and blonde, bone-dry grass. Only the glimpses of the Peaceful Sea to the west broke the drudgery.

Dee continued her slow decline. On the fifth day, clouds moved in from the southwest and the air grew clammy, both signs of a coming storm. Without warning, cloud-to-cloud lightning crashed overhead, spooking Dee's horse. It took off into a meadow. Percival climbed on his horse and took off after her. Then the rain came, buckets worth. He was soaked to the skin within minutes, but he ignored his discomfort as he called out for his sister. After a few minutes, he lost the trail as raindrops pelted him like pebbles. He was near panic when he spotted Dee's horse without its rider. Percival galloped to the scene, and he found Dee lying on her side.

"Gaia in Heaven. Dee, can you hear me?"

Dee groaned. Her hair was plastered to her head by the rain. "I got the horse to stop, but I fell off. I'm so tired." She shivered.

Percival fought back his emotions. His twin was in serious

danger. Her bones and flesh looked intact, but had she suffered internal injuries to compound what the procedure back in Cassanti had done to her? He coaxed Dee in his saddle and climbed up behind her. With the reins of Dee's horse in his hand, he headed back to where he had left Roz.

Gaia bless the woman! She had set up her tent under a tree, out of the worst of the downpour, and Percival put Dee inside. Percival helped the barely conscious Dee out of her soaked clothes while Roz unpacked a cold-weather sleeping bag and wool blankets. Percival set up the battery-powered stove and heated water for soup. Dee managed a few sips before falling asleep. Roz climbed into the bag with her to add her body heat.

Percival passed the night under a rain tarp. The image of Dee's pale skin, sunken eyes, and blue lips when he found her in the meadow haunted him. Competing thoughts warred in his mind and heart. The procedure in Cassanti had hurt Dee somehow, but he had no way of knowing what kind of damage or what he could do to fix it. When he or Roz tried to help, Dee pushed them away, but he couldn't help the feelings of guilt and failure that never seemed to ease. Dee couldn't be forced to do anything, but he was responsible for her. He was responsible for Ben, for Roz, even for Poddle, because he'd agreed to take him on. Everything always broke when he was involved. He struggled to keep from sobbing.

The rain stopped just before dawn. The sun peaked over a distant mountain range, and birdsong filled the air. Percival realized that in the semi-arid desert, the rain would bring forth wildflowers in a day or two. He imagined the once dry meadow covered in color. The thought lifted his spirits.

Roz screamed.

Percival jumped and opened the tent flap. Roz was curled in a corner, terrified. Percival approached the sleeping bag with trepidation, already knowing what he'd find. Dee's face was as a gray as the clouds that brought the previous day's rain. His sister had died.

Percival roared in grief and pain. He pulled at the blaze of his red hair, clumps rising through his fingers like flames. His heart broke into a thousand pieces as he cradle Dee's lifeless head against his chest, begging Gaia to make this a nightmare and wake him up. Nothing answered his prayers except his own sobs and Roz's crying. He hated the sounds, and he hated Cereris for bargaining the Grail for his sister's blood and her life. Percival cared no more for the grand mission of saving his country with a ball of flashing lights that might not even work. What did Merlin know? All Percival wanted now was his sister, his stubborn, crazy, sarcastic, beautiful, intelligent, most wonderful sister a man could have. Everything was injustice and unfairness and stupidity and nothing mattered anymore.

CHAPTER 22:
PERCIVAL RETURNS

Lina received the text from Percival as she was clearing up her workspace for the night.

Home in three days.

Her com nearly slipped out of her fingers as she read and re-read the text. She had to call him. She punched in his voice tie, but all she saw on the screen was a "failed connection" message. Then another text arrived.

Call my mother. It's bad news.

Lina cursed her com and the com system when she tried to reach Percival and got another connection failure message.

Meet me at the border.

Lina froze. No one had heard anything from Percival after he left Aurelia on a ship bound for Cassanti, and that news had come from the Viridian ambassador. Why hadn't Grenwick said anything when Percival came through again on his way home? It didn't feel right.

Nothing felt right these days. Mordred made more threats. Arturus issued counter-threats, officially declaring Mordred a rebel against the state. That made him an outlaw. Knights and soldiers were shooting each other and lopping off arms and legs with swords. Everyone in the palace was on edge.

What should she do? Of course, she should contact Eleanor Rathkeale, but Lina didn't know if Percival had reached anyone else among his friends and at the palace. And what about Dee? How come she hadn't sent any messages? The bad news. What could that be? Had the Last Grail been another myth?

Lina texted Guinevere first. The queen would tell Arturus and Merlin. She might even organize a welcome escort. Guinevere responded that no one else had heard anything. Why had Percival contacted Lina first? Lina had no idea, but her heart warmed. He hadn't forgotten about her. He'd probably tried a dozen people, but he also tried her. While they were texting, news arrived from The Keep. A cadet had heard from Roz, one of Percival's retainers. She confirmed his immediate plan of getting to the border, but the message added little else.

Nothing had arrived from Ben, the other retainer, or Dee. Guinevere said not to worry.

Lina called Eleanor, using the voice tie Percival had included with his text. Lina had never spoken to Eleanor, and when she answered, Lina felt a little nervous, and she wasn't quite sure what to say.

"I'm a friend of Percival's, Ms. Rathkeale. He asked me to contact you. He's on his way home!"

The voice on the other side was mature, but wary. "What else did he say?"

Lina swallowed. "He said there was bad news. But I haven't heard anything more."

The line went silent. "Did he mention Dee?"

"No, I'm sorry."

"Lina, I'm coming to Camelot. I'll let you know when I arrive."

The line closed abruptly, but Lina sensed Eleanor's shock. Percival wouldn't ask Lina to call his mother and mention bad news unless the news had to do with family, not the Grail. Gaia in Heaven, had something happened to Dee?

* * *

The next morning, Lina joined the royal party traveling to the border to meet the returning expedition. Arturus led the group himself, a fact that set the news chans on fire. For days, the capital had overflowed with rumors about a coming showdown between Arturus and Mordred. The rebellious lord's soldiers were probing Camelot's defenses. Leaving the capital now seemed risky, even reckless. The timing of Percival's arrival was at once exciting and suspicious. The government wouldn't talk about his location or what he might have discovered. Speculation ran rampant. What if Percival had succeeded? It would boost Arturus' popularity, and thus his chances at keeping his throne and avoiding a war. What if Percival had failed? Mordred would take advantage of the country's anger and disappointment. More people might join him. Was Arturus on his way to the border to greet a hero, or to escape destruction?

Arturus said nothing to quell the speculation. Guinevere herself was uncertain why Arturus wanted to meet Percival instead of waiting for his arrival in Camelot. Perhaps he simply couldn't wait, like everyone else.

Lina cared little about the rumors and talking heads. She was mostly concerned about Percival and Dee, and she begged Guinevere to let her go to the border. Guinevere said yes. Eleanor had called Lina the night before. She would arrive in Camelot in two days, promising to meet Percival, Dee and Lina when they came home to the city.

Flanked on all sides by his household guard, Arturus' company arrived at the border crossing, a little town called Ash, which sat below a spur of the Range of Needles. The mayor, alerted only an hour before the king's arrival by a herald, could barely contain her terror. She never expected a visit by the king, queen, and what appeared to be an army. Arturus calmed the mayor and asked where they might find a place to bivouac without causing too much fuss. They'd only be here for 24 hours or so. The mayor showed them to a small park on the edge of a fir and hemlock forest. The captain of Arturus' household guard declared the park adequate for security. Just to be safe, they set up checkpoints on the highway leading to Ash and beefed up security at the border crossing.

The camp at Ash included a large pavilion for Arturus and Guinevere, as well as smaller shared tents for Lina and other aides, including Merlin. Of all the courtiers, Merlin appeared the most excited about Percival's impending arrival, like a child anticipating ice cream. While they waited for the expedition, Arturus and Guinevere received local elected officials and leading citizens. Everyone was searched for weapons.

Just after dinner, a messenger handed a note to Arturus. The setting sun spread a golden glow on the park, while ancient firs within and on the edge of the park cast long shadows, reminding Lina of columns in the Great Audience Hall. Hundreds of people from the town and the surrounding countryside had filtered to the park, giving the moment a festive atmosphere. Lina smelled spiced meats and bought roasted vegetables from a food cart. While she sipped an iced drink, a herald asked that the tables in the pavilion be moved aside.

Silence gradually fell on the crowd, including the nobles, knights, and men-at-arms. The throng slowly split in half, making room for two riders to pass. Lina recognized Percival, and her heart leaped into her throat. He wore his light battle armor, a little worn, but clean, its decorative chromed fastenings reflecting the sun's last rays. Lina resisted the urge to call out and wave to him, but he was several meters from her, and nearly everyone, even the children, made almost no sound. Percival's eyes were fixed on Arturus, as if no one else mattered to him. He'd allowed his beard to grow, and though well-trimmed, it covered all of his face and neck, with a full mustache. The beard was darker than his flaming red hair, which had lost some of its luster. His face was serious, careworn, and lonely. Her heart ached for him. Had she had changed in the months since his departure?

A horse followed Percival on a lead. It carried a crate on its flank, balanced by a pannier on the opposite flank. Behind the horse was another rider, Roz, dressed in threadbare, but clean traveling clothes, with a similar tired look as Percival's. She also had a pack horse on a lead. Lina waited for Ben and Dee to appear, but they didn't. Lina's heart beat hard against her chest. She felt as if something was crushing her, despite her joy at seeing her lover.

Percival halted at the entrance to the pavilion. He glanced

back at Roz, waiting until she caught up. They dismounted as one and approached Arturus. He met them halfway, his expression a mix of relief and fear.

"Percival. Cadet Goodread." Arturus extended his hand. "We are overjoyed to see you both."

"My lord king." Percival bowed his head and took Arturus' hand.

Roz echoed Percival's words and actions.

Where was Dee, Lina wondered. And Ben?

"Sire, I wish to report that we have retrieved the Last Grail from Cassanti." Percival glanced at Roz. Together, they detached the crate from the pack horse and laid it at Arturus' feet. People in front of the crowd nearest Arturus strained to look. Percival took a small crowbar and pried off the lid. He and Roz lifted a glittering object within a gold frame encrusted with jewels. The reds and oranges from the half-sunk sun bounced off the objects as water caroms off rocks in a falls. The crowd gasped.

Merlin chomped at the bit to get his hands on the device.

Percival returned the Grail to its crate and closed the lid.

"Percival, Cadet Goodread," Arturus said, "I cannot express the depth of my personal gratitude and your country's gratitude for what you have accomplished."

Percival bent his head in thanks. "My lord, I must also report…" He halted, unable to continue. Lina's heart nearly burst as she waited for him to say what she feared most.

"My lord, I must also report the loss of your cadet, Ben Playa. He died of an illness aboard ship on the way to Cassanti. He was buried at sea."

Arturus sighed. "I am greatly saddened by this, Percival. He is a hero to all true Viridians."

"I must also report…" Percival cleared his throat. He almost choked on the words. Lina wanted nothing more than to stand next to him and hold his hand to give him strength. But she held her place.

"My sister, Dindrane Rathkeale, was lost as well. She died giving life to another, so that Cadet Roz and I could bring this gift to you and to her people."

All was silent. The slight breeze through the park had dropped to nothing. The birds had grown quiet. The children had grown quiet. Only a few sobs broke the stillness. Guinevere cried openly.

Arturus said, "There is no greater sacrifice, my dear friend. I am so sorry for your loss. We will find a way to honor your sister, I promise."

In the midst of the devastating emotion felt by Dee's loss, a thought came to Lina. She'd been working hard at completing as much of the mural in the Great Audience Hall as possible, leaving the portions that had vexed Dee alone. She was stuck because she couldn't see the ending of the story. More importantly, she couldn't see that she would never finish the mural, at least then.

In that instant, everything fell into place for Lina. This was the moment envisioned by Dee in the mural she designed for the Great Audience Hall. Despite her frustration, she had heard the future tick of the clock, played out in a small-town park, bracketed by snow-capped mountains, guarded by the forest, illuminated by a sun dimmed by a troubled atmosphere. Lina saw the completed work in her minds eye. Arturus, regal despite his persistent illness, empathetic, grateful. Guinevere, beautiful, emotional, with a stubborn intelligence. Percival, loyal to the core, persistent as a tiger, heartbroken at a terrible loss. Dee saw nearly all of it, and she committed her vision to light, maybe to last for generations, if civil war or the failure of the Great Machine didn't destroy it. Lina had already felt the weight of honoring Dee's dream as an artist. Now the work took on new meaning for Lina. She'd have to finish it for her friend.

The impromptu ceremony ended, Merlin and an assistant descended on the wooden crate and its precious device. Percival and Roz shared a moment with the king and queen, but Lina was done with courtesy and deference. She ran to Percival, shouting to him. He turned and for the first time since arriving, he smiled. Lina practically jumped at him, kissing him without a word of greeting, whispering "I missed you" and "I love you" to him. She pressed her body into his, wanting to hold him so that he would never doubt that she had chosen him as her lifelong partner.

Percival gazed at her, as if disbelieving that she existed. "Lina, I was hoping to see you. My com hardly worked. I didn't even know if you received my texts."

Lina stroked his cheek tenderly. "I got the important ones. Your mother is coming to Camelot."

Percival's face fell. "I know. I managed to reach her this morning. I wanted to tell her about Dee before she found out some other way."

"How did she take it?"

"It's hard to tell with her. I think she knew something like this would happen, but..."

"Darling, I'm so sorry. Dee was the most important person in your life."

A family group, from elders to a baby, surrounded Roz. She had relations near Ash. The reunion offset Percival's sadness. The security people, nervous that Mordred had operatives in the crowd, kept people away from Percival, who was a new celebrity.

Lina said to Percival, "Do you feel up to telling me what happened?"

"It's been weeks now. The shock has worn off, but it still hurts like hell."

Percival told the story of Dee's donation to the Cleric Cereris, and the trade she'd made. "I thought Dee was alright, but she got sick quickly. Getting soaked in a cold rain was probably the worst thing that could happen." He sighed for a long moment. "I couldn't bring her home. Roz and I buried her on a hill with a view of the sea. I think she discovered a love of the ocean. We marked her grave with a cairn of stones if Mother or I want to visit."

"If you do, please take me with you."

Percival nodded, then took Lina's hand. "I'm glad you're here. I've hardly thought of anyone else after Dee died. I couldn't think of anyone else to talk to, not even Mother. I wanted to talk to you every day."

"You can now. I'm not going anywhere."

"Percival!" Merlin elbowed his way through the line of soldiers. His eyes were wide with excitement. "My dear boy, I'm glad I found you."

"Is something wrong, sir?"

"No, nothing at all. Everything is right, I'd say. The Grail you brought back. It's the real thing!"

"It works?"

Lina squeezed Percival's hand. Maybe all his sacrifice was worth the cost.

"Everything about it checks out," Merlin said. "The technical manual is just what we needed. It has tons of information about the Great Machine. I want you to come with me."

"Where, sir?"

"To the Great Machine, where else? You can help us install it." Percival was incredulous. "Me? I'm not an engineer. I know nothing about the Grail or the Great Machine."

"It doesn't matter. I want you there when we restart it. You deserve to see it in operation first hand."

Percival glanced at Lina. "But I must see my mother. She's come to Camelot—"

"Your mother can wait." Merlin hinted at irritation.

"I need to talk to her about my sister."

Merlin caught himself. "Yes, well, I see. Look, this is the most important thing to happen to Viridiae since its founding. You are the hero of the moment. You are a dutiful son and brother, and I'm truly sorry for your loss. But this is a once in a lifetime opportunity!"

"Dee would want you to be there," Lina said. "I'll explain it to Eleanor. You know she'll understand."

Percival thought a moment. Lina watched his mood change from sorrowful to excited. "When do you want to leave, Merlin?"

"First thing, tomorrow morning."

Lina nodded in encouragement.

"Very well, sir. I'll go with you, for Dee's sake."

CHAPTER 23: A KIDNAPPING

Just after midnight, most of the Viridian company returned to Camelot, leaving a small contingent of men-at-arms to escort Merlin, his assistants, and Percival to Apparatus Montis, the location of the Great Machine. Percival regretted his decision to go with the scientist by the end of his first day. The man wouldn't stop talking. He asked question after question, mostly about Cassanti. Percival didn't want to think about the place any longer. It brought up too many painful memories.

"Tell me again about the spear you saw during the temple ceremony, Percival."

"It was a javelin."

"Indeed. I didn't know there was a difference."

"Javelins are a type of spear intended for throwing."

"What was it made of?"

"I don't know. I didn't examine it."

"I've read that ash is often used for these kinds of weapons because of its density."

"Pine is lighter and easier to work, but it's the tip that matters more. It needs to be sharp and strong to penetrate shields and armor."

"Could you tell anything about the tip of the javelin in Cassanti?"

Percival shook his head. "It was golden, but gold is too soft for a spear tip. The best are made of carbon steel."

"It's possible that it was gold leaf or gold paint covering a steel tip?" Merlin said. "One thing that wasn't lost after the Dissolution was knowledge for making good steel. Now, about the artificial light you saw..."

"Please, sir, couldn't this wait until a formal debriefing?"

"Oh, that's coming. But I'd rather have a nice informal discussion under a clear blue sky than in a dingy palace office. Agree?"

After two days, Percival and Merlin's party started an easy climb through foothills below Apparatus Montis, which Merlin said were two ancient words meaning Machine Mountain. After an hour or so, one of the soldiers came down the trail as fast as his animal could carry him. He stopped in front of the burly, scar-faced sergeant at the head of Percival's column and spoke quickly. Sending the soldier back up the trail, the sergeant signaled a halt and came down to Merlin's side.

"Do you know another route to the Machine's outer gate, sir?"

"No, I don't. What's wrong?"

"The scout sees signs of another party. Do you know if there's others in the area, people you know?"

"No. The Machine's compound should be empty, except for a few caretakers."

All at once, a dozen horsemen and women in black uniforms emerged from the dense forest. The Viridian sergeant drew his sword, but a knight in light armor pointed his pistol at the sergeant's chest. Aware of his sword's pommel within inches of his hand, Percival held steady, not wanting to provoke the knight.

"I'm Sir Dexter Capp. I'm pleased to make your acquaintance. On behalf of Lord Mordred of Lothia, I promise not to hurt any of you, if you cooperate."

"Gaia in Heaven, Sir Clapp, or whatever your name is," Merlin said. "We are on a scientific mission. We are bringing the Grail to the Great Machine, hoping to repair it. Why are you blocking our way?"

"My Lord Mordred supports your mission and wishes you success... in good time."

"What in hell is that supposed to mean?" Merlin said.

"I've been instructed by Lord Mordred to escort you and the Grail to his encampment. He wishes to learn more about the

Grail before you install it."

"That makes no sense, man. I can just as well explain it after I've tested it and connected it to the Great Machine's systems."

"Mordred isn't interested in the Grail's scientific value, Merlin." Percival had spent a couple of hours in Ash catching up with Arturus about Mordred's rebellion. "The rebel wants the Grail because of the prestige it brings."

Merlin scrunched his face. "Prestige? What kind of prestige?"

"He thinks if he has the Grail, people will follow him," Percival said.

Capp said, "You must be Sir Percival, gallant knight, intrepid adventurer, and hero of Viridiae. I congratulate you on your success. This is only a short detour, my friend. Mordred only wants to examine it, document it, and allow you and Merlin to finish your work."

Merlin laughed, "Are you saying he wants his picture taken with it?"

Capp shrugged. "You must admit its propaganda value is immense."

"At least you're honest, for a highwayman. I'm a scientist, not a public relations agent. Every moment we waste on stupid requests is a moment that makes the climate worse. Can't you tell that our environment is suffering? Don't you have eyes to see?"

Merlin swept his hand, and even to Percival's untrained eye, the forest looked sickly, like someone who hadn't eaten or slept in days.

"As I said, Dr Ambrosius, it's only for a few days."

"Capp," Percival said, "I didn't lose my sister and one of my friends so that Mordred could score points with the masses. Back off and let us go."

"I'm afraid that's not possible." Capp gestured, and the dozen Lothians moved closer. "Hand it over, and Dr Ambrosius too."

"I'll not be your hostage," Merlin said.

Percival almost laughed at the irony. The Lucians invaded Viridiae to find Merlin and bring him to Lucana. Mordred apparently had the same general idea.

"Very well, Dr Ambrosius, if that's the way you want it." Capp motioned two of his men into position behind Percival. Others drew pistols and threatened Merlin's escort. Two more dismounted. One took the lead of the pack horse carrying the crate containing the Grail. The other checked Merlin for arms, found none, and tied his hands. Merlin complained the entire time. Meanwhile, Capp took the reins of Merlin's horse.

"You're a kidnapper as well as a thief!" Merlin said to Capp.

"Think of it as a pleasant detour, Dr Ambrosius." Capp turned to Percival, his expression flat. "If you follow us, I'll kill you and Merlin. And keep the Grail."

Percival watched helplessly as Capp and his soldiers led Merlin away at a trot. The Viridian sergeant, a man named Meddish, asked Percival what they should do.

"Rescue Merlin and the Grail, what else?"

* * *

Percival couldn't let Capp get far, or he might lose his best chance at retrieving Merlin and the Grail. He certainly couldn't let Capp reach Mordred, or he'd face the impossibility of rescuing Merlin from the midst of an army. The only chance was to intercept Capp before he left the area. Fortunately, Meddish knew the local landscape from previous assignments guarding the Great Machine.

"Capp might know the area, too," Percival said.

"I doubt it," Meddish said. "Lothia is distant, so it's unlikely he's spent much time down here. And I didn't recognize any of his people. If one or more of them was local, or served with the guard unit, I'd know."

"I've never been here myself," Percival allowed.

"There's only two practical routes to the Great Machine, the one we used, and one through a narrow canyon to the northwest." Meddish pulled out his tablet and got a surprisingly good connection for a remote area. "Capp could try bushwhacking, but it would slow him down, and there's a good chance he'd get lost. He's almost certainly going through the canyon."

Percival grinned. "I'm betting you know a third route."

Meddish adjusted the map on his tablet. "There's a series of trails that follow this cut to the east of the canyon. The trails come out at its head. We can get him there."

"He's got twice as many soldiers as we do, and we have all this baggage and civilians."

"We'll have surprise and the terrain, not much more, except for good men-at-arms."

Percival nodded. "When do we leave?"

"Now. He's got a head start, and we have farther to go."

While Meddish organized his soldiers, Percival explained the plan to Merlin's assistants. Meddish left two of his soldiers to escort the civilians to the Great Machine compound, gambling that they wouldn't encounter trouble. After lightening his destrier of unneeded gear, Percival followed Meddish and three of his troopers down the trail Capp had arrived on only hours before. After a kilometer or so, Meddish took a nearly invisible cut to the east, and they increased their pace.

The light was good and the air crisp, but not cold. Meddish trotted, then cantered through a meadow blanketed with succulent grass and wildflowers. Percival could almost hear his horse's longing to stop for a long snack. Fording a creek, they climbed a steep trail. The view at the crest was magnificent, clear as glass, with the peak of Apparatus Montis behind them and a series of deep valleys ahead.

Remembering the cross-country trek on the island of Koda on his second, failed expedition to find the stolen Viridian Grail, Percival reflected that the feelings that accompanied his failures —anger, depression, loss, self-pity—had faded. After all, he'd finally succeeded at finding an operating Grail, and he determined not to lose it to a thief. Lina's presence, too, soothed his sorrows. Dee's death left a gaping hole in his heart, but the pain wasn't as sharp as before. When it came to Lina, he doubted that he could ever live more than half a life if he somehow lost her.

They descended into dense understory of sword ferns, flowering bushes, and young firs, perfect cover for an ambush. Meddish, leading the column, halted near a wall of rock. Percival trotted up to him.

Meddish pointed toward the rock wall down the slope. "Capp will need to pass through that gap. We should position half our people on the other side of the trail."

"Can you be sure we've beat them, that they haven't already passed through?"

"We'll know shortly."

Percival placed his trust in Meddish's knowledge of the terrain. Percival took three of the soldiers across the trail, leaving Meddish behind with the balance of the squad. Everyone dismounted, tying their horses behind them in the thick brush. Percival spotted poison oak, and hoped he'd avoid a painful rash.

Thirty minutes passed, then forty-five. Percival watched Meddish closely, as well as kept his eye on the gap. As the wait crept close to an hour, Meddish waved his hand in a prearranged signal. Percival passed on the signal to the other Viridians and patted the pommel of his battle sword. It was better suited for open country on horseback, but he hadn't brought all his weapons. At least he had his good light armor.

The sounds of horse sighs and clanking metal filtered through the still air. Percival heard voices, and he swore he made out Merlin's high-pitched gravelly tone. Using surprise, Meddish and Percival wanted to separate Merlin from the rest of group quickly and spirit him away, avoiding a general melee. Meddish would grab the pack animal carrying the Grail. It was a decent plan, but they were ready for anything.

The first of the Lothian riders appeared, one of the ordinary soldiers. Percival held still, waiting for his quarry. Another Lothian soldier passed. Both were relaxed, perhaps convinced they had made good their escape, and not expecting trouble. Percival heard Merlin's voice again, followed by a gruff order.

"Can you not be quiet, man?" Capp was annoyed. "You have more words than a library of textbooks."

"I can't help it, Sir Nap, or Clapp, I can never remember. I get talkative when I'm nervous."

Percival felt like a cat ready to pounce. He'd picked out a point on the trail where Merlin would have to pass. When the scientist got there, he'd bolt for him. Meddish knew the place as well, and when Percival moved, Meddish would attack and scatter the Lothians.

A horse nickered. The sound came from one of the Viridian animals, and a Lothian turned his head and shouted. Their cover was blown.

Merlin hadn't reached the predetermined point, but Percival took off on his destrier. He raced through the brush and snatched the reins from Merlin's bound hands. He needed to get Merlin away from the action. The horses started climbing the secret trail, but Merlin's animal wasn't used to the extra effort. It caromed into a tree and tumbled, throwing Merlin to the ground. A pad of fallen needles broke his fall.

Behind them, shouts and screams pierced the quiet forest. Pounding hooves and the clanks of steel signaled duels. Percival dismounted, amazed that Merlin hadn't broken anything. Merlin got on his hands and knees.

"Percival? How did you—"

"We have to get out of here." Percival lifted Merlin by his shoulder and started up the trail, but it was too steep. He decided to find a hiding spot.

Capp cut him off. "Stupid Viridian. Trying to run from a man on horseback. Is that what they teach you at The Keep?"

Percival drew his sword and put himself between Dexter and Merlin. "You want to see what I've learned? Get off your horse and I'll show you."

Capp, sword in hand, charged Percival, who dodged the blow. With his free hand, he snagged loose chain mail at Clapp's waist and pulled him down to the ground. The horse's twisting hind quarters knocked Percival aside and ran off.

Capp scrambled to his feet. "You're going to lose, Percival. Mordred has sent more soldiers in this direction. They could be here any minute. They'll cut you to pieces."

Was he bluffing? Percival and Meddish hadn't seen anything to suggest more Lothians. "Nice lie, rebel. Give up now, and I'll say good things about you when you go on trial for treason."

Capp charged again, and their swords clashed. They found themselves in a small clearing, almost like an arena, and they circled each other like panthers. Sword on sword, parries, thrusts, and Percival was cut on the shoulder. He cried out, more in surprise than pain, but the man who drew first blood always had the advantage as the fight progressed. Capp sensed it, and he pressed harder.

Percival, aware of other sounds of fighting, kept Merlin behind him, by turns defending the scientist and attacking Capp. Merlin shouted advice like a boxer's cornerman.

"Watch your left, Percival! He likes to step forward when he parries. Sword up, man!"

Percival wished Merlin would shut up.

As they spun, Percival slipped, and Capp came down hard on Percival's crown with his fist. Stunned, Percival fell back, then got to his feet. His head cleared enough to see the exhausted Capp hold back. Percival fell forward, out of breath, hoping to knock Capp down. Instead, he pushed him into Merlin.

"Get off me," Merlin barked. "You smell like horse."

"I swear to Gaia I will cut out your tongue, Ambrosius, when I'm done with this fool knight."

At that instant, a bloody stain formed under Capp's chin. He dropped his sword and grabbed his throat. Blood leaked from his mouth as he reached around to get hold of something. He couldn't, and he fell face first on the ground. A knife stuck out of the back of his neck.

"I'll shut up when I damn well feel like it," Merlin said, his hands bloody. "You, however, will hold your tongue from now on."

Capp lay dead at Merlin's feet.

Percival heard the pounding of hooves and got to his feet, ready to fight off other Lothians. Meddish appeared with his soldiers. The horse with the Grail was on a lead behind him.

"Hot work, eh, Percival?" Meddish said.

"Hot enough, but you can thank Dr Ambrosius for finishing the job."

Meddish gaped at the scientist.

"You military types are always surprised when a civilian, especially an old man, defends himself successfully. I was young and strong once, and learned a few things over my lifetime, including how to kill a man if necessary."

Percival and Meddish looked at each other, and laughed.

"Now, let's get the Grail to the Great Machine." Merlin brushed dirt off his pants, leaving streaks of blood like paint stains. "I've had enough of pointless distractions."

CHAPTER 24: THE GRAIL AND THE GREAT MACHINE

The machine built to save the world hummed behind a double door the height of a man on a horse. Percival had seen photos of the entrance, stained by algae and age, and set in from the surrounding cliff face, but he expected something grander, more impressive. It should awe him, he thought, like the nine towers of the old wall surrounding the inner city at Camelot, or the soaring height of the groves of fir in the King's Forest near his mother's home. But the entrance had an unexpected element. He felt a mild vibration through the ground, like the hooves of a horse on a wooden platform. The earth was alive, almost breathing.

"That's a fair description of the Machine's purpose, to help the earth breathe," Merlin said. "Without the Grail, it's wheezing, and badly."

"Are you sure the Grail will fix it?"

"Who knows? We have to take it on faith that Joseph Arimathea knew what he was doing."

They arrived at the Viridian compound late in the evening, as the purple sky turned to inky black, the only light coming from the Milky Way and battery powered lights. Merlin's assistants and the small escort met with no trouble, as Percival had hoped. By the time Percival and Meddish arrived, Merlin's team had already set up various instruments and tools to prep the Grail for installation. Meddish had delivered Capp's body to his Lothians, telling them to deliver the rebel to Mordred with a warning to stay away from Apparatus Montis. Two of his men trailed the Lothians for a few kilometers until they were convinced that the rebels had taken the message to heart.

Percival slept well that night in a cabin that sheltered the year-round caretakers of the Machine. He dreamed of his sister. They sat on a log in the forest near his mother's cottage. It was in this secret childhood hideaway that Dee showed him her power to kill with thoughts, nearly snuffing the life of an innocent spider. Later, she had conjured a lightning strike that had killed their father, Sir Adnan de Grosse, after Percival had wounded him with a javelin.

"I can't protect you any more, Perce." Dee's face was relaxed and calm. Golden thread in her outfit caught the reflection of the campfire.

"You will anyway, despite yourself," Percival said.

"I'm gone, you know that."

"Yes, but I'll hear your voice in my head, scolding me for one thing or another, warning me about things I can't see for myself. We're a team. That doesn't change just because you're dead."

"You're such a moron."

The scene changed to the Great Audience Hall in Camelot. Hundreds of people surrounded him. He wore the dress uniform of a Round Table knight. Lina glowed like an angel in her wedding dress. Percival thought his heart would burst with feeling for her. He took her hand, her fingers delicate but strong, and they proceeded down a central aisle. He noticed a problem. Many of the chairs among the applauding crowd were empty, though he couldn't imagine who might have begged off or failed to show. Who would—

"Percival! We can't wait for you forever!"

Percival opened his eyes to Merlin's unshaven face.

"You've got five minutes or we're starting without you."

"Starting what?" Percival drew his hand over his face.

"Doing what we can here for, you fool!"

Five minutes later, after dressing and grabbing a breakfast pastry from the kitchen, Percival sat next to the driver of a small electric cart with a flat bed. Under a tarp was a squarish shape, which Percival surmised was the Grail. Merlin and his team drove in another cart ahead of Percival. The doors of the mountain were open, like the maw of a beast. Percival's stomach tightened.

The carts eased down a tunnel at a walking pace. A string of electric lights along the wall illuminated the passage and its vaulted ceiling. Tiny stalactites and water stains marked cracks in the vault. The cart's tires splashed through shallow puddles. They came to another double door, the same size as the first door, covered with streaks of mildew. Merlin stepped out and punched a code into a keypad of Viridian make. A status bar turned from red to green, and an electric motor whirred, sliding one door to the left and one to the right.

The pitch darkness of the interior surprised Percival. Was the Great Machine completely inactive? As Merlin disappeared into the darkness, Percival again felt the ground vibrate, more intense this time, as if he were nearer the source. Then the lights came on.

His cart moved forward, then turned onto a ramp. Percival was enveloped in a web-like maze of metal girders, trusses, pipes, and electrical wiring. All of it floated in the center of a cavern, really a hollowed-out ball, an artificial space so large that Percival imagined all of Camelot's citadel enclosed by it, like a jar. They must be in the center of Apparatus Montis, he thought. The only way he knew that a wall lay on the opposite side was a dim light that marked another set of doors.

The cart stopped at a room that could hold both carts and a dozen people comfortably.

"Welcome to the control room, Percival," Merlin said. "At least, that's what I call it. I don't know what Joseph Arimathea called it."

Merlin flipped a light switch. A harsh bulb illuminated a wall and a console set at an angle. Indentations and bumps covered the wall, while the console had squares etched into a metal Percival couldn't identify.

"Let's see what we've got," Merlin said. "It worked the last time I was here."

The scientist consulted a palm-sized tablet in his left hand. He touched two of the control panel knobs simultaneously, which began to glow. He placed a finger on one of the indentations, and the consoles awakened with an eerie blue light. Merlin stepped back, and in a few seconds, three of the walls, glittered red, blue, and green, each the soft intensity of a sunset.

Merlin's technicians examined various portions of the panels, some of which showed the characters Percival saw in the technical manual Cereris gave him. He could only make out a few of the characters, none of which meant anything to him.

"You're disoriented by this point, eh, my boy?" Merlin said. "When I first saw this, I couldn't make head nor tails of it. But I managed to figure it out with a little bit of research and experimentation. Fortunately, the builders guessed it might need some adjustments, and it was forgiving to my poking and prodding."

Percival said, "You called it a control room. So this could be the nerve center of the Great Machine?"

"Correct, my friend. It's actually one of several control rooms throughout the complex."

"Several?"

"Oh yes. What you see here and out there," Merlin pointed out a window toward the spider-work in the cavern, "is perhaps five percent of the Great Machine. There may be some nooks and crannies I haven't discovered yet."

"Where is the rest of it?"

"Mostly below us, going down several levels."

"As large as this level?"

"Larger, filled to the brim with compressors, heat exchangers, water-based coolers, and a half-dozen other technologies I can't even begin to guess at. But it's all wired to this room. This is the brain of the Machine."

Percival had trouble grasping the scale of it.

"What's more, this brain is tied to all the other eleven Machines scattered over the planet. I believe, though I haven't been able to prove, they communicate with each other through artificial satellites overhead." Merlin glanced up, as if he could see through the solid rock.

"And they've all been running and talking to each other for a thousand years." Percival was stunned. "The ring communicator / com reader combination on my finger and in my pocket will last me three years, maybe four, if I'm careful."

"Arimathea was a genius, perhaps the greatest in Earth's history. There was a lot at stake. The planet was dying. This was the Old Civilization's last chance, and he made it work."

"Until recently," Percival said.

"Yes, the Grail in this Machine failed, as did the Lucian Grail. No design is perfect. I don't know about the other Machines, but I expect they're having trouble too."

"Why now?"

"I don't know. Perhaps they're reached the end of their designed life. Or perhaps Arimathea believed humanity would solve the Warming problem by the time the Machines wore out. The Dissolution happened within a few decades of the Machines coming online, and the collapse of the Old Civilization meant no more research. After a while, people forgot how to care for the Machines."

"Until you came along," Percival said.

"Don't be silly. I've found records of men and woman who've tried to work out the Machine's secrets over the last few centuries, but I've been lucky enough to build on their work. The Grail is the key."

A terminal on the console flashed green.

"The Grail is a kind of basal ganglia. These are important concentrations of nerve cells in the brain, controlling information pathways. The Grail is glue that holds everything together, and not just in our Machine, but with all the other Machines."

"In other words, it's a node in an enormous, planet-wide network."

"Among other things."

"And if a node of the network goes down, the entire network is weakened."

"Which is why we need to get it back to full strength, or the Warming will return. We're already seeing it."

One of the technicians handed Merlin his tablet. He turned to study the green readout. "Excellent. It's just as I'd hoped."

"Hoped?"

"Time to save the world again, my dear boy."

Merlin led Percival to the cart with the Grail, leaving assistants to monitor the Machine in the control room. Other assistants lifted the tarp off the gold frame that held the device, which appeared inert, unlike other times he saw it.

"Is it broken, Merlin?"

"Not to worry. It was connected to a self-charging battery system, probably meant to keep it ready when needed. We don't think taking it off the battery will harm it. Here, take this." Merlin handed Percival a heavy box with a thick handle.

"What's this?"

"You don't think I'd go anywhere without tools, do you?"

Percival was glad he had something to do. He was beginning to feel that he was in the way.

Two assistants lifted the Grail carefully from the flat cart bed. The Grail and its frame rested on a platform secured with ropes. The group stepped onto a suspended walkway leading to an open, circular room partly enclosed by sheets of metal. A few lamps in the room glowed, but shed little light. Merlin approached a small console and touched it, tracing a round pattern. Invisible doors about a man's height in an otherwise blank wall of metal slid open, and the four Viridians stepped inside.

Merlin touched the wall, and a warm light filled the small space, about the size of the kitchen and dining space in Percival's Camelot apartment. He perceived a change in the attitude of Merlin and the assistants. Perhaps it was the light, which resembled candlelight, without the flickering. It was bright enough to see the strange symbols of the Old Civilization language on the walls, but not so harsh that you blinked. You'd entered a different world, a holy place, almost like a temple to Gaia during the solstice, when worshipers sent prayers to the goddess for good health and fertility. The only thing missing was the smell of incense. Instead, Percival noticed a metallic, musty smell. He set Merlin's tool box in a corner.

A platform about the height of Percival's waist rested in the middle of the room. With care, almost reverence, Merlin loosened fasteners at the corners of the frame while an assistant held the Grail steady. The sage-scientist and technicians said little, as if they'd had rehearsed these moves a dozen times. After a pause, Merlin lifted the device out of the frame. Percival almost reached out to help Merlin, remembering the dense weight of the Grail, but the old man held it steady. He hefted it to the raised platform, and with his technicians guiding his hands, set it into four long, thin pegs, which fit into the body of the device. With the Grail secure, Merlin connected two thick cables emerging from the platform to the device. The scientist stepped back, and a cover lowered from above, as if on cue. The cover resembled the gold frame protecting the Grail on the trip from Cassanti.

"Take your places, my friends. Percival, you stand there." Merlin pointed to a place out of the way.

Merlin and his assistants swiped tablets and called out readings. Percival heard references to temperature, voltage, and other parameters he didn't recognize. Handing his tablet to one of the assistants, Merlin stood in front of the console. He touched it in a discernible pattern, and waved his hand over several bumps of different shapes on the wall. The nearly imperceptible vibrations Percival had noticed intensified further, and the warm light in the room grew brighter.

Then, everything stopped.

"Dammit!" Merlin barked. He pushed Percival aside and opened the toolbox. Metal tools clunked as Merlin pushed them aside. "Why is it the tool you need is never on top of the pile?"

The assistants shrugged.

"Aha!" Merlin removed a rubber mallet. He approached the

platform and its cover protecting the Grail, studying the seam where the cover met the platform. Taking careful aim, he smacked it with the mallet, not too hard, not too soft. The warm light returned, brighter and more intense.

"A thousand years will take anything out of alignment," Merlin remarked.

The Grail began to glow. Percival had seen this before, first in the lab in Lucana, then in the shrine in Cassanti. The device shone like a jewel with a thousand facets, shooting beams of light in all directions. Then something new happened. Pieces of it turned, some clockwise, others counterclockwise, as if aligning in a certain way. Parts rotated inward, others out, always smoothly and under control.

Merlin laughed. "It's working!"

The vibrations intensified, but Percival felt no danger. Merlin left the room, and his three companions followed. Merlin ran out on the walkway into the lattice of girders and beams. Percival stopped cold. The whole structure gleamed, humming in low tones like a musical instrument. Percival started to laugh, as if seeing the birth of a new foal. The Viridians had resurrected the Great Machine.

Handshakes and hugs all around.

That evening, in the kitchen that served the outdoor compound, Percival, Merlin, Meddish and the technicians and soldiers celebrated their success. Measuring instruments placed inside the complex and in strategic spots around the site sent nothing but good news. Despite the positive results, Merlin worked hard to maintain his scientific skepticism.

"It may be too early to celebrate." Merlin sipped on a bottle of ale. "The Great Machine is a millennia old. A lot could go wrong. It might not have the ability to reverse the failing climate."

"How long until we know?" Percival said.

"I'm not sure. It might be years before we'll notice a change in rainfall or average temperatures, or the health of harvests."

"I'm not a scientist, Merlin, but I feel pretty good about the future. One success, even if it's temporary, makes up for a lot of failure."

Merlin set down his bottle, and he invited Percival to walk with him.

"The difference between good people and bad people," Merlin said, "is that the good try to fix their sins. The bad don't."

"What do you mean, Professor?" Merlin was again in a talkative mood, but Percival didn't mind this time.

"Have you ever wondered, Percival, how the Grail was lost? By that I mean, why it disappeared? It started when I tried to fix something. Let's see, that would have been around the time you were admitted to The Keep."

CHAPTER 25: MERLIN WARNS PERCIVAL

Nearly four years before Percival departed for Cassanti, the research season was nearly over, and soon the fall snows would make travel to the Apparatus Montis compound impossible. Merlin and his engineers and scientists had been studying the newly discovered Grail for weeks. Taking baby steps, they shut down the Great Machine system by system, removed the Grail, and left the Machine in hibernation. The earth beneath them beat like the heart of an enormous, entombed beast while they examined the Grail in the compound's lab, learning how it got power and data from the main control systems.

After 14 hours poking, prodding, and examining every micron of the spherical Grail's surface, Merlin sent his team to bed. He stayed awake, guarding the Grail like a parent worried about a sick child. He marveled at the beauty of its workmanship and despaired at its mystery. He had learned virtually nothing, except that it likely had an internal mechanism. Had an internal part failed? He could not find a way inside.

Another worry of a different kind plagued his thoughts. Lady Morgause had sent one of her agents, Sir Gawain, to speak to him. Morgause had financed his personal research, particularly the Old Civilization's DNA manipulation technology. He was working on a way to create a questing beast, but success was years in the future. Morgause had a hold on Merlin, but he guessed that Gawain's visit had little to do with science, and everything to do with court politics. Mordred, her dark, resentful, brilliant son, was likely at the heart of it.

Trouble was, Gawain was late. Merlin expected him early in the day, but the knight had not shown up.

Merlin wasn't one to worry about a spy's safety. Gawain could take care of himself. More than anything, Merlin wanted to know how the Grail worked. All the research and testing of the Great Machine's mechanisms showed that the Grail, the heart of Joseph Arimathea's design, was broken. Could Merlin fix it?

What would Arimathea do? Merlin had no idea. For more than seven decades, ever since Arturus the Great appointed the sage-scientist his chief science advisor, Merlin had chipped away at the great man's secrets. Every year, through the administrations of three monarchs, he oversaw four months of excavations, interpretations, and reconstructions at the Apparatus Montis site, even as the Machine continued its business of regulating the climate, along with its eleven sister machines around the world. The Viridian Great Machine was Merlin's life's work. He'd deciphered the incomprehensible symbols and icons in the control rooms, figured out the unique circuitry built to last hundreds of years, and untangled the systems logic that made everything work together.

The key to the Grail itself, however, eluded him.

Rubbing his century-old eyes, Merlin fingered the new piece of equipment he'd brought from his lab at Camelot. It magnified surfaces up to a thousand times in various wavelengths. Merlin thought it might show a hidden seam or a locking mechanism. Arimathea demanded manufacturing tolerances down to a few microns for critical components. A way inside might be hidden from the naked eye.

Merlin spent all day examining every micro-millimeter of the device. Sitting in the semi-darkness, doubtful of ever realizing his plan of repairing the Great Machine and restoring Viridiae's climate, he decided on one more pass before bed. Recalibrating the instrument, he positioned it over an interesting pattern in the abstract engravings on the device's surface. They served as decoration and as instructions, though Merlin still could not read large swaths of them.

Setting the magnification of the new tool to its maximum, he passed the camera over the region. Five minutes elapsed, then ten. His eyeballs felt as if they would fall out of their sockets. Another ten minutes and the pass would be complete. With only a few millimeters to go, he spotted what appeared to be a crack. Was the Grail damaged in some way? No, the crack was too regular with a nice smooth curve. He followed it, and it kept going, following a circle around the roughly spherical Grail like a high-latitude line on a globe of the Earth. How could he have missed this?

In his excitement, Merlin forgot about his exhaustion. The more he looked, the more the seam appeared as if it were inviting him to open the device. He knew he should wake up his team, but he couldn't wait. He found a knife with a tungsten blade that sharpened to a single atom. It slipped into the space nicely. By sliding it slowly around the seam, Merlin happened onto a fastener that looked much like a sunken clasp, but only just big enough to see with the naked eye. Merlin pried the fastener loose, and the tiny hatch gave way. Lifting it a few millimeters, and the top of the Grail came off, leaving an opening eight centimeters wide. Merlin whooped with happiness. Even after nearly a hundred years of scientific research, he still found joy in the unexpected.

He peered inside opening and spied a thin, rectangular shape that resembled a power cell, but with the color of frosted crystal. Maybe it was a programming chip. Next to it, a tiny light burned amber. A voice told Merlin to wait, but his curiosity overwhelmed his judgment. Using a pair of thin tongs with rubber tips, he grasped the crystal rectangle and tugged with the slightest pressure. The object moved, slipping out of its space as smoothly as a silken thread. Merlin gazed at the perfectly formed battery—if that's what it was—about a half-centimeter in width and six centimeters long. He turned it over, examining every corner and surface.

And then he dropped it.

When it hit the floor, it bent.

* * *

Merlin cursed himself. How could he have been so stupid? The Grail was already broken, and he'd made it worse. If the battery or whatever was damaged, Merlin had no spare parts. They'd never found any during the site surveys. Maybe they'd been stolen, though they'd found no evidence of a break-in or a theft. The Great Machine had all kinds of taboos against pilfering or vandalism. It took them four months that first season to open the outer doors. One of Merlin's archaeological digs turned up evidence of guard posts and small forts with garrisons.

Merlin licked his lips and lifted a corner of the battery or chip and calculated the angle of its new kink mentally. It was almost exactly in the middle of the object. How could something meant to last a millennium bend so easily? The angle was only a degree or two. He didn't dare try to bend it back into shape, but he feared the consequences if one of his people discovered that he had wrecked the Grail with his impatience.

He decided to try something. Using the tongs, he slipped the edge of the part into its slot. The minuscule indicator light was off. The object fit its slot, but it snagged when it reached the crook in the middle. Gritting his teeth, Merlin gave it the tiniest of pushes, and the part slid down with some extra resistance. The indicator light flashed green, and Merlin thought he was witnessing a miracle. Had he accidentally repaired the Grail and the Great Machine? He let out a sigh when the light turned a solid amber. The sigh turned into panic when the amber light began to flash once a second. Merlin held his head in his hands. He had no idea what the flashing light meant, except that he'd screwed up in the worst way possible.

"Having a bad day?"

Merlin turned at the unfamiliar voice. Sir Gawain Lothian, Lord Mordred Lothian's brother, darkened the lab's doorway.

"Gawain." Merlin's mind raced. "I'd nearly given up on you."

"I thought it best to show up when I'd cause the least disruption."

"In the middle of the night? Did you intend to wake everyone up to serve you?"

Gawain stepped into the light of the overhead lamp. The dark-faced knight wore the cloak of the Regarders Order, Viridiae's intelligence service that masked as enforcers of the King's forest laws. "Not exactly a warm welcome, Professor."

Merlin glanced at the Grail. "I'm just finishing up for the day and I'm tired. I sent my assistants to bed. Why are you here? Your message didn't say why you were coming."

While Gawain cast his eyes around the lab, perhaps looking for threats, Merlin replaced the covering on the Grail. Merlin kept his movements easy and slow, as if he had done the same thing every day for weeks. He glanced at the screen showing the camera view of the clasp. As if on cue, the clasp gripped the lid without a sound.

"I've come on a matter of state security. I've come to take possession of the Grail device."

Merlin gaped. "You're insane. It doesn't belong to you. Who put you up to this?"

"Lord Mordred has decided that the Grail is too important to be left in the hands of a person acting in an advisory role."

"What in hell are you talking about?"

"I'm ordered to take it to a safe place, where the Order's experts will examine it."

"Don't be an idiot. You're nothing but a glorified policeman. I've been working on this project twice as long as you've walked on this earth. I know more about it than anyone."

"I'm not here to argue with you, Professor." Gawain drew near, smelling to Merlin of menace and horse sweat. "I'm taking it this evening."

Merlin's heart beat like a galloping destrier's. He wanted to keep the Grail in his possession, but more importantly, he didn't want his foolish mistake discovered by amateurs. His standing at court was solidified by only one thing, his reputation as an eminent scientist. He had no faith in humanity's capacity to forgive mistakes. He'd seen other scientists who'd failed, accidentally or deliberately, and they'd disappeared from the public eye overnight, along with their court support and funding. It didn't matter that he was Merlin Ambrosius, Viridiae's most brilliant mind, if he couldn't hold a six-centimeter battery carefully with a pair of tongs.

"You can't have it, Gawain. You tell Mordred that the Grail belongs with me. I work for Arturus, not for him."

Gawain put his nose into Merlin's face. "Don't make me threaten you."

Merlin gulped, but it was partly for show. In his frenzy of alarm, an idea had come to him. "If you take it, how will I explain it to Arturus?"

Gawain backed away. "He doesn't need to know the details. Mordred made it clear that my visit is intended to be clandestine. I didn't expect you to be guarding it."

That confirmed Merlin's guess. "You intended to steal it."

The knight fingered the hilt of his dagger. "I figured that I would have to dispatch a guard, but I can't kill you. That would be... messy."

"I don't have to say anything. I fell asleep while working." Merlin glanced at a corner desk piled high with tablets and papers. "Someone broke in and took the Grail."

Gawain stared at Merlin sideways. "You sound as if you're eager to get rid of that thing." The knight's eyes flicked to the Grail.

"Nonsense." Merlin swallowed. "I don't want to see it damaged, that's all. It's priceless and irreplaceable. And I'm in no position to get into a fight with a warrior in his twenties."

Gawain tapped the dagger's hilt and spoke thoughtfully. "I think you're holding something back, but I don't think I care." He glanced around the lab. "Do you have something I can carry it with? So it won't be damaged?" He snickered.

Merlin placed the Grail in a wooden box his team had used to transport it from the Great Machine. The box was lined with cotton batting. The seven-kilo Grail sat on a cradle to keep it from rolling around. Merlin locked the lid with four hasps.

Gawain lifted the box with both hands. "Awkward, but I'll manage."

"Please be careful."

"Not to worry, Professor. I'll keep it safe. Just remember your story. And don't follow me."

A moment later, Merlin heard Gawain's horse clopping out of the compound.

* * *

More than five years later, after a half-dozen expeditions to find the Grail, Percival sat with Merlin on a log in the darkness at the edge of the compound. He absorbed Merlin's story, but his feelings ranged from puzzlement to sympathy to anger.

"I don't understand, Merlin. Why did you lie? Why did you cover up what happened?"

"To protect myself, of course. Isn't that why anyone lies? I'm not proud of it, but like all lies, it was a gamble."

Percival put his emotions in a bottle, for the moment. "You gambled that if the Grail surfaced, you could simply return to your work, repair the Great Machine, and all would be forgiven."

"That's oversimplifying, but yes, you're correct."

"Oversimplifying? A dozen people died searching for that thing, including Dee."

Merlin paused. "If I had foreseen so much loss, I would've found some other way. Even old men fail to gauge the consequences of their actions before doing something stupid."

Percival sighed. "Did you know where Gawain took the Grail?"

"No, I did not. He may be a thug, but he's good at keeping a secret. I think the only person who knew was Morgause. She was his true controller, not Mordred, but I have no proof."

Morgause was at least as ruthless as her son, perhaps more so, Percival judged.

"I'd discovered the Grail, then I'd lost it. Finding it was the only thing I cared about, not just to keep my secret and my reputation, but to fulfill the thousand-year-old mission it represented. I operated on the assumption that the Grail was hidden. I sought out any clue on its whereabouts. I didn't expect that Arturus would turn it into some kind of spiritual quest, a way to show Viridian pride. It's just a device, though it's important. It did lead Galahad to find the False Grail in Perditon, which we used against the Lucians. My research also led to the Last Grail in Cassanti."

"What about the Koda expedition?"

"Remember that Mordred revealed information about the Grail's possible location on the island right after you returned from the expedition led by Sir Kevin." Merlin shrugged. "I've concluded Mordred let it slip because he was mad at his mother for creating this mess. Their relationship is the strangest I've ever seen."

"But the Grail was taken from Gawain by the Lucians."

"I expect Morgause had a hand in that too. Again, I have no evidence, but her motivation would've been to destabilize Arturus' status as monarch, creating an opening for Mordred."

Percival folded his arms. He didn't know how to think about this wizened, but vigorous elder who behaved like a child as much as he did like a man with a hundred years of experience. Percival found it hard to grow angry with Merlin when it came to Dee. His sister had made her own choices, though they were based on false premises. And they really did need to find the Grail, because Percival had lost the Viridian Grail before the Battle of River's Bend. Her loss wasn't in vain, but Merlin's lie colored an entire chapter of Viridian history. How many other falsehoods had the man promoted?

Merlin patted Percival's knee. "What will you do now, son?"

"Return to Camelot. See my mother. Marry Lina Catalpec."

"She's a beautiful young woman, and talented. What about work for yourself?"

"I don't know. I'm thinking of leaving the Round Table, but afterward…" Percival shrugged.

"I'm not getting any younger, son. Someone will have to take over for me, to keep an eye on the Great Machine. Think about it." Merlin pursed his lips. "Another thing. You will be called upon to defend your king, and soon."

Percival shook his head. "I hope not. I'm finished with adventuring and politics."

"I sympathize, but Mordred is a troubled man. He and his mother tried to use the Grail to their personal advantage. They are both selfish, driven only by a lust for power. Take my advice: Be ready. When Mordred comes for Camelot and Arturus' throne, you and everyone you love will be a target."

Percival nodded, more with politeness than agreement. On the other hand, an inner voice advised him to heed Merlin's warning.

CHAPTER 26: WAR THREATENS CAMELOT

Lina met Eleanor Rathkeale at a tea room a few blocks from the palace. She wondered if she was greeting her future mother-in-law. Percival had not broached the idea of marriage, and although Lina was not above asking her lover for what she wanted, she was not 100 percent sure of his feelings on the subject. Talking about it too soon might preclude it for months or years. Although their brief time together was nothing but blissful, Lina knew love often blinded the unwary.

Eleanor impressed and intimidated Lina from their first "Hello." Eleanor was a tall, serious woman in late middle age who dressed in the fashion of Camelot as if she were an executive. There was no mistaking Eleanor's grief over the death of her daughter; Her makeup and clothes were muted but they did not hide her drawn look and shoulders that sagged ever so slightly. She was a proud woman who'd sustained a devastating loss. Lina offered a polite, but sincere embrace.

A servant brought Nihon tea and cakes. Fresh flowers decorated the glass-topped table. They sipped and made small talk about Eleanor's journey. She was staying at a hotel known for treating its guests with discretion.

"I haven't been to Camelot in so long, I've forgotten how beautiful it is, despite the destruction of the war. I understand your father is participating in its reconstruction."

"Yes, he's been awarded several contracts."

"I have an interest in property development. I own several buildings in the town near my country holdings."

"Perhaps I could introduce you to my father sometime. I'm sure you'd find much to talk about."

"You're very kind."

An awkward silence followed. Returning to Camelot had brought back painful memories, as well as good ones, for Eleanor. They shared grief over Dee's death, but they did not know each other well enough to express it, beyond social niceties. How could Lina break the ice?

"You must be very proud of Percival."

Eleanor glanced out a window. The street was busy with pedestrians, horses, and public cars. "I had to learn to be proud of him, at least of his choices in career."

"I don't understand."

"I opposed his decision to go into the military. I wanted him to do almost anything else."

Lina wasn't sure how to respond. Did Eleanor's attitude have something to do with Sir Adnan deGrosse's assault on her? Lina didn't feel comfortable asking the question.

"Dee also ignored my wishes," Eleanor said. "I'd hoped she would pursue a career in science and technology. Instead, she became an artist."

"She is—was—brilliant."

"So I've come to understand. Sometimes it's a good thing when children ignore their parents. Don't you agree?" Eleanor offered a slight smile.

"Respecting your parents doesn't mean always agreeing with them. My parents also wanted me to go into some kind of profession, one that paid more than art."

"This reminds me. I knew your mother slightly when I was at court, before Percival and Dee were born. Your mother is well, I hope?"

"She asked after you only yesterday, when I called her after returning from Ash. She extended an invitation for dinner, if you have time while you're in Camelot."

Eleanor seemed to consider the offer, but didn't respond. "I imagine you saw my son when you were in Ash."

Lina gulped. They were getting closer to uncomfortable territory. "I did, Eleanor. I know he wanted to see you right away, but Merlin whisked him away."

Eleanor almost laughed. "Merlin is a character, brilliant, almost to a fault. If I may ask, how well do you know my son?"

Here it was. Even though they had never spoken about Percival, except in passing, Lina felt as if Eleanor knew every detail about their relationship. Mothers just seem to know things by instinct, and Eleanor was ready to judge her. Would she pass the initial test? "Percival and I, well, we haven't known each other long, but I would like to say we are friends, even close friends." Lina paused. "He's the kind of man every woman hopes for: courteous, courageous, humble, loyal. I know first-hand that Arturus loves him."

"Really? The king loves him?"

"He wanted Percival to go to Cassanti and find the Grail. He never mentioned anyone else, apart from Dee. As soon as word reached us that Percival had returned, the king decided to meet him himself at the border."

"And you were invited to go there?"

"Guinevere invited me."

"The queen?"

"I'm fortunate that she sees my service as useful."

Eleanor leaned back in her chair. "Before he left for Cassanti, Percival said to me that he had met a wonderful girl named Lina. He was as happy as I've ever heard him. He said a part of him wanted to quit his quest to Cassanti so that he could be with you."

Lina flushed.

"He decided to go anyway, for Arturus' sake and the country's. He told me he might not come back." Eleanor swallowed. "I never imagined Dee would be the one that was sacrificed."

Lina stared into the thin remnants of her tea. She heard bitterness in Eleanor's voice, but also resignation. How did she not break down into tears?

"I wish we could've met under happier circumstances,

Eleanor."

Eleanor reached for Lina's hand. "So do I, child. Percival is all I have left of my family. It may take a while for me to learn how to share him. Will you be patient with me?"

Lina nodded as she wiped away tears.

* * *

A few days later, Percival texted Lina that he was on his way home. The news chans had reported Merlin's success installing the Grail, and pundits speculated endlessly on how the next few months might play out. Would a normal, healthy climate return? Lina welcomed the news like every other Viridian, including Mordred, who put out a statement praising the scientist and his team, not mentioning Percival or the expedition. Perhaps he wanted nothing to reflect well on Arturus' decision-making. After all, he was trying to usurp him.

Lina poured herself into finishing the mural in the Great Audience Hall. She kept her memory of the moment at the border when Percival delivered the Grail to Arturus in the forefront of her mind. When Dee started the project before the Lucian war, she'd seen almost every detail in her imagination. It was almost clairvoyant. But Dee was too literal. Lina added extra, almost idealized meaning in the gestures she designed, such as Arturus' benevolent face and Percival's falling to one knee as he presented the device. Dee had forgotten—or ignored—one thing: herself.

It was up to Lina to interpret Dee's role in the mural's drama. What could she do? She wanted to be true to the history, but showing her friend's death in a far-off land seemed to minimize her sacrifice. This is where Lina, in frustration, felt the limits of her talent. She could never know exactly what Dee might have done, so she let herself make the decision. She placed Dee next to her brother, her hand on his shoulder, gesturing toward the Grail with the other hand. Of course, she wasn't there in reality, but she was there in spirit. Let the historians say that the mural is not perfectly accurate. Lina's job was to capture the emotion and the meaning of the moment.

"Yes, that is how I want to remember it."

Lina turned and found Guinevere. "My lady, I didn't see you there."

"I hadn't seen you in the palace apartments since we returned from Ash. You haven't been answering your com. I was worried."

"I'm sorry, my lady. With Percival coming home and the Grail installed, I felt the need to finish Dee's mural quickly."

"She truly had a gift. You as well."

Lina wanted to disagree, saying she didn't deserve the comparison, but she said nothing. "Thank you, my lady."

"I see Dee found a role for Mordred, lurking appropriately in the crowd, envious eyes flicking between Arturus and the Grail. It's almost comical."

"Dee's gifts went far beyond color and composition."

"She had a snarky edge. That was one reason why I liked her." Guinevere took a seat on a bench. "Sit with me, please, Lina. I want to ask you for a favor."

"Anything, my lady."

"I'm going to be leaving Camelot in a few hours. The public will be told that I'm going home to Cameliard for my safety, which is true, but only half the story."

Lina waited for Guinevere to explain the other half, but the queen kept her eyes on Dee's rendering of Mordred. "Why are you leaving, my lady, if I may ask?"

"That man there, lurking like a cat in the brush. New intelligence has come to us. He's planning to attack Camelot in the next week or so. Arturus will order an evacuation soon. He's already called up reserves."

A spike of fear hit Lina's breast. War was coming to Camelot again. Until now, the war between Mordred and Arturus had been limited to border skirmishes. A few soldiers and knights had died, and Mordred had threatened invasion, but nothing had come of it.

"Mordred feels he has waited long enough to act. Maybe his mother's constant nagging finally broke him. Perhaps the recovery and installation of the Grail weakens his position. We know he tried to steal it and kidnap Merlin."

Lina startled. Percival mentioned nothing about an incident.

"It doesn't matter at this point. Mordred is coming, but we have a plan. Arturus is going to intercept him."

"Intercept him? Where?"

"I can't say. We don't know. It will depend on Mordred's route with his main force. He has three or four choices, but Arturus won't let him near Camelot."

Lina took in the situation. "I'm sorry, my lady. I don't see how I can help. Do you want me to go with you?"

"No, Lina. I want you to find a way to go with Arturus."

Lina understood Guinevere's meaning, and she didn't like it. "You want me to spy on your husband?"

"I want you to be an observer and tell me what you see. I can't be there. Arturus is adamant. He wants me out of the way, that is to say, out of danger's path."

Had Guinevere let slip something? Lina wracked her brain to discern it. Maybe Eleanor could help her. And how could she get herself attached to a military column? She had no connections to Arturus, other than Guinevere.

"Could you suggest to him that I go?"

Guinevere was firm. "No, he will not agree to it. You'll have to find another way."

Lina didn't have a choice in the matter. "I'll do whatever I can, my lady. I promise."

* * *

As it happened, Lina's mother, Isra, had invited Eleanor to dinner at her parents' house that evening, and Eleanor had accepted. The two women instantly hit it off, telling stories of their time at Arturus II's court to Lina, Kenric, and her father, Reuben. Kenric had strengthened into a boy on the cusp of an athletic adolescence. He loved team ball games and horses. Eleanor said he reminded her of Percival at his age.

A knock on the door interrupted their dessert of ice cream and apple pie. Lina answered and shrieked. The rest of family came running, but she was already in Percival's arms, kissing him deeply. She didn't care that his mother and her family were watching. Their brief time together at the border was nothing compared to having Percival in her own house, at least her parents' house.

"Well, then," Reuben said. "You've already reacquainted yourselves."

Lina finally let Percival go.

"I'm sorry I didn't call or text first," Percival said. "I got into Camelot only an hour ago after hard riding from the Great Machine. The palace told me Lina was here, so I thought I'd surprise her." His eye caught sight of Eleanor. "Mother, I didn't expect to see you here."

Eleanor stepped out from behind Isra and reached out to her son, holding his face in her hands. "My goddess, Percival. I thought I'd never seen you again." Mother and son embraced.

"I wanted to tell you about Dee in person, but the Grail…"

"I know, Percival. I forgive you. You had to go. I'm so proud of you."

Lina held back her tears and went to her own mother, who enclosed her daughter in loving arms. Kenric knew Dee had died. Reuben laid his hands on his son's shoulders to steady him.

Eleanor said, "I apologize, Isra, Reuben, to your whole family. You've been wonderful hosts. I've never felt this welcome in Camelot. You'll want to spend time together. Perhaps it's time I should leave."

"Nonsense!" Isra said. "We are all family here. Let us set another place for Percival. He's probably starving. Can't let him leave hungry."

The two families gathered at the dinner table. Percival told the story of the Grail and the Great Machine, and Merlin's escape from kidnappers. Throughout the conversation, Lina held Percival's hand, as if letting it go might mean he would again disappear from her life. She feared she might flush red, because of her growing desire to bring him to her bed.

"I have more news." Percival withdrew his hand from Lina's. "Arturus had sent out a call for reservists and knights on leave, which covers me. I received the text on the way here from the Great Machine. I have to report to the citadel the day after to-morrow."

Eleanor sighed. "So much war. When will it end?"

"When Mordred is defeated, Mother. That's the only way peace will return to Viridiae."

"Spoken like a soldier." Eleanor appeared ready to complain further, but she stopped herself.

Lina saw this as the right time to ask a question she'd been holding back. "I've also been told to follow Arturus." She relayed most of her conversation with Guinevere.

"What?" Isra said. "How is this possible?"

"The queen asked me to find a way to follow the king to wher-ever the battle with Mordred will take place."

"That's insane," Isra said. "You're not a soldier. You're not a re-servist. You have no training."

Eleanor looked at Lina with a serious expression. "What's does Guinevere want?"

"I probably shouldn't tell you this, but she wants me to report what I see to her."

"A spy?" Isra said.

"Guinevere doesn't trust Arturus. Or Mordred, for that mat-ter," Eleanor said. "This is a difficult situation for everyone. Lina, did you agree?"

Lina nodded. "What could I say?"

"You could've said no," Percival said, suddenly upset.

"That's not for you to decide, my love. Guinevere trusts me. I think I should return the favor."

"That doesn't mean putting yourself in harm's way," Reuben said.

"I have an idea," Eleanor said. "Even though I've been away for a long time, I still have a few contacts. Once it's clear where the armies will meet, civilians will stream out of the area. There's a group of volunteers that follows the army to help refugees. I know one of the organizers. She'll accept you. You don't need to say exactly why you're there, but you'll get a chance to get close to Arturus."

"Do you think it will work?"

"I don't want you to go," Isra said.

"The queen has asked her and she's agreed," Reuben said. "She can't back out now."

Eleanor said, "I think she'll be relatively safe. Both sides understand that the refugee service people are neutral. Lina won't be in serious danger, as long as she stays away from the battlefield."

"You're quiet, Percival."

"I've seen battle. None of you have. Nowhere is safe within a hundred kilometers of a battlefield. We all know the history of civil wars. They're bloody and awful."

"All Viridians have a duty to their country," Reuben said. "You and Lina have been called. The country needs you."

"But not for the next 24 hours or so," Lina said. She took Percival's hand. "Perce, I'm tired. Very tired. Will you escort me home to the palace?"

Percival stared at Lina for a moment, then his features softened. He'd got the message. "Of course I will, Lina."

"Thank you for your help, Eleanor. Will you call your friend and see if volunteering is possible?"

Eleanor nodded, but not so much to Lina's request, but because she understood that Lina wanted to be with her son, and this time, Lina would let nothing, not even an incipient war, stand in her way.

CHAPTER 27:
MORDRED ENCAMPED

Lina reported to the Marshal of Refugee Relief office the day Percival left the city. Eleanor put her in touch with Nira, the organization's frazzled volunteer coordinator, who asked what Lina wanted to do.

"I want to be close to the front lines, to help the people who are most in danger."

"My job is to keep you safe, among other things." Nira had a weariness that underlined long years of experience. She had run some of the relief efforts before and after the Lucian War. "Have you ever volunteered for this kind of thing before?"

"No, I haven't." Lina remembered a volunteer experience at a veterans' home as a teenager, but it was a requirement for graduation.

"Why do you want to volunteer now?"

What could Lina say? Because Guinevere needed her to watch her husband? "My boyfriend is fighting for the king. I want to do something more than text him my love and support. We're probably going to get married."

"Probably?"

It just seemed inevitable. The day and night they spent together before he reported for duty felt like they had been together since the dawn of time. Saying goodbye to him was as painful as lying to Nira, though it wasn't a total lie. Lina thought by getting close to the coming battle, she might see Percival.

"I apologize if I seem skeptical, Lina. I've seen too many eager-looking people step up, only to disappear the next day when they see how much work there is to do, and how thankless it can be. I'll be honest. Eleanor told me you have connections at the palace, and we need those as much as we need money and donations. Thanks for helping." Nira extended her hand in welcome.

After a day of drudge work organizing bags of secondhand clothes, Nira invited Lina to take a job she described as moderately dangerous. Lina would help set up and run first-aid stations only a short distance from Arturus' military encampment. The stations were meant for displaced civilians, but soldiers and knights often came through. As well as recruiting volunteers, Nira managed these stations.

Lina texted Guinevere the news with a special encryption app on her com.

Arturus' army was on the move, and Lina followed ten kilometers behind with her team led by Nira. They traveled in a convoy of three electric trucks emblazoned with the MRR logo and colors. Refugees were already streaming out of the region between Camelot and Lothia known locally as Crookbank, which older people called "Camlann."

"There's a strategic bridge across a gorge," Nira said. "Mordred would have to cross it to get to Camelot. Arturus wants to block him."

"How do you know so much, Nira?"

"I studied at The Keep. I was invalided out of the army after an incursion by the Lucians long before the war."

Travel slowed as military columns going toward Crookbank and refugees fleeing the area clogged the road. The MRR team set up a temporary aid station at their overnight camp, and they were quickly overwhelmed. They had to close early to avoid depleting their supplies of food and medicine before reaching their assigned station the next day.

Early in the morning, a column of knights on horseback cantered by the MRR convoy, which was stalled behind a disabled cart. Lina swore she recognized Percival, whose flaming red hair made him easy to pick out. But the man's back was to her, so she couldn't be sure. They hadn't contacted each other since he'd said goodbye, saying that security would make it impossible. With all her heart, she begged the man to turn his head, so she could know. When he did, it wasn't Percival, and the red hair was a loose bandanna.

"Something wrong?" Nira said. "You look disappointed."

"I thought I saw Percival, my boyfriend."

"Percival? Sir Percival Rathkeale? He's yours?"

Lina nodded.

"Lucky girl."

The MRR convoy reached its assigned encampment point a couple of hours before sundown. They were about eight kilometers south of Crookbank town and its bridge across the River Cam. Lina again told Guinevere where she was and what she was doing. She hadn't heard any response from the queen, and she had no idea if her messages were received or if they were useful. All she could do was keep her promise to stay in touch.

The MRR trucks attracted refugees into the pasture where they were parked. The displaced people packed horses and small carts with belongings. They came alone or in family groups. Many had nothing but the clothes on their backs. Some had food, but most didn't, and even fewer had water. Lina and the MRR volunteers pitched a pair of tents that served as a mobile kitchen and eating area. They handed out glass bottles of water and sandwiches wrapped in paper packaging that would decay and disappear after the next rain. One of the trucks transported a mobile sewage recycling unit. Another vehicle carried a portable shower.

The MRR unit alone could never serve the volume of refugees coming down from Crookbank, but that didn't slow the volunteers. Lina registered people by name, address, identification number, and com contact. By midday on their first day, she had taken down hundreds of names from the town and surrounding villages and farms. The MRR's supplies of food and clothing were already halved.

Just after lunch was served to the refugees, Nira made an announcement to the volunteers. "MRR headquarters back in Camelot wants us closer to Crookbank. They're evacuating the town and the mayor wants us to process the refugees and move them out of the area."

"How close will we be?" Lina said.

"They've got a site for us three kilometers from town on the main road. We leave tonight."

"Will we get more supplies?"

"I've requested them, but we're low priority."

They packed after dinner and they were on the road by sundown. Traffic choked the two-lane road, and in the darkness, Lina feared they might hit someone. It took the MRR unit two hours to drive the five kilometers to the new campsite. Exhaustion overcame everyone. Lina, Nira and the rest of the volunteers slept in their seats.

Lina awoke to a knock on her window. A stranger moved her hand to her mouth, asking for food. Lina donned her blue MRR vest. Nira woke up the other volunteers and soon ready-to-eat breakfasts were filling hungry bellies, including Lina's. Dozens of men, women and children lined up for bulbs of fruit juice.

The MRR campsite gave a clear view of the rising valley to the market town of Crookbank. The arch of the bridge across the Cam was visible on the other side of town, which was split in two by the road. On the other side of the valley, across a broad green pasture, Lina saw hundreds of tents and pavilions, all flying the green flag of Viridiae. Percival would likely be there.

"Wouldn't be my choice for a battleground," Nira said.

"Why not?"

"Once Mordred comes across that bridge, it's all downhill. That's always an advantage in an open field. I don't want to think about the casualties when the battle comes."

"Is it going to happen here?"

"As likely here as any place."

"But all Arturus has to do is block the way to Camelot, right? The road is the main route. That shouldn't be hard."

"Mmm. In theory."

Around mid-morning, after a rain, a handful of refugees

turned up with bleeding wounds. One of the men had lost two fingers to a sword. Lina guided the refugees to the truck with the medical supplies and a volunteer nurse. When Nira asked who had attacked them, the man pointed across the bridge to Mordred's camp on the other side of a hill.

Shouts and a gunshot interrupted. Eight or ten men and women in black armor on horseback galloped into the center of the compound knocking over tents and tables and slashing at the MRR canopies. Nira ran up to one of the raiders. She held out her jacket, pointing to the red and white MRR logo. Her movement spooked the horse and the rider, who brought down her sword on Nira's unprotected head, killing her. Lina ran over to her, shaking with shock. They were only trying to help the refugees get away, just giving them food and clothing. She cried over Nira's startled and lifeless eyes. More shots and screams punctuated the slaughter as refugees defended themselves with stones and a few old swords.

"You! I know you."

Lina looked up from Nira's corpse. One of the MRR trucks was on fire.

"What's your name?"

The voice came from behind her. The voice belonged to a burly, gruff man who strutted about as if he owned the place.

Lina collected herself. "I'm Lina Catalpec. I'm a volunteer here. I've never met you. Why did you do this?"

"You're Dee Rathkeale's assistant. You're part of Guinevere's circle."

"How do you know so much about me?"

"Our intelligence is very good."

Lina couldn't tell him that she was spying on Arturus for the queen. "Like I said, I'm a volunteer."

"You're coming with us."

"No! I'm needed here. You killed Nira. Someone has to help these people."

One of the knights shouted. A half-dozen riders from the Viridian camp raced toward them.

The gruff officer pointed to the knight who killed Nira. "We're bringing this woman back. Maybe she can help us reach Guinevere."

The knight reached down from his destrier and pulled up Lina, nearly wrenching her arm out of its socket. The raiders galloped up the road, through Crookbank, and over the wooden bridge. Lina held on to the anonymous knight, fearing she'd fall off the sweating horse's rump. They crested the hill and Mordred's camp lay before them. Hundreds, maybe thousands of tents and horses packed a plowed field. Men-at-arms and knights milled among the tents, sharpening weapons and cleaning guns. They were getting ready for an attack.

Later, Lina would remember the stench of latrines.

Despite the surprise at the sight of so many soldiers, Lina smiled at her own cleverness. She had dropped her com, deliberately, on the road to Crookbank.

* * *

The knight carrying Lina stopped in front of a large pavilion flying the black and white Lothian flag. He dropped Lina to the ground as the gruff man arrived. The knight identified him as General Yama, Mordred's chief of staff. She was surrounded by enough warriors to overrun a small nation, making escape impossible. She winced when Yama grabbed her sore arm and escorted her inside the pavilion. Soft light filtered through the heavy canvas. Mordred sat at a camp desk studying papers. Morgause, his elderly mother, lounged in a chair at the back. She perked up when she saw Lina.

Mordred finished reading a document before he looked up. He cocked his head.

"Yama, you've brought a guest."

"She's close to Guinevere. She's assigned a room in the palace and works with Dee Rathkeale."

A pained expression crossed Mordred's face. "What's your name, girl?" His voice had a hiss to it, slow like a snake's, but intelligent.

"I've already told General Yama." Lina yanked her arm, but the bruise hurt.

Morgause said, "Careful with her, General. She's delicate."

"Lina Catalpec, my lord Mordred," Yama said.

"I know your family, Ms Catalpec," Mordred said. "Your father owns a large construction company, does he not?"

"What difference does it make to you? I want to know why you attacked a defenseless refugee camp. My lady," Lina addressed Morgause, "one of your son's men killed the person who was organizing relief efforts. It was blatant murder!" Lina had never felt so much burning anger, but neither had she ever witnessed Mordred's kind of brutality.

"A serious charge, Lina," Morgause said.

"Yama?" Mordred raised his eyebrows at the officer.

"A sentry was killed last night. Signs pointed to the town."

"And you had to exact punishment."

"Yes, my lord."

"There, you see, Ms Catalpec? A justified defense of my man. I would've expected nothing less."

"How can you justify such a thing?"

"We're at war, in case you haven't noticed."

Lina had noticed. In fact, she almost felt a sense of shame. Prior to this, all she knew of war were the reports on the news chans and the occasional glimpse of a wounded veteran on the street. The vets she met in high school were elderly and harmless. Now she understood better Percival's need to join Arturus to defend against Mordred. The prince's callousness disgusted her.

Morgause added, "War is a terrible thing, Lina, even if it is in service to a just cause."

Lina ignored the elder. "What do you want from me, Lord Mordred? I'm volunteering with the MRR. I need to go back to the victims of your raid."

"My lord," Yama said, "it occurred to me she might be a way to reach the queen."

"An interesting idea, my son," Morgause said.

Mordred set his papers on the desk, thoughtfully, as if they had great value. "Ms Catalpec, let me ask you something. Would you have any insight as to why Guinevere does not respond to any of my requests to speak with her?"

"I have no idea, my lord. Perhaps because you're a rebel and traitor?"

Mordred came around the desk and snatched Lina's injured arm. She cried out in pain. Mordred dragged her to the tent's opening.

"Look at that, Ms Catalpec. Five thousand knights and soldiers. You tell them they are traitors. They rebel because they are patriots. They support my rightful claim to the Viridian throne. Arturus is destroying this country and I will save it."

"By killing your king?"

"You're a puny little girl who knows nothing about leading a great nation. But you might be what I need to bring Guinevere over to me. Contact Guinevere. Tell her I want to talk."

"I don't know how. I mean, I can't. I lost my com during your stupid raid."

Yama threw a com onto the table. "Her com, my lord. She dropped it while we were on our way here."

Morgause laughed again, this time with enthusiasm.

Mordred snatched the com and gave it to an embarrassed Lina. "Contact Guinevere."

"Why would she answer? I'm just a palace artist."

"You don't give yourself enough credit, Lina." Morgause rose from her seat and moved nearer. "You think we're idiots? We've intercepted all your messages."

Mordred's nose nearly touched Lina's face. He poked the com with his finger. "Tell her I want to speak to her. Tell her if she doesn't answer, I'll kill you."

Lina couldn't help but whimper. "Lady Morgause, you know I can't betray Guinevere's trust."

"You'd better do as my son asks."

Lina was terrified. She saw what the knight did to Nira. The same thing could happen to her. Lina's hands shook as she entered the contact information. "She only gets texts. We don't speak by voice. We—"

"Stop talking. Tell her what I said."

Lina's fingers could barely tap the keys. Why did she agree to help Guinevere? Percival, help me! She didn't speak the words, but wished them. It was all she could do to keep from completely breaking down. "There, I've sent it."

Mordred relaxed. "That wasn't so hard, was it? All we do now is wait. Are you hungry? Thirsty? I have some very good Napene wine in my stores."

Mordred's sudden change in tone upset Lina more. She shook her head.

"Too bad. It would calm your nerves."

Ten minutes passed. The com lit up and buzzed.

"Answer it, Lina," Mordred said. "Put it on speaker."

Lina touched the answer button. "Hello?"

"Lina! Is that you?"

Mordred grabbed the device from Lina. "Everything is fine, my lady. It's a pleasure to speak with you."

"Mordred! Where's Lina? What have you done?"

"Lina is here with me, healthy and safe, for now."

"She'd better be, or you'll answer for it."

"My lady, I've been trying to reach you for weeks. Messages, letters, calls. General Yama has tried back channels. Nothing has worked. Why won't you speak to me?"

"Isn't it obvious? You're a rebel. Stop threatening and attacking my husband."

Mordred laughed. "I think you're avoiding me for another reason. You don't want to talk about our mutual interests. You certainly don't want to talk about why your husband sent you home."

Silence filled the tent. A slow smile crossed Mordred's face. Lina thought it a cross between a sneer and one full of secret knowledge. Yama echoed his boss's smirk.

"Arturus is afraid of you, isn't he, my lady? He wants you

away, far away at Cameliard, where you can't do him any harm. I'm not the only one who has a claim to the throne. Mine is the strongest, but you have one, too. Remember, a long time ago, before the Lucian War, I suggested we partner? That would be Arturus' worst nightmare."

Lina couldn't believe her ears. Had Guinevere, the woman whom she admired as strong, kind, supportive, agreed to ally with a traitor who threatened Camelot?

"I know someone else who ought to fear me, Mordred." Guinevere's voice was even. "If you and I partnered, you'd be the junior partner."

Mordred's grin left him. "Any alliance would have to be of equals. Otherwise, we're enemies."

"If I did act against Arturus, he would die."

"Ah, that's more like it."

"You're assuming I want him dead. I don't. When we married, he promised me a partnership, a true partnership. Viridiae would thrive, and Cameliard would thrive with it. He's kept that promise, even more so now, with the repair of the Great Machine. And believe it or not, I love him. Perhaps not with a burning passion, but it's a love built on mutual respect and shared goals. What do you have that can best that?"

"You're not reigning as equals, Guinevere. You deserve that kind of treatment. Anyone can see that. Beside me, you'd be a true equal, in every way."

"Until you got tired of sharing power. Weak men always do."

Morgause looked as if she were contemplating her next move in a game of chess.

Mordred fought to control his frustration. He had too much at stake, Lina thought.

"You misjudge me, Guinevere. You need me. I need you. Join me. Together, we'll take the country to places Arturus cannot dream of."

Lina wanted Guinevere to scream no, or hang up without saying a word, or do something else that would send Mordred a clear message that she wanted nothing to do with him or his twisted thinking. Instead, no sound came out of the com for several seconds.

"Mordred," Guinevere said, "you haven't asked what I want, which is proof of your selfishness. On the other hand, leadership requires a certain amount of selfishness. I need to consider what's best for me and for Cameliard. I'll send you my answer to your proposal when I'm ready."

The com went silent. Lina stared at it, gape-mouthed. What did Guinevere mean?

Yama coughed. "In my opinion, you got as much from her as she could give you, my prince, at least for the moment."

"I disagree, Yama. She's hedging her bets, which is why we have to destroy Arturus here, at Camlann. She'll join me when I'm done with the king. She won't have a choice, because if she resists, I'll destroy her too."

"What should I do with her?" Yama indicated Lina.

"She's a nothing. Turn her loose."

Lina sat with her hands on her lap, her head down. She'd been used, like a game piece. Did Guinevere send her on this mission because she wanted her captured? Or was it an accident of fate? Lina didn't care. She wanted nothing more to do with plots and intrigue, war and the threat of death. She wanted only to be with Percival, and to make art.

Morgause sniffed. "Stay safe, my child."

Mordred kept her com.

Yama ordered a knight to escort Lina to the edge of camp. The knight pointed the way to Crookbank. The bridge was only a few hundred meters distant. A wide, shallow river flowed beneath the bridge, which had a lovely double-arch on either side of the deck. Her shoes clopped on the planks. She wished she had her tablet. She'd make sketches of the arches and the landscape with the pretty village below gentle hills. She wanted to forget Mordred and Morgause. They were evil, as far as she was concerned.

What about Guinevere? Lina thought she knew her, but doubts filled her mind.

Lina followed the main road through town to a roadside

shrine to Gaia. She sat on its stone bench, meant for travelers. Down the slope, she made out the tents and pavilions of Arturus' camp, with their banners of green flapping cheerfully in the breeze. Percival might be there. The sun touched the top of the valley rim. It would soon be dark, and the refugee camp was cloaked in smoke. Taking a deep breath, she set off for the Viridians.

CHAPTER 28: THE BATTLE OF CAMLANN

Lina's heart stopped when she spotted Percival speaking to a soldier in the camp. She called out to him, and Percival took charge of her from the sentry, but not before a long embrace. When she told Percival that she had come from Mordred's camp, Percival escorted her to Arturus' pavilion. Lina told the king her story of the raid, her capture, and Mordred's call to Guinevere.

Ganieda was also in the pavilion, an eerie echo of Morgause's presence in Mordred's tent. The elder nodded in greeting to Lina, but said nothing.

"How is my—that is, Lord Mordred?" Arturus stopped himself from saying what everyone knew, but never discussed, that Mordred was his illegitimate and unacknowledged son by Morgause. Sitting in an upholstered chair, Arturus appeared stronger than usual, true to his reputation for vigor when he was campaigning. Most people thought he was slowly dying of an unknown or unidentified disease. Some people thought his health was directly tied to the smooth operation of the Great Machine, and that he was getting better after its repair. In the lines around his bleary eyes and his pale skin, Lina saw a man tired of worrying, tired of fighting, and fearing that he would be the cause of more death and destruction.

"Your Majesty, Lord Mordred and his mother are safe and healthy." What else could Lina say?

"Did they speak of me and what's coming?"

Lina hesitated. Arturus was known to accept bad news, but she had never delivered any to him before. "They are still your enemies. They mean to destroy you."

The contrast between Arturus' calm demeanor and Mordred's surly attitude was striking. "I expected as much. What about Guinevere? What did she say?"

Lina felt on firmer ground with this question. "Majesty, she refused to declare for Mordred's side. She regards him as untrustworthy. She also said that she loves you."

"Did she? I mean, it's encouraging to hear about her loyalty, but a wife's love is a priceless treasure."

Lina left out Guinevere's pledge to think about Mordred's partnership offer. Perhaps she should have mentioned it, but she suspected Arturus already knew. He was not a stupid man.

Arturus excused Lina, inviting her to visit the officer's mess tent for food and drink. Percival took her to his tent, which he shared with Sir Bors, the one-armed knight, who was one of Percival's best friends. They had sought the Grail together on the island of Koda.

"I'm happy to see you, Lina. I wish we could have some privacy, but that's hard in bivouac."

Bors had departed as soon as Percival introduced Lina.

"I love you, Percival, but I'm not staying long. Tomorrow, I'm going back to the refugee camp."

Percival folded his arms. "I have bad news about that. Arturus ordered the refugee relief team away from the area. It's too dangerous for them. They've already left, along with the refugees. We heard that one of the workers was captured, but we never guessed it was you."

Lina sighed. "Can you take me to them?"

Percival shook his head. "It's too risky right now. Arturus has patrols out. Mordred has spies in our camp. Everyone is triggerhappy. It's safer to stay here, despite…"

"What is it?"

"We're going to fight tomorrow. Probably early. Everyone can feel it. Mordred sent an ultimatum today. Leave the area or be attacked in the next 24 hours. Dawn tomorrow would be the ideal time for him. The weather is forecast to be clear. The sun will be at his back and in our eyes."

Percival's sad tone frightened Lina. "You don't seem very confident."

"It's not a bad place to fight, but not a good one. And it just feels, well, ominous. The Lucian War wasn't like this. I was nervous, but I never thought I might not survive. This time, I'm not so sure."

Lina covered her mouth to hold in her emotion. She had just got Percival back after a long absence when she was unsure whether she'd see him again. Losing him forever after so short a time together was to much to think about.

"Whoever wins this fight will rule," Percival said. "Arturus believes it. I believe it. That's why he has to win."

* * *

A retainer assigned Lina to a tent, where she found Ganieda waiting for her. "I'm surprised to see you here, Ganeida."

The leader of the Society of Theurgists smiled warmly. "Me too. I know you and Percival are close, but following him here was a mistake."

Begging for Ganieda's confidence, Lina explained Guinevere's request.

Ganieda said, "The woman is shrewd indeed."

"Why are you here? This isn't a place for art teachers."

"I'm here because of Morgause. I'm more and more convinced that she is attempting to support her son with dark forces. She is full of hate for Arturus, which makes her a serious threat."

"What can you do?"

"I've known Morgause for decades. I believe I have some... power to blunt her. Normally, I would never use my understanding of the invisible world to help one side or another in a war, but I'm fearful of a Lothian victory. It would be terrible for Viridiae."

Lina sat on a camp chair and covered her face with her hands.

"You're exhausted, my dear." Ganieda stroked Lina's tangled hair. "You need rest. Tomorrow will be a difficult day. You may not see me tomorrow, but I'll be by your side."

Lina gazed up at her teacher, uncertain at her meaning.

* * *

Anxiety jolted Lina awake every hour or so. No one in the camp rested easy, given the occasional groan, horse's neigh, or clank of sword and armor in the inky darkness.

An hour before dawn, activity outside the tent picked up. Servants rose, and before long, Lina heard the sounds of cooking: pots, pans, utensils. Arturus' personal valet and the pages assigned to help him with his armor were already at work. The smell of fresh biscuits drew Lina out of bed like a magnet, but her hunger was short-lived. After a few bites, she joined the cooks and helpers feeding Arturus' household guard.

The soldiers' faces were grim. Few of them smiled or talked to one another. Lina had never spent time in a military camp, but wouldn't men and women-at-arms be excited about the upcoming fight? These Viridians had none of that feeling. They were nervous and apprehensive. Then she heard an off-hand remark by one of the soldiers: Mordred had twice as many soldiers and knights as Arturus.

A two-to-one advantage.

It didn't take a military strategist to understand the ratio's significance. Lina remembered Nira's observation, that Mordred would be fighting downhill. Lina got that too. She once played a ball game with Kenric, and he charged at her down a grass slope. Even though he was a quarter her weight, he bowled her over when he collided with her. It was all in fun; they fell down laughing. If Mordred attacked Arturus in the same way on the field at Camlann, no one would laugh.

The commanders had ordered all the electric lights doused as a security measure, which made cleanup harder for Lina and the kitchen staff in the predawn hours. They cheated by using portable lamps to operate the stoves and fill the basins with water. By the time they were finished, most of the guard in their section of the camp had left, leaving only a pair of sentries. Lina and the others waited for the carts and electric vehicles to evacuate them.

No one came. Lina volunteered to find someone who could tell them what they should do. Maybe they had misunderstood the order. She wandered through the camp, still in her apron, looking for someone in authority, but the entire camp was empty, save for a few dogs. The only place with any activity was the medical pavilion, where men and women in white tunics made last-minute preparations or simply waited by the tent entrance with their arms folded. None of them had information about evacuating servants.

She found herself at the camp's perimeter, marked by loops of concertina wire. An opening served as a gate. To the east, the sky lightened to the pale purple of the loosestrife flowers by the road. Below the horizon, the sun sent orange light bouncing off high clouds toward a wall of men, women, and animals to the west, flying the green banners of Viridiae. Observation drones floated over the line. Opposite the Viridians, perhaps a half-kilometer up the valley, but still in shadow, lay Crookbank and its bridge. Lina saw movement, and she heard voices, carried by a light breeze descending the hills. A tower over the community hall dominated the center of the village, and Lina watched the tip of the tapered roof brighten as the limb of the sun peeked over the eastern hills. Dust in the air scattered the yellow light, and Lina made out the line of Lothians, black flags flapping, like dogs eager to run.

Shouts echoed across the field from the Viridian line. Moving as one, the line surged forward at a leisurely pace, then picked up to a slow march. The camp sat on a piece of lifting ground, which gave Lina a view of the line moving across the field like the wave of the ocean, trailing layers of fighting men and women like foam. After a few seconds, the line's pace built to a fast walk.

Up the valley, in front of Crookbank, the Lothians moved as well, down the gentle slope, as the sun peeked halfway over the hill. The full power of the star hadn't quite hit the faces of the

Viridians, but Mordred apparently couldn't wait for the clash. He sent his knights immediately toward Arturus' force at a full gallop. Lina watched with a terrible combination of excitement and fear, knowing full well the outcome of a collision. She couldn't take her eyes off the moving fortresses of humans, machines, animals and weapons as the distance between them shrank. The air was rent with war cries and pounding hooves.

Then, without missing a beat, Arturus' line split in two, as if it had hit a giant rock jutting out from an invisible shore. One side moved left, the other right, opening a gulf in the middle. The momentum of the Lothian charge, only a hundred meters away, carried hundreds of knights in full battle armor through the gap. The Viridian flanks resembled the jaws of a giant snake, and as the Lothians poured into the snake's mouth, the jaws began to close shut, even as the flanks of the Lothian line collided with the upper and lower jaws of the beast.

Lina sought out Percival in the morass, but things moved so quickly, she could only guess at who was fighting where. Plumed helmets and decorated armor marked some of the knights. She recognized the ermine-spots on Sir Bors' shield, the red cross on white of Sir Galahad's coat of arms, and several other knights made famous by their war records, Grail quests, or prowess in the lists. With no time to retrieve and repair his battle armor before he was told to report to his reserve unit, Percival blended in with the mass of lesser-known knights and soldiers. Arturus, on the other hand, stood out on his snow-white war horse. He wore a crowned helm, topped by a crest in the shape of a mythical beast.

Lina could not find Mordred's armor and shield. She knew what to look for, because she had seen his coat of arms in his tent with its golden eagle painted on black.

The noise intensified with pops from single-shot pistols and the clang of sword against armor. War cries morphed into screams. But as soldiers and horses fell, the jaws of the Viridian beast closed, and its teeth—the Viridian knights against the gristle of the Lothian host—began to chew. Arturus' plan was clear. He used Mordred's eagerness against him. He drew him into a net that closed like a purse. Mordred's force was cut in two, evening the odds. Arturus hoped to surround and destroy half of the Lothian army, and frighten or demoralize the rest. It worked. The Lothians on the outside of the Viridian trap scattered like birds. Lina didn't understand why, until she saw Mordred fighting like a demon in the center of the trap. The abandoned Lothians had lost their leader, and they lost their heart for the battle.

Lina's fascination turned to horror. The Viridians and Lothians mixed in a gory stew of blood and limbs, screams and challenges. What started as an orderly attack disintegrated into a melee with survival as the main reason for each slash or shot. Dying and living were all that mattered. Standing by the gate, as blood-soaked soldiers and knights stumbled toward the medical tents, sometimes carried by slashed animals, she could not tear her eyes away from the whirlpool of killing. She was witnessing an event people would talk about for a thousand years. Her artist's mind was already at work capturing the intensity and meaning of the moment.

The fighting raged for an hour, then two, contained on the broad field that had once nourished cows a local farmer milked for a famous cheese. How would the blood-soaked ground change the cheese's taste? The scattered Lothians managed to regroup for a counterattack, which was repulsed by Arturus' reserves. That's when Lina discovered Percival, charging a group of Lothian foot soldiers, killing two at a single stroke of his broadsword. She stifled a gasp, as the man who was her tender lover suddenly became a murderous hybrid of human and horse. He resembled the fantastic beasts brought to life by the DNA manipulators of the Old Civilization, and in modern times by Merlin, with his disastrous demonstration of the lab-grown questing beast at the Camelot fair.

In front of her, it seemed that more Lothians stood over the bodies of Viridians than the opposite. She feared Mordred might have the upper hand as he wasted his opponents right and left. Then Lina heard a noise that did not come from this universe, or so she felt, because it forced her to cover her ears to blot it out. The tinny roar stopped everything as the fighters on both sides paused, amazing and terrified. Out of a line of trees galloped a single figure on an enormous white mare, each covered in chrome-plated armor, with the figure holding a broadsword and a shield with three diagonal red stripes on a white field.

"Gaia in Heaven," Lina whispered to herself, "it's Lancelot."

The Viridians raised a cheer, and the fighting resumed. The Viridians pressed forward into a ragtag line of Lothians. Lancelot rode straight for the Lothian line.

"Mordred, you dog," Lancelot screamed. "You're mine. I'm going to kill you now."

Out of nowhere, Lina felt a presence, but it wasn't Lancelot. Nor was it Arturus, Percival, or any of the fighters on the torn-up field. It was calm, determined, full of concentration, and it enveloped her like a fog. Ganieda? Lina looked about, thinking her teacher had appeared nearby, but she saw nothing.

In front of Lina, the soldiers and knights around Mordred gave way, though one brought him a dark destrier without a rider. He mounted, pushed onto the saddle by three men. He gripped his broadsword, its blade painted black with blood. He spurred the animal and it sped at a gallop toward Lancelot. He swung, but Lancelot parried the blow, bringing her blade down on the small of Mordred's back. Lancelot's helmet came loose, and she threw it off. Her blond hair streamed out, unkempt and missing its usual tight braid. Her eyes flared, like the eyes of a raging beast, as she spun her horse around.

"Come back, Mordred. You're a traitor and a coward. You're a dead man!"

Mordred spurred his horse to a gallop, its breathy pants carrying across the field strewn with bodies and weapons. He ran his armored animal directly into Lancelot, and as she struggled to keep control of her warhorse, he pulled out his pistol and fired point-blank. Lancelot and the horse fell. Lancelot managed to swing her leg clear before the animal landed on it, and she scrambled off. Blood streamed from a wound on her neck, streaking her hair.

Mordred dismounted, running toward the stunned Lancelot. He swung his broadsword, which Lancelot parried with her shield. She was badly hurt, dropping to her knees and losing the grip on her sword. Her gloved hand clutched at her neck, trying to staunch the blood, and she didn't see Mordred approach her from behind. With one stroke of his broadsword, he decapitated her.

Mordred exulted. "Lothia and justice!"

A massive groan exhaled from the Viridian camp, including from Lina's lungs, as if half of the Viridian lives had left the earth with Lancelot's death. Viridiae's greatest warrior, Arturus' peerless champion, undefeated in every battle she had ever fought, lay dead on the field at Camlann. Everyone thought she was lost to the country, driven mad by Guinevere's rejection. The queen had tried to bring her back to the fold, but Lancelot's fury could not be assailed. Then she appeared, albeit late, on the field at Camlann, perhaps plagued by doubts about her decision to withdraw from the world. No one would ever know, and with her gone, nothing could stop Mordred or the Lothians. Camelot was lost, Lina was sure, to a usurper, a small, angry man who cared more about a grudge than his country.

"Mordred!"

Once again, a voice brought everyone to attention, Lothian and Viridian. The free-for-all quieted, and the two sides separated, as if by a magic spell. On Lina's left, Mordred stood over Lancelot's body, panting after striking the death blow. Ten meters away, standing in his green tunic streaked with gore, was Arturus, helmeted, visor up.

"Mordred," the king said. "I say we finish this."

Mordred lifted his visor. Dried blood streamed from his nose and mouth. "Agreed. There's been enough death today. When you die, it will end."

"Defend yourself." Arturus lowered his visor.

Again, Lina discerned a presence, but it was different, not in quality, but in quantity. Two distinct instances, things, but immaterial. They struggled, pushing against one another like tectonic plates, invisible deep in the bowels of the earth. Lina's feeling that Ganieda was near returned. The other presence? Angry, hurt, hateful, protective.

In the midst of this swirl of emotion, Lina saw the climax unfold. This was the moment both men, father and son, feared and wanted in the same breath. She concentrated, committing to memory every color and sound, even the coppery taste of the air. King and usurper circled each other, looking for weakness. Mordred nearly stumbled over a corpse, and Arturus made to charge, but Mordred recovered. His foot touched something, and he bent down, lifting a javelin from the ground. Arturus froze. A second later, the javelin was in the air. Arturus moved, but not quickly enough, and the spear struck his breastplate. It penetrated just enough to jam itself so that Arturus could not remove it. Blood trickled down the shaft.

The javelin jutted forward like a strange appendage, but Arturus took advantage of Mordred's unbalanced stance to lunge. The point of his sword pierced Mordred's chain mail and entered his belly. Mordred screamed, and Arturus drove the blade home, but not before Mordred wrapped his hand around the javelin and pushed with equal force. Arturus growled, blood gurgling in his lungs and throat, but he managed another push, driving his sword out Mordred's back. Both men, face to face as the Viridian and Lothian hosts watched, dropped to the ground.

Arturus exhaled and went limp. A few seconds later, Mordred followed his father into the void.

The outcome stunned Lina. No one on either side of the battle moved. Nothing had prepared them for this outcome. Everyone assumed one or the other would prevail. Viridiae would belong to either Mordred or Arturus. What was supposed to happen now?

The struggling shadows had vanished as well.

A woman screeched. Morgause, the one-time lover of Arturus, mother to his bastard son, stumbled out of the Lothian host, keening like an anguished bird. She knelt first over Mordred, cradling his head in her hands, begging the heavens to let her son live. Then she reached over and stroked the head of Arturus, declaring her love for him, that she never meant for him to die. Why, she asked the sky, could they not love each other as she loved them both?

The sun reached its zenith, pouring midday heat on the field, raising a stink from death like a horrible maisma. No one knew what to do. A figure on a gray mare, without armor or shield, appeared on the distant road, followed by two retainers. All the fighters, Lothian and Viridian, watched the woman and her female guard tread over the broken ground. Guinevere sat high in her saddle, wearing a tunic of blue satin, with a white linen wimple and gorget. The queen looked ethereal, ghost-like, as if she were a soul that had materialized to share secret wisdom. Little emotion played on Guinevere's face, except for sadness and perhaps disappointment, as if something she had foreseen had come true, despite a wish to the contrary.

When she reached the weeping Morgause, she dismounted. Lancelot's body lay a few meters away. Guinevere called out for General Yama and Sir Galahad, Arturus' second-in-command. After a moment, both appeared, Yama holding an injured arm, Galahad with his mail in shreds. Galahad was in shock. He'd seen his mother killed.

"My lords, no, let me say, my friends, because we are all equals on this ground, equals in anger and sorrow," Guinevere said. "I grieve for all of us, for everything we've lost today. Some of you wanted me to fight on your side, others on their side. I saw no point in it, because no matter what I did, or didn't do, thousands would die. No one is made noble by this kind of destruction. In my heart of hearts, I wanted no part of it."

Lina's eyes filled with tears. Percival, dirty and bloody from head to toe, but unhurt, stood next to her, and touched her hand. She leaned into Percival's shoulder, but kept her attention on Guinevere, who knelt beside Arturus' body.

"Oh my dear husband, how you hurt, every day, first from your illness, and then from your son's betrayal. But you saved your country, by sacrificing yourself. And now I carry your burden."

Yama spoke up. His face twisted in skepticism. "What do you mean, my lady?"

"Think about it, General. Lord Mordred wanted the crown, but he has no wife, no heirs, no other family apart from Lady Morgause. My husband and I never had children, and no one has stepped forward with any other claim to the throne that would be accepted by the Round Table."

"Leaving you, of course," Yama sneered. "How convenient for you."

Galahad tensed. The sword in his hand quivered.

Yama continued, "And why should we accept your claim? You may be queen, but no one has ever chosen you as ruler."

"You speak the truth, General Yama, but I doubt you have the means to prevent me from taking Arturus' place until a new monarch can be chosen." Guinevere raised her hand slowly, delicately pointing to the blue sky overhead.

The open field at Camlann was surrounded by thick forests on the north and south. As Guinevere lowered her hand, thousands of Cameliardian knights and soldiers emerged from the woodlands, fresh and ready for battle. Yama looked about nervously. Galahad face hardened, ready to join Guinevere in taking revenge for his mother's death, until he saw the queen's withering stare.

"Gentlemen, stand down your armies, or I will annihilate them both."

Galahad spoke first. "But these Lothians are traitors, Your Majesty."

Yama hesitated, seeking out support from his side, but none of his officers or men would look at him. "Very well, Your Majesty. We stand down."

"Galahad?" Guinevere said.

The commander studied the field. The war lust had faded. He glanced down at his mother's corpse. "Yes, my lady, for Lancelot's sake."

Lina's shoulders relaxed with relief. Percival shouted, "Long live Queen Guinevere!" In a few seconds, both hosts joined in the chant, some individuals more enthusiastic than others, but all welcomed the peace.

CHAPTER 29: PRESENTATION OF THE GRAIL

Lina ran out of time. She had a bad habit of tinkering with a project until the last minute, but she doubted she would ever get a similar commission. She had spent night and day for two weeks putting the finishing touches on Dee's monumental light tapestry, but workers would soon arrive at the Great Audience Hall to prepare the space for the official unveiling. The first guests would show up at noon. She turned off the projectors and put the control system into standby before rushing to her room at the palace to shower and change.

The fingers of her right hand quivered from nervousness, and she had to hold them with her left hand to apply her makeup without streaking it. She wanted so much to honor Dee's designs and artistic vision, but she had to add numerous details Dee couldn't have foreseen, even with her clairvoyant gifts.

At dinner the previous night with Percival at Ganieda's house, the elderly artist tried to reassure Lina.

"It's inevitable that critics and purists will pick the piece apart," Ganieda said. "It goes with the territory."

Ganieda adjusted the blanket over her legs. She was still recovering from the Battle of Camlann. Lina had found the elder in her tent, shivering, on the verge of passing out. Later, Ganieda explained that she had struggled to suppress Morgause's dark energy, which almost turned the battle in Mordred's favor.

Lancelot's unexpected arrival distracted Morgause enough to tip the balance, but the effort had cost Ganieda the use of her legs. The paralysis was slowly receding, but Ganieda was confined to a wheelchair.

"I don't want people to say I just parroted Dee's work," Lina said over vintage Napene wine. "I have my own style, but people's expectations—I don't know what they expect."

"Probably too much," said Eleanor, who had remained in Camelot to spend time with Percival and attend the unveiling. "No one is ever satisfied with public art, because the vast majority of people don't really know what they like."

"Dee would be intensely proud of what you've done, Lina." Percival touched her hand. "She never expressed any doubts about your abilities."

Lina had plenty of doubts, but at this point, she had to set them aside and launch the work into the world. When she returned to the audience hall, the workers had already placed most of the folding chairs and installed the PA system. A raised dais contained chairs with upholstered seats meant for the dignitaries. At one end of the long hall, the lights overhead turned down, was the throne of Arturus Strong-Arm.

Inside a curtained area, Lina made last-minute adjustments to the unveiling system, and she kept seeing tiny details in the tapestry that could stand improvement. That color should be sharper, she thought, or that form should have a smoother curve. Her urge to tinker was interrupted by fragrances brought in by the caterers: basil, cardamon, cinnamon. Florists placed small bouquets on the serving and eating tables.

Percival and Eleanor arrived first. After kissing Percival, Lina touched cheeks with Eleanor. The two women were still feeling out their relationship, though Eleanor showed no signs of resistance to her relationship with Percival. Eleanor offered a small box to Lina. "I wanted to give you something to celebrate the unveiling. It's a ring that Dee gave to me when she was a child."

Lina opened the box. "This must be a treasure to you. I

couldn't possibly take it."

"Nonsense. Dee would be pleased."

Ganieda arrived next with her brother, Merlin. Lina had never seen them together, and their sibling resemblance was striking.

"I had to drag him away from his new toy." Ganieda, the older sister, could not help teasing her little brother. "His social skills have always been marginal."

Merlin ignored the jibe. "Percival, I've learned more about the Great Machine every day. I'm fine tuning it to the specifications listed in the Grail manual. I'm convinced that the climate is already showing signs of stabilizing."

"So our problems are solved?"

"Not so fast. This kind of science doesn't deal with absolutes. Manipulating the climate is not like describing the motions of atoms."

"But you're optimistic."

"Indeed, I am."

Sir Bors de Gannes and his family entered the hall, as did Sir Galahad du Lac-Corbenic, his arm in a sling. He wore a black armband in memory of his mother, Lancelot, but he proudly presented his protege, Penny. Percival trotted over to his friends. Other leaders of the Round Table, elected and appointed, turned up. One thing Lina asked the queen's household to avoid was turning the unveiling into a wake for Dee. But the public feeling of sadness over the loss of a great artist before her prime was unavoidable.

The country also reeled over the loss of Arturus III. Bors, Galahad and Percival carried his body off the field at Camlann. Lina did not see what happened to Mordred's body, though she heard the Lady Morgause had taken it back to the Lothian family estate for burial. Galahad sent a detachment of Arturus' household guard with Lancelot's body to her estate. Arturus lay in state in the Great Audience Hall for three days as thousands of Viridians paid their respects. Guinevere buried him temporarily in the military cemetery next to the citadel, promising to inter his body permanently in the audience hall next to his father and grandfather when an appropriate tomb was prepared.

While the guests took their seats, Lina's nerves almost overwhelmed her, and she clung to Eleanor's side. The time for the unveiling was here, but Guinevere had not arrived. Eleanor reassured Lina that a queen is required to be late, lest she be thought in thrall to someone else's needs, instead of the country's. Lina accepted Eleanor's odd rationalization, but her knees weakened by the minute.

Finally, two household guards in polished ceremonial armor signaled Guinevere's imminent appearance. She walked through the hall's main entrance dressed in a smart, but feminine business suit, dark in honor of her dead husband, but not morose. A black armband showed that she mourned a family member, though Lina thought it might also signal mourning for Lancelot. On her shoulder was a jeweled representation of the Viridian flag. Everyone stood when she entered, and a few applauded. She shook hands with guests, making brief small talk. A few looked at her sideways.

"I don't understand their attitude," Lina said to Eleanor.

"She's queen of Viridiae, but she's not the monarch, at least not yet. Some delegates to the Round Table believe she had always planned to take the throne from Arturus, and the war with Mordred simply provided an opportunity to fulfill her ambition. They don't want to endorse that kind of behavior."

Lina remembered Guinvere's conversation with Mordred in his camp. She promised to respond to his offer of joint rule. Did she? It was unclear. And why didn't she intervene on Arturus' side during the battle? Lina thought she would never understand politics.

"The vote to confirm her as the monarch is a formality, I guess. Why can't they just get it over with?"

"Guinevere doesn't want to be seen as trampling on Arturus' body, so to speak, while climbing to the throne. She can afford to wait a while."

Guinevere spoke to Percival for a moment. He bowed slightly. Later, Lina learned that Guinevere had dropped the investigation into his behavior at the Battle of River's Bend. As far as the queen was concerned, Percival had redeemed himself by finding the Grail and fighting bravely at Camlann.

When she reached the dais where Lina and Eleanor waited, Guinevere embraced Lina like a sister.

"I'm sorry I'm a little late, but I wouldn't miss this for anything, my dearest Lina."

Lina's heart pumped wildly. The queen had seen the tapestry's progress, but would she like the final result? Disappointing her was unthinkable.

"Lina, I'd like to speak with you after the ceremony," Guinevere said. "I have a job for you."

"Yes, of course, my lady."

Guinevere took her seat on the dais, as well as Lina and a few palace functionaries. The government's minister of arts and culture, a wild-haired man with a touch of the dandy, briefly told the story of the tapestry's inception. He left out Mordred's role, instead recounting Dee's rapid rise from obscurity to a leading light of Viridian arts. He asked for a moment of silence to remember her. After a deep sigh, he introduced Lina, who stood and bowed in thanks. The applause died down, and Guinevere took the lectern.

She had made only a few public appearances since returning from Camlann with Arturus' body, including the memorial and his burial. But over the weeks, Camelot's people had invested in her their relief at surviving another war. Mordred never attacked the city, but people had fled in fear. When they returned, Guinevere among them, all the main threats on the country had receded. Mordred was gone. The Lucians were still mired in murderous internal plots. As Merlin sent in his optimistic progress reports, even the long-term threat of a failing climate fell away. Despite grumbling at the Round Table, the people viewed Guinevere as a force for stability and normality.

At the lectern, the queen said a few words of praise and thanks for Dee and Lina's hard work. She pressed a button, and the lights lowered. A moment later, Dindrane Rathkeale's *Pre-*

sentation of the Grail to Arturus shone like a morning sunrise, full of intense, but soft color, the tiny animations making each figure alive and present. The audience fell silent. Lina thought she heard sobs. A few people shifted in their seats. Lina nearly choked. They hated it!

Slowly, individual people applauded, first politely, then intensely, as if a shock had worn off, replaced by joy and laughter. Percival and Eleanor, sitting in the front row, beamed at Lina. Guinevere returned to her seat next to Lina and clasped her hand. She urged Lina to her feet, and presented her again to the audience, which erupted in cheers.

Lina spent the next quarter hour accepting congratulations from the attendees. Guinevere took her aside, guiding her away from the mob for a private conversation.

"Lina, I'm so proud of you. People are going to remember this day for a very long time."

Lina thanked Guinevere.

"I want to show you something." The queen swept her hand across the wall above the columns opposite Dee's tapestry. It was covered with an ordinary fresco of an unidentifiable landscape. "What do you see?"

"Nothing important, my lady."

"You're wrong, my dear. I see your next work. I would like to commission a light tapestry from you as monumental as Dee's. We need to remember what happened at Camlann. Will you do it?"

Lina studied the wall and then Guinevere's face. In a flash, she understood the woman's ambition, for herself, and for her country. Camlann was perhaps the most important event in Viridiae's history since its founding, and Guinevere wanted people to know her role. The commission was as much about Guinevere's ego as it was about Viridian history and culture. Lina didn't mind. She loved the queen, but she vowed to show the battle in all its violence, as well as its heroism.

"My lady, I'm honored by this commission. When should I begin?"

EPILOG

Ten years later, Percival found Dee's bones buried under the cairn where he had laid them. Spring lingered on the bluff above the Peaceful Sea, with green grass and orange poppies surrounding the cairn. *Dolphin*, still captained by Michael Libb, had brought him to Port Morris with Lina, their eight-year-old son Dean, and his six-year-old sister Aila to find her. He wanted his children to see where his aunt had died saving Viridiae. They rode for a week along the coastal road, each kilometer bringing back hard memories of Dee's decline after Cassanti, the rainstorm, and her burial. He asked Roz to come, but she was too busy with a new garrison command in the unruly town of Bell's Ham. His mother argued that Dee should be allowed to rest undisturbed by the Peaceful Sea, but Guinevere believed she should come home to Camelot. Dee was more than a lost daughter and sister. She was a national hero.

Percival could've sent a professional with experience in exhumations, but he felt compelled to do it himself. A week before he died, a month after Ganieda passed, Merlin gave him personal instruction on how to excavate a grave. Percival brushed the dirt off Dee's bones with the same care he might if he were brushing her hair, which she allowed him to do when they were children. He collected every fragment he could find, down to the smallest bones of her fingers and toes. They seemed to hover in a space between life and death. He wept more than once, letting his tears drop on what he thought of as hallowed ground. When the bones were carefully packed in a specially built casket, he rebuilt the cairn, thinking he might revisit it again someday. Maybe Dean, Aila or their children would want to see it as well.

Dolphin returned Percival and his family to Grey Harbor, and the trip to Camelot was uneventful. Camelot's news chans, their drones hovering overhead, covered their arrival as if they were bringing home the relics of a saint. Percival disliked the way they praised Dee as a kind of superhuman creature. She was his sister, that's all. Yes, she had done an amazing thing. On the other hand, they disagreed, they fought, they laughed. She made mistakes. She had a biting tongue. She was Percival's best friend. But the media and the public had already anointed her, and there was little he could do to change that.

Guinevere had ruled for nearly ten years, brushing aside the doubts of opponents at the Round Table. The people loved her, and time had been kind to her. Gossip about her private life occasionally flared on the tabloid chans, but she declared in more than one interview that she would never marry again. Even if her mate was only a consort with little or no power, independence for a woman of means and power was always preferable. This was a painful lesson of history.

On the day of the interment of Dee's remains, Percival, Lina, Dean, Aila and Eleanor sat in the first row of the Great Audience Hall. On one wall, Dee's *Presentation of the Grail to Arturus* danced in figures of light. On the opposite wall, Lina's *Death of Arturus* hovered like a ghost, dark and moody. Between them, a simple, black-draped catafalque supported a small casket of polished rosewood inlaid with gold. The assembly stood on the slab of granite that protected the final resting place of Arturus III's remains, moved after the tomb was completed two years after his death.

For Dee, Guinevere had ordered a niche added to the eastern wall of the hall, near the throne of Arturus the Great. A choir sang a dirge as hundreds of Viridians from across the country witnessed the ceremony. The news chans broadcast it nationwide. A priestess of Gaia said a blessing and Guinevere made a short speech. Percival barely heard her words. Dee would think of all the hubbub as silly and wasteful.

As the pall bearers placed the casket into its green marble

sarcophagus, flanked by huge bouquets of flowers, Percival could only think of the time he spent with Dee in the secret forest hideaway near their mother's house. He had wanted to be a knight, though his mother disapproved. Dee was unsure what she wanted then, but destiny had marked a path for her. Though she was gone, destiny still had plans for her. Percival imagined pilgrims, scholars, and the curious visiting her grave, hoping to find inspiration. He pitied them, because they would never know her the way he had.

Percival thought back to the installation of the Grail in the Great Machine, where Merlin asked to be buried. Percival could almost hear the hum of the sparkling device, still revealing its secrets to a cadre of scientists and engineers working in the depths of Apparatus Montis. They had shared what they discovered with their Lucian counterparts, who then repaired their own Great Machine. As far as anyone knew, all 12 of the machines around the world were functioning normally, and if one failed, the caretakers knew what to do. Perhaps humanity could finally live up to its responsibility to care for the earth. The dream of the Grail might yet come true.

AUTHOR'S NOTE

Thank you so much for reading *Return of the Green Land*, the third book in my fantasy trilogy, *The Future History of the Grail*. Like many young boys, I thrilled at the King Arthur stories, starting with T.H. White's *The Once and Future King*, published in 1958, the year before I was born. I also loved any movie with Arthurian themes. I'll never forget watching John Boorman's 1981 classic *Excalibur* at a theatre in Seattle's Northgate Mall in 1981. Frankly, I found these versions of Arthur, Guinevere, Lancelot, and all the other Arthurian personalities far more compelling than other rising interpretations of medieval fantasy, such as Dungeons & Dragons. The inventions of Geoffrey of Monmouth, Sir Thomas Malory, and various French and German storytellers are timeless, universal and cross-cultural, available to any modern storyteller willing to take them on.

Today's challenge is finding a new approach to the characters. I've written science fiction novels that take place in a relatively near future affected by climate change, which is one of my major themes. I believe humanity faces an existential threat from a warming climate, and I wanted to speculate on how people might adapt in the next century or two. For this new project, I wondered how could I combine the Arthurian legends with the reality of an unfolding environmental disaster. Most modern interpretations of the Arthurian stories place them in a historical past or a more-or-less realistic present. I decided to project my Arthurian characters into the future, a thousand years, to be exact. To my knowledge, very few writers have tried this. I'll leave it to you to decide whether I was successful.

Figuring out the problems with this strategy took some research. Of course, I watched *Excalibur* again. I also picked up a few volumes from Powell's Books in Portland, Ore. The books included *Arthurian Myth & Legend: An A-Z of People and Places*, a reference I went to again and again. I also purchased John Matthews' *The Arthurian Tradition* and *The Grail Tradition*, which provided invaluable structural and plot help, as well as explaining the original spiritual meaning of the Grail legend. *Life in a Medieval Village*, by Frances and Joseph Gies, provided some ideas about setting. A video lecture series by Prof. Dorsey Armstrong of Purdue University was priceless in helping me understand the Arthurian narrative tradition. The series is part of the Great Courses, which I accessed through the Seattle Public Library. And then there are countless online articles and websites. A good list of sites is available at the Best of Legends. I found the lyrics for the traditional songs used in chapter 14 of *Fall of the Green Land* and chapter 21 of *Return of the Green Land* at the Traditional Music Library. I also took inspiration for the characters and culture of the Lucians from Shakespeare's *Julius Caesar* and the HBO series *Rome*. And what would writers on deadline do without Wikipedia?

Of course, I had enormous help with the project along the way. Editor Melanie Austin helped with structure and characters. My wife Edith Follansbee proved again that I have a habit of forgetting to insert certain words, thinking that people won't notice them if they've gone missing. My friends at South Seattle Fiction Writers read early drafts. More friends at Two-Hour Transport in Seattle suffered through readings of my works-in-progress. Numerous friends and relatives volunteered as beta readers, not knowing what they were getting into. Thank you all!

I'd like to hear your feedback. Please take a moment to review my book on Amazon, Goodreads, or your favorite book review site. You can follow me on Facebook (@AuthorJGFollansbee), Twitter (@Joe_Follansbee), and Instagram (@jgfollansbee). You can also follow me on my personal blog. Tell your friends!

The three novels in the *Future History of the Grail* are intended to be read in sequence. *Fall of the Green Land* is followed by *War for the Green Land* and finally by *Return of the Green Land*. Of course, you can read them in whatever sequence you like, as long as you read them.

Thanks again!

– Joe Follansbee, Summer 2020

MORE BOOKS BY J.G. FOLLANSBEE

Tales From a Warming Planet
The Mother Earth Insurgency
Carbon Run
City of Ice and Dreams
Restoration

The Fyddeye Guides
The Fyddeye Guide to America's Maritime History
The Fyddeye Guide to America's Lighthouses

Young Adult Historical Fiction
Bet: Stowaway Daughter

Maritime History
Shipbuilders, Sea Captains, and Fishermen: The Story of the Schooner Wawona
Blowing Out the Stink: Life on a Lumber and Cod Schooner, 1897-1947

ABOUT THE AUTHOR

J.G. Follansbee is an award-winning writer of thrillers, fantasy and science fiction novels and short stories with climate change themes. An author of maritime history and travel guides, he has published articles in newspapers, regional and national magazines, and regional and national radio networks, including National Public Radio. He's also worked in the high-tech and non-profit worlds. He lives in Seattle and blogs at https://jgfollansbee.com/blog/.

www.ingramcontent.com/pod-product-compliance
Lightning Source LLC
Chambersburg PA
CBHW060908250626
47159CB00008B/2914